WICK＿ＭPIRE

KNIGHT'S RIDGE EMPIRE #3

TRACY LORRAINE

TRACY
LORRAINE

Editing by Pinpoint Editing

Proofreading by Sisters Get Lit.erary

Photography by Wander Aguiar

CHAPTER ONE

Stella

I don't feel the stones and sticks on the ground as I fall to my knees. The only pain that assaults my body as I reach for both Seb and Toby, who are lying on the ground in the darkness, is that of my heart shattering in my chest.

"No, please. No."

It's too dark to really see anything, and while I might be silently praying that something else happened here, I know deep down that I'm not going to witness a miracle.

A rattling breath comes from one side of me as a hand on the other grips mine.

"It's okay, Sis," Toby forces out, his eyes closed, pain etched across every inch of his face.

"I'm so sorry. I'm so sorry."

Taking Toby's hand, I squeeze it tight as my head continues to swim from whatever it is that's in my system.

My body wants to shut down, to give in to whatever it is. But I can't.

"Baby, none of this is your fault."

The sound of Seb's voice fractures something inside me, and the second I look at him and find his dark eyes staring up at me, I break.

Falling onto his body, I cling to him as my tears soak his shirt along with the blood.

I'm completely unaware of anyone else around us, so I startle when a large pair of hands wrap around my upper arms and pull me away from both of them.

"No," I cry, fighting to break free.

I kick my legs, trying to make contact, but my body barely complies, my limbs flailing uselessly, all my years of training nothing but a distant memory as I'm forced to watch a mass of zombies surround my boys, blocking them from my sight.

"NOOO!" I scream, trying to up my efforts to get away, but my body is having other ideas, shutting down faster than I can control.

"They're helping, Stella. They know what they're doing," a familiar voice says in my ear.

He brings us to a stop on the edge of all the action, and I sense two others come to stand beside us. Ripping my eyes from the scene before us, I find Nico and Alex standing there, shadows making their somber expressions even more harrowing.

A sob rips from my throat, reality slamming into me.

Sensing that I've given up fighting, I'm released, although only for a few seconds because strong arms wrap around my body, holding me.

"It's going to be okay," Theo breathes in my ear. The serious tone of his voice stops me from arguing despite every inch of my body screaming, 'How? How can this possibly be okay?'

Falling back into him, I make use of his strength as my legs damn near give up.

In a move that I'm sure as fuck isn't planned, both of my hands are grasped, both Alex and Nico squeezing, helping hold me together.

Men move around in front of us, some disappearing through the trees, searching for the shooter, I'm sure, as others focus their efforts on Seb and Toby, who could well be fighting for their lives right now.

Silent tears streak down my face as I wait for a sign, anything to tell me that they're going to be okay.

Someone looks over and gives Theo a nod, and my heart sinks.

"What does that mean?" I demand.

"Come on, Princess. We need to move so the paramedics can do their thing."

"No. I'm not leaving them. I'm not I—THEO," I scream as he throws me over his shoulder and pins me in place with firm hands on my waist and marches through the trees, right as two ambulances come to a screeching halt right in front of us.

But it doesn't matter how much I kick, punch, and

scream—his hold on me doesn't loosen, and his steps don't falter.

Someone opens a car door, and finally, Theo sets me on my feet, but being upside down for so long after drinking whatever I drank, my legs are nothing more than spaghetti and I immediately plummet.

Thankfully, the boys aren't as wasted as I thought they were, or maybe the events of the past thirty minutes or so have sobered them somewhat, because they manage to catch me before I hit the floor.

"Come on, Princess. We need a head start to the hospital so we can be there for them."

Knowing that Alex is right, I allow him to manhandle me inside. They pile in after me, but not before I spot Emmie running toward the car.

"Wait," I cry, stopping Theo from closing the door.

"What's going on? Someone said there were gunshots."

"Get in or fuck off," Theo grunts.

"Get in," I cry.

She takes in the state of me before glancing at the full seats, but Alex is on my wavelength and drags her inside, depositing her on Theo's lap.

"Seriously?" he grunts.

If the situation were any different, I'd be amused by his reaction... but as it is, I feel nothing but dread.

Ignoring her human cushion, Emmie twists around so she can look at me.

"What's going on?" Her eyes are wide and full of fear as she looks between mine.

"S-Seb a-an—"

"Seb and Toby have been shot," Nico says matter-of-factly, as if it's not affecting him, which I know is bullshit because he's feeling it just as intensely as I am.

"Holy shit, are they okay?"

Clearly my reaction to that question says it all, because she just reaches out and takes my hand.

"They'll be fine. They're mafia; they're like immortal or some shit, right?"

"Something like that," Alex mutters sadly.

His words don't help at all.

Seb lost his dad in a gunfight. They are most certainly *not* immortal.

"It'll be fine, right?" She glances at Theo, pleading for him to say that it will.

"Of course," he breathes, studying her a little too closely.

"Where's Calli?" Nico suddenly asks.

"Um..."

"Emmie," he growls.

"I left her dancing with some guy. I came as soon as I heard, I don't know where—"

"Fucking hell," he barks, dragging his cell from his pocket.

"Shit, I didn't—she'll be fine."

"I'll get one of the guys to grab her and bring her to meet us."

Silence settles around the car, the dread that's already sitting heavy in my stomach only growing with every second that passes.

With my eyelids closing, I rest my head on Theo's shoulder, soaking up the support from Emmie through her warm hand.

"I think I was drugged," I confess, my eyes closing as my body shuts down.

CHAPTER TWO

Sebastian

The second I open my eyes, realisation hits me. My brain might feel like it's been pushed through a mincer, but not even that, or getting fucking shot, is enough to make me forget the sound of her voice down the line when I answered her call.

The fear.

A violent shudder shoots down my spine.

"Where is she?" I demand when I find only one person in the room with me.

Dragging his head up, Theo blinks at me a couple of times, seemingly more dazed and confused than I am.

Lifting his hand, he pushes his hair back from his brow and rolls his shoulders.

"She's fine. She's in her own room being checked out."

"Why? What happened? Is she hurt?"

He shakes his head, and relief like I've never felt hits me, knocking me back to the bed. All the air rushes from my lungs as reality swamps me.

I could have lost her tonight. If she didn't call me when she did, he could have got her.

She could be the one with a bullet through her shoulder and lying in a hospital bed.

Or worse.

"Toby?" I ask, more memories hitting me.

"He's going to be okay. He came back from surgery about an hour ago."

"Fucking hell," I mutter, tipping my head back and staring at the ceiling.

That motherfucker saved my life, there's no doubt in my mind.

The cunt's aim might have been off with his first shot, but the second one... if Toby hadn't barged into me, pushing me out of the way, then that surely would have hit me.

"Is it bad?"

"Nah. You're both gonna have kick-arse scars to impress the ladies with, though."

I appreciate his need to lighten the tone, but it falls a ways from the mark.

"This is such a fucking mess." Silence falls around the room, the pain in my shoulder almost too much to bear, but I'm alive, so there's no fucking way I'm going to be a pussy about it and insist on more pain relief. The fucking sling they've got me in is bad enough.

I'm not staying here any longer than I need to.

I need to be with Stella. I need to keep her safe.

Look what happened tonight. I wasn't there and she—

"Why's she being checked if she's okay?" I ask, remembering his words from earlier.

"She was drugged," Theo confesses, scrubbing his hand down his face.

"He was at the party?"

Letting out a long sigh, he stretches his legs out before him. "I dunno, man. Either that, or he's got one of our guys working for him."

"None of them are that fucking stupid."

"Well, you'd like to think not, but the evidence might suggest otherwise."

"Do we have anything on the shooter?"

"Just the bullet pulled from Toby's chest." I wince, guilt swamping me that he literally took that bullet for me. Selfless motherfucker. "Dad's sending it for analysis. We'll find this guy, Seb. We will."

"I know. It just needs to be before it's too late. Tonight was meant to be fucking safe."

"Fuck, I'm glad you're okay, man," Theo confesses, sitting forward once more, seemingly unable to sit still for more than two minutes.

"I need to see her. I need to see with my own two eyes that—"

"I know. I wouldn't expect anything less. I'm not

fucking carrying you, though," he states, lifting a brow at me.

"It'll take more than a hole in the shoulder to stop me from walking," I state stubbornly.

But I regret it the second I throw the covers back. I might be using my good arm, but fuck me does it hurt.

"Oh yeah?" Theo asks, clearly seeing the grimace on my face as I fight it.

"Fuck off. It hurts a bit, that's all."

"A bit," he quips.

Gritting my teeth, I swing my legs over the side of the bed. The sight of the hospital gown someone wrestled me into not long after the ambulance dropped us into the ER makes me groan.

"Let's go before Janice comes back to give you a bed bath."

I grunt the second I hear the name. "Tell me she's not on shift tonight."

"No can do, bro. She was thrilled to see your ugly face too."

Yeah, I bet she fucking was.

All the arguments I had with her while Stella was in the hospital come back to me.

"No wonder this hurts. I bet she fucking stitched me up without any pain relief."

"Well, that would explain why you kept blacking out."

"I did no— fuck off," I bark when I catch sight of his smirk as he rounds the bed to help me.

"You sure you can do this?" he asks, holding me around the waist.

"I need to see her."

He helps me shuffle across the room and pulls the door open.

"Jesus fucking Christ. I leave you two alone for five minutes..." Sophia says, sounding exhausted.

"I ain't arguing with the stubborn arse," Theo says by way of an excuse. "You know he won't stop until he gets what he wants."

Sophia looks over her shoulder in the direction she just came from.

"She's asleep."

"I don't care," I spit.

"Fucking hell," my sister sighs, tentatively taking my other side, being careful of my strapped-up shoulder and helping me down the short hallway.

"See," Theo says when we pass the small window to where Stella is. "Still as hot as the last time you saw her."

A growl rumbles up my throat at his words, but I can't deny that they're true.

She might not be looking her best right now—her skin is pale, her makeup is smeared all over her face, and she's got obvious tear tracks down her cheeks—but she's beautiful. She always will be to me.

Movement at her bedside drags my attention away from my girl, and I find Galen sitting there, his face pulled tight. The lingering zombie face paint does little to hide the pain etched into his features. Calvin, his security, and their housekeeper are sitting on the other side of the room, frowns pulling their brows together.

"We should get you back," Sophia says.

"No. I need to talk to him." I surge forward, forcing the pain aside as I reach for the door and use the handle to keep me upright.

Galen startles, his eyes going wide when he sees me standing there.

"Shit, you should be in bed."

Ripping my eyes from his as he stands, I look back at Stella.

"I know. I just needed to..." I trail off. Something tells me he doesn't need the words. "What did they give her?"

"GHB. Come sit down," he says in a rush, moving aside. "Although you should be in a bed."

"We're gonna wait outside," Calvin says, he and Angie slipping out of the room to give us some privacy —but not before Angie squeezes my good shoulder in support.

Ignoring Galen, Theo and my sister behind me, I shuffle forward, lowering myself to the chair and reaching out for her hand.

She moans as we connect, and my heart aches knowing that she's aware that I'm here.

"Everything's going to be okay, baby," I say, rubbing across her knuckles with my thumb.

I only managed to get five minutes with Stella before my favourite nurse came to drag me back to my own room.

The look on her face when she saw me sitting there was pure death.

I'd have told most people where to go when they started ordering me around, but Janice... there's something about her that makes me listen. I have no idea if she's got kids, but fuck, I feel for them if they exist.

Sophia and Theo escorted me back to my room and helped me into bed before I quite swiftly passed out again.

It might have only been a bullet to the shoulder, but whatever pain meds they have me on are killer.

The next time I come to, there's a scent filling my nose that makes my heart rate increase.

"Baby?" I whisper, not entirely sure if I'm still dreaming or if she really is here with me.

"Hey."

Goose bumps erupt across my whole body at her voice, and a shiver of need races down my spine.

Dragging my eyes open, I'm greeted by the most incredible sight.

My chin drops as I stare at her lying right beside me, sharing my pillow.

She looks a million times better than when I saw her in her room, however long ago that was. Her makeup has been washed away, leaving her beautiful skin clear, her hair has been fixed, and she's no longer wearing her costume.

"How are you feeling?" I ask, continuing to check her over for injuries despite the fact that I've been told she has none.

"Me? I wasn't the one who got freaking shot, Seb. What the fuck?" There's an edge of anger to her tone, and it startles me a little.

"I-I didn't mean—"

"Shit. I'm sorry."

Leaning forward, her warm hand cups my jaw as her brow presses against mine.

"Do you have any idea how fucking terrifying that was?"

A flashback to when she was stabbed hits me. "Yeah, actually. I do."

Tears fill her eyes as she stares at me. "I thought you were both dead," she whispers, emotion cracking her voice.

"It'll take more than—"

"No," she begs. "Please. No jokes."

I nod, helpless but to do anything she asks.

"Have you seen Toby?"

She shakes her head. "Not yet, but the guys are with him. I made them leave us alone."

"Hmm," I hum, rubbing my nose against hers. "I like the way you think."

"Sebastian, you're in the hospital."

"A guy still has needs, baby."

"You're insufferable."

"And you're incredibly hot. I can't help it if I get hard every time I look at you."

At my words, she glances down. "Oh my God. Don't let Janice see that, she might start to think you're softening to her."

"It'll definitely go soft if she comes anywhere near it, don't worry about that."

"Jesus," she mutters, a smile playing on her lips.

Wrapping her arm around me, she snuggles into my good side and we just lie there in silence, appreciating that tonight didn't go as badly as it could have.

Stella's breathing evens out, and I start to think she's drifted off to sleep. But just as I close my eyes to do the same, my name floats through the air.

"Yeah, baby?" I whisper back, caressing her arm with my thumb.

She shifts so she's looking up at me once more.

"I love you."

My chin drops, and all the air rushes out of my lungs as I stare down at her in disbelief.

I know she feels it. I see it within her when she looks at me. I saw it in the way she wanted to react to me when I told her how I felt.

But hearing the words?

Fuck.

It makes me appreciate her holding back from saying it as a reaction to me doing so because knowing just how much she means it... Fuck, it makes my heart shatter in all the best ways.

"Stella, I—" Her fingers press against my lips.

"Rest."

Unable to do anything but what she says, I close my eyes once more, drop my nose to the top of her head, and breathe her in.

CHAPTER THREE

Stella

"Hey," I whisper when Theo and Alex slip into Seb's room, finding me curled up with him on the bed. Neither of them looks overly shocked by the move.

"He's awake," they whisper back, following my orders to tell me the second Toby came to.

It's been a little under twenty-four hours since both of them were brought in.

Toby was wheeled straight through to surgery, and Seb was sent to be stitched up.

We all ended up on the same ward where I was after I was stabbed. A ward I've since discovered is totally funded by the Cirillo Family.

I don't know why I didn't figure that out before.

The level of care I received during my first stay was incredible, so it makes total sense really.

Both of them now have private rooms to recover in, and despite the fact that Seb wanted to discharge himself the second he was able to, we've all managed to convince him to stay another night after ripping his stitches during his little quest to see me while I was out of it yesterday morning.

As gently as I can, I try to climb from Seb's side.

My body aches, but I have no memory of why.

The only things I can remember are running from a dark, hooded figure, finding Seb and Toby on the ground, and then waking up in the hospital to find my dad, Calvin and Angie at my side.

Dad's face was a welcome sight until I registered the cuts and bruises that covered him.

He refused to explain everything to me while I was laid up, but with the zombie costume and the lingering face paint, it didn't take a genius to figure out that he'd been at the party working security, and I assume he was one of the guys who went out searching for the shooter.

"Where are you going?" a deep, sleepy voice rumbles behind me as a hand grabs me around the waist.

"I'm going to see Toby. Don't worry, I'm not running away."

"I should fucking hope not," he groans.

"I won't leave you alone. You've got some playmates."

Dropping a kiss to his pouty lips, I pull myself from his hold and stand up.

Thankfully, my legs—hell, my entire body—seems like it's ready to cooperate now.

I have no idea how I managed what I did with the amount of GHB in my system, but it's safe to say that it took a fair bit of time for the lingering effects to subside.

"You good?" Theo asks, looking a little concerned as I let go of the bed.

"Yeah." I take a couple of steps toward the door but stop when I'm beside him. Throwing my arms around him over his shoulders, I lift up on my tiptoes and hold him tight for a few seconds.

"Thank you," I breathe in his ear.

"Anytime, Princess."

Dropping a kiss to his cheek, I release him before the possessive asshole in the bed starts complaining.

Shooting a look at Alex, I smirk when I find a knowing smile playing on his lips.

"I'm going. Rib him as much as you want for that. I'm pretty sure I saw the nurse with some kind of lube earlier."

I slip out of the room before any of them can respond. Despite everything, I've got the biggest smile on my face as I make my way down the hall to Toby's room.

Everything might be shit right now, but the guys I once thought I hated make all of this that little bit better. The fact that we can still have some kind of normal makes it all a little easier.

The second I push the door open and look around, Toby's eyes meet mine and a smile curls his lips.

"Hey, Sis. How's it going?"

I have no idea where it comes from. I was feeling good, strong, but the second he speaks, the floodgates open and I start sobbing like a baby.

Through my tears, Toby stares at me with a completely helpless expression on his face.

"I'm sorry. I don't know what happened," I confess, walking over to his bed and taking his outstretched hand.

"Hey, it's okay," he whispers. "I'm going to be okay."

Lifting his hand, his fingers brush my tears from my cheek as I sniffle.

I thought it would be Seb that broke me, but clearly not.

"I thought you were dead," I say, repeating the same words I said to Seb when he first looked at me.

He doesn't even attempt a witty comeback, sensing that I can't handle the jokes right now.

"As long as you're not."

Dropping my head into my hands, I blow out a long breath.

"That was too close."

"It was. But also, it was the closest we came to catching him. He's taking more risks. Which means he's more likely to make a mistake."

I get what he's saying. But at the same time, sheer fucking terror washes through me as I think about what will happen the next time this guy takes a risk. Two of us were shot. Three of us ended up in a hospital bed. What happens next?

"We're going to beat him, Stel. I fucking promise you that."

He pulls my hand from my face and holds it tightly.

"He's not going to get to you. Not when he's gotta get through us first."

"That's what I'm scared of." I'd rather he just kill me than hurt everyone around me. It's me he wants for whatever reason. Not them.

"Maybe I should just—"

"No," he spits out, his voice hard and stern despite the state of him. "You do not get to make decisions alone about this. And you're not putting your neck on the line in the hope to save the rest of us. We're family. We do this together."

"Fuck, Toby. I hate this."

"So do I, but we can hate it together. Yeah? We're not alone anymore."

The sincerity in his eyes makes tears well in my own all over again.

"What did I do to deserve you?" I ask as his door opens behind me.

I don't turn to look, assuming it's going to be a nurse or one of the guys.

But the second Toby looks over my shoulder, his entire body tenses, his lips turning down in a grimace.

"Dad, what are you doing here?"

All the air races from my lungs.

Dad?

Fuck.

Toby squeezes my hand, letting me know that it's

going to be okay, but his cunt of a father is the last person I wanted to run into today. Or any fucking day, for that matter.

"My only child got shot, am I not allowed to visit him?"

"O-of course. I just wasn't expecting to see you. I know you're busy with Mum and all this bullshit."

His shoes squeak against the floor as he rounds the bed.

Tingles—and not the good kind—race over my skin as his eyes take me in. Or the back of me, at least.

"I didn't know you had a girlfriend, Son. Are you going to introduce me?"

'I'm sorry,' Toby mouths quickly.

I squeeze his hand back and turn to face his father.

The second our eyes lock, anger crosses his face.

He knows exactly who I am.

Straightening my spine, I plaster the best smile I can muster up and swallow down any apprehension about meeting this motherfucker.

"It's so nice to meet you, Mr. Ariti."

"Estella, how wonderful to meet you after all these years."

My skin prickles, disgust rolling through me as I stare at the man who's done his best to single-handedly ruin both my mother and brother's lives.

My teeth grind as I fight to plaster a smile on my face.

What I really want to do is grab any kind of weapon I can get my hands on and not let the fucker up until I watch him take his last breath, but I know I can't.

So instead of acting on it, I allow that little fantasy to play out in my head while I continue to glare at him.

As much as I might want to hurt him, I know it's not my place.

After everything he's been through, Toby deserves to be the one who gets to land that final blow.

"You too, Jonas. Although, I must admit that I haven't heard too much about you."

"Yes, well. It seems that you and Toby have connected."

"He needs all the support he can get right now, don't you think?"

"Of course. Toby has great friends."

Yeah. Shame about some of his family.

"Well, as you can see, I'm alive," Toby damn near hisses at his father. If I didn't already know exactly how he felt about his sperm donor, then I've seen all I need, to fully understand his hatred of the man he's expected to call 'Dad.'

Suddenly, everything I've been through recently with my own father seems to pale in comparison.

So he didn't know about a stalker that I never even hinted to having? So what, he's kept secrets? At least he's never physically hurt me, and I know for a fact that he never would. Or anyone I love.

I study Jonas as he looks down at his son with what I'm sure is fake concern in his eyes. Unlike my father, and Nico's, who I've finally met, Jonas shows no signs of being part of the chase for that scumbag on Sunday night.

"Were you at the party, Jonas?" I ask him, my voice sickly sweet.

He nods. "I was, yes. It was a great night before... well... you ruined it."

My brows rise in shock.

"Oh, right. Well, yes, I guess I did help to put a dampener on things. I'm not sure it's entirely my fault though."

"Hmm..." he mumbles, clearly not agreeing with me. "Forgive me, Estella—" I bite the inside of my cheeks to stop myself from demanding he calls me Stella. I might not be a fan of my full name, but this cunt has no right to call me by the same name as my friends, as people I actually like. "But before you arrived, none of our events have ended in gunfire and with our soldiers in the hospital."

"With all due respect, Jonas, you're part of a criminal organization. I'd put money on that not being true."

A weird noise rumbles up his throat while Toby's hand squeezes mine, amusement and pride flashing in his eyes. Although, the underlying fear never seems to leave.

"I'll leave you to catch up. I'm sure you've got loads to talk about."

Bending over, I kiss Toby on the cheek. "I'll send one of the guys down."

There's a part of me that wants to make a massive pain in the ass of myself and stay, but I'm not sure I can be in a room with that man any longer, knowing what I know.

It's not until I slip out of the room and suck in a huge gulp of air that I realize that I wasn't actually breathing.

Shaking off the revulsion from having to look that motherfucker in the eyes, I make my way back down to Seb.

"What's wrong?" he asks the second I walk in. Both Theo and Alex jump to their feet immediately.

"Uh... what makes you think something is wrong?" I ask, not sure if I'm horrified or impressed with how quickly he can read me.

"You're as white as a sheet."

"I'm okay. I just had the pleasure of meeting Jonas."

"He's here?" Alex asks, looking shocked.

Seb and I share a look. As far as I know, it's only the two of us who are aware of how bad the situation is with Toby's family.

"Y-yeah?"

"That fucker never turns up when Toby needs him. He's up to something."

He's gone from the room before I can even get a word out.

"Come here, baby," Seb says, holding his hand out for me.

It's not until I move toward him that I notice he's dressed. "Going somewhere?"

"Yeah, home with my girl."

My stomach flutters at his words, and my lips twitch in a smile.

"At least he's out of action for a while. I might get some peace," Theo mutters, but we both ignore him.

"Are you sure you're okay to leave?"

"Princess," Seb warns. "You discharged yourself after being stabbed and got on a long-haul flight. I've got a clean bullet wound—"

"And ripped stitches," I add, just to make a point about his stubborn streak.

"And ripped stitches," he repeats. "And I'm just going home to be looked after by my private nurse."

"I see. And what are you expecting this nurse to do for you exactly?"

"And that's my cue to leave," Theo says, pushing from the chair and walking toward the door. "I'll be waiting in the car."

Seb doesn't even look up as his friend leaves.

"So I was thinking," he says, walking his fingers up my thigh. "If I ordered you one of those little nurse uniforms, you could—"

"Nice try, asshole."

"I saved your life, baby. A little appreciation would go a long way right now."

A laugh rips from my throat. "Yeah, sure, big guy." I pat him on the chest—the non-injured side—but before I manage to pull it away, he captures my wrist and brings my palm to his mouth.

"You need me, baby," he growls, his eyes holding mine as his lips and then his tongue brush over my skin.

My stomach clenches as heat blooms between my legs.

Damn him.

"Almost as badly as I need you."

"Seb." It's meant to come out as a warning, but it's nothing more than a breathy moan.

"If I didn't think that Janice was due back any minute with my meds then I might suggest you do something about this." He pushes my hand lower until I have no choice but to wrap my fingers around his hardness.

"Sebastian." This time there's a little more strength to his name.

"It's been days, baby. I'm dying over here."

Rolling my eyes at him, I jump up and drag my hand away just in time for Janice to join us.

She takes one look at our guilty faces and shakes her head, amusement playing on her lips.

"Ready to get out of my hair, young man?" she asks Seb, keeping her knowing eyes on his.

I don't know what his issue is with her—she's always been lovely to me. But then I didn't like Seb when I first got to know him either, so maybe I shouldn't be surprised. He can be an arrogant prick when he wants to be. And I can only imagine what a pain in the ass he was when I forced him to live in the hallway.

Regret floods me for how I treated him during my hospital stay, but then I remember all the things he did to me and it starts to ebb away a little.

Yeah, we're pretty much as bad as each other.

"I've got your pain relief, which you *will* take," she states, pinning him with a knowing look.

"Yes ma'am," he responds sarcastically

"Don't worry, I'll make sure he takes them," I tell her.

"Good. Listen to her, Sebastian. She's got a good head on her shoulders."

"She's got a lot of good things on her body, Janice."

"Jesus Christ," I mutter, grabbing some of his things that are still littered around the room and stuffing them into his bag.

"You're a brave woman, you know that?" she asks me, passing me the bag from the pharmacy.

"Brave or stupid. Jury's still out."

She chuckles as she heads for the door.

"Your paperwork is all good, young man. You're free to leave. And," she adds before she disappears around the corner, "I'll be happy to never see you two in one of my beds again." She pins us with a stern look before leaving us alone again.

"Like I'd willingly be back," Seb mutters as he drags himself from the bed.

"You love her really."

"Hmm. Come on, girlfriend. Let's go home."

"Sounds good to me."

I might not have had much choice about spending the first night here, but there was no way I was leaving while he was admitted, no matter how much everyone insisted I do. I guess I was just lucky that he didn't give me a taste of my own medicine and leave me to sleep on the chairs out in the hall.

CHAPTER FOUR

Sebastian

"Thought you were waiting in the car?" I ask when Theo emerges from Toby's room.

"I was, but Jonas left as I was heading out."

"Wow, he really put the effort in there," Stella mutters beside me.

"Is everything okay?" I ask, not liking the darkness in my best friend's eyes.

"Y-yeah. Come on, let's get you home."

When I glance through the window to Toby's room, I find Alex still sitting beside him, but Toby is out cold.

We need to have a conversation about what went down on Sunday night, but now isn't the time.

"Yeah," I agree, taking a step forward as Stella wraps her arm around my waist as if she's going to be able to stop me from falling should my legs decide to give out.

It's amusing, but I don't deter her. Any excuse for her to touch me.

Theo is silent the whole way home, and it doesn't help settle the dread that's sitting heavy in my stomach.

The second we pull up outside the coach house, Stella pushes the door open and hops out, ready to help me.

"Bro, what's going on?" I ask quickly, in case he doesn't want to say whatever's nagging at him in front of Stella.

His eyes find mine in the mirror.

"Nothing."

I know he's lying, but the second Stella opens my door, he climbs out and disappears inside the house before us.

"What's got his panties in a bunch?"

"Fuck knows. But it looks like you're going to have to carry me up the stairs yourself, Princess."

She looks me up and down once I'm standing before her.

"Yeah, that's not happening," she scoffs. "I'm sure you've got this covered."

Theo's already disappeared into the room by the time we both get upstairs. Following his lead, we do the same. And we don't emerge until Stella slips out to grab our takeout and to get drinks.

I smile as I listen to Stella laughing in the living room with Calli and Emmie. They turned up a little over an hour ago to rescue her from my grumpy arse—their words, not mine.

As much as I might want to lock her in here with me to ensure she's safe, and of course to look after me, I know I can't.

She hasn't even suggested leaving the house, which makes me happy, but I know I'm on borrowed time. She might seem a little more concerned after the events of Sunday night, but she's never going to be the kind of person to shy away from danger. I know she wants to catch this fucker as much as we do. I just fear she's going to do something stupid to make it happen.

The door opens and I look toward it excitedly, hoping to see her white-blonde hair poke inside. Only, I quickly realise I'm not that lucky.

"Hey, how's it going?" I ask Theo as he closes the door behind him.

When he turns to me, I see the same dark and tormented look in his eyes as on the way home from the hospital yesterday.

He slumps into my chair after dumping the abandoned clothes on the floor.

"You knew, didn't you?"

"About what?" I ask, needing a little more information than that.

"About Jonas. Maria."

"Uh..." I hesitate, guilt swamping me for keeping something like that from him. Theo, Alex, and I don't have secrets—or at least, we never used to. But now with Stella, things are different. "It wasn't my story to tell, man," I say, rubbing the back of my neck.

"I know, I get that. But shit. How didn't we fucking know?" he asks, pain evident in his tone, his face pulled tight as he thinks about what Toby's been through alone.

"Because he didn't want us to. The same way only you guys know the truth about my mum."

"Fuck. I hate this. I knew Jonas was a prick, but fuck..."

"I know. Toby needs to find a way to put an end to that fuck. I have no idea what he's got over him, but it can't be enough to keep him fucking breathing."

"Agreed."

Theo chews on his bottom lip, deep in thought.

"Spit it out," I demand.

"Do you think Jonas has something to do with all this shit with Stella?"

"No," I say confidently. "If he wanted her dead, if he wanted to punish Galen, then he just... would. This isn't his style."

"Torture isn't his style? Did you not listen to the kind of control he has over Toby and Maria? I think this is exactly his style."

"I know, but... this is different. I just... no."

Theo studies me as I consider this line of thought once more.

"Okay," Theo finally concedes. "But who is it?"

"Million fucking dollar question," I mutter as another howl of laughter comes from the living room.

"This is fucking weird, man. There are chicks hanging out in my house."

"You love it," I say, waving him off.

"Do I?" His brow quirks as he stares at me.

"Calli is cool. It's nice to see her actually leave her bedroom for once. And Emmie seems—"

"Like a royal pain in the ass," he finishes for me.

"Seriously, what is your deal with her? You usually go for that type."

"I do not," he argues.

"Sure," I breathe, sliding off the bed and heading toward the bathroom, pissed off with the sling holding my arms that Stella insists I keep wearing. "Hot emo girls are totally your thing." I close the door behind me before he can come up with a response, although something suspiciously hard does collide with the wood a few seconds later.

Touchy fucker. He's totally imagining banging her six ways from Sunday.

I expect to find my room empty when I emerge, so he startles me a little when I discover he's standing at my window.

"What is it? Is there something out there?" I ask, a little panicked.

I've been trying to play it off a little for Stella's sake. I know Sunday night is still haunting her—I see it every time I look into her eyes—but I'd be lying if I said I wasn't a little on edge, waiting to see what comes next from this motherfucker.

"Nothing. Everything is fine."

I come to stand beside him, looking out into the

darkness beyond. The house in front of us is lit up, his family inside doing whatever they do. Or more so, his mum and the kids. I'm sure Damien is nowhere to be seen, as per usual.

"I wish I knew what his next move is going to be."

"You and me both."

My eyes scan what little I can see, but there's nothing. No one. Not that I was really expecting to. He has to be a real fucking stupid cunt to try something at the boss's home.

But then, I guess he is going up against us all. He must think he's really something special if he believes for even a second that he's going to win.

"Hey, what are you doing?" Stella asks, bursting through the door behind us.

"Nothing," I say, turning my back on the window and pushing my free hand into my pocket, running my eyes down the length of her.

She's wearing one of my hoodies and just a small pair of shorts underneath that have vanished. The level of tease is almost unbearable. And if I didn't trust Theo explicitly, or was pretty convinced both Calli and Emmie are straight, I'd be demanding she change. Because damn.

"Stop getting ideas, bro. You're still on a sex ban, remember?" Theo quips, sounding way too fucking happy about it.

"I haven't forgotten," I grunt. How fucking can I when she walks around like that?

"You coming to hang? Emmie brought doughnuts."

"I'm in," I say, unable to refuse the offer of being with my girl and doughnuts.

Pushing from the window, I walk right up to her, threading my fingers through her hair at the nape of her neck, and slam my lips down on hers.

"Mmm, tastes like you've started without us," I whisper, licking across her bottom lip.

"You get the leftovers," she confesses.

"You taste like heaven, baby."

Sweeping my tongue into her mouth, I drag her body against mine, ignoring the pain in my shoulder. It's so fucking worth it.

"Fucking dying for you, Hellion."

She moans into my kiss, letting me know that the feeling is most definitely mutual as she sags into my hold.

Something hard hits me around the head, forcing me to release her.

"What the fuck, man?" Theo stands behind me, unable to get out of the room because we're blocking the doorway.

"Sex ban."

"You need to get laid, bro. Seriously, all this stress is bad for your health."

He stares at me, his face impassive.

"Get out of the fucking way."

With a snorted laugh, Stella takes my hand and leads me down to the living room, where Calli and Emmie are sitting on the sofas around a huge box of doughnuts.

My stomach growls at the sight.

"You've looked better, Seb," Emmie deadpans.

"I got fucking shot. What about it?"

"I see they didn't install any humour while you were in the hospital."

I flip her off and reach for one of the chocolate-covered doughnuts.

Her lips part as if she's about to give me some more sass, but Theo joins us, and the second she looks up and spots him, whatever biting remark that was about to fall from her seems to shrivel up and die.

Pulling her mask on along with her usual grimace when she looks in Theo's direction, she reaches out for the pinkest doughnut left in the box.

"Here, take this one." The way she says it makes my teeth shiver, it's so sickly and fake.

"Why? Laced it with rat poison?"

"Yep. I'm looking forward to watching your insides melt."

"And they say romance is dead," I mutter around my mouthful of sweetness.

Stella and Calli laugh, but both Emmie and Theo scowl at each other.

He must decide the risk of poisoning isn't all that great, though, because after a couple of seconds he reaches for the offending doughnut and stuffs almost the entire thing in his mouth, much to Emmie's disgust.

"Thanks," he mumbles, marching to the kitchen for a drink before disappearing to his room and slamming the door behind him.

"You should go cheer him up," Stella suggests.

"Fuck off. His attitude is not my issue."

"I dunno, I reckon you could probably help each other work out some stress," I say, feeling brave with there being a coffee table between us.

"What the fuck are you trying to say?" she growls.

"That you look about as uptight as him."

She huffs in frustration. "I'm not uptight."

"No? Do your dad and Miss Hill keep you up all night with their—"

"Shut the fuck up," she hisses, her face twisting in anger.

"What? They are banging, right? I knew it was her with some rough looking biker in the car park last week."

"He's not rough," Emmie spits while both Calli and Stella laugh.

"No, he's not. He's hot as fuck is what he is."

"I'm sorry?" I ask, my brows lifting, and I rear back and look at my girl through new eyes.

"Emmie's dad. He's hot," she confirms.

"He's like... forty."

"Hardly. You need to look closer."

"So what are you saying, then? That I'm too young for you?"

She thinks for a moment, and I brace myself for what's going to come next.

"I mean... you're okay for now. But you know, never say never. Emmie's dad might get bored with Miss Hill and might be willing to trade for a younger model."

An unamused laugh falls from my mouth while Calli falls about giggling. Even Emmie cracks a smile, making me wonder if there actually is something in the doughnuts.

Throwing the rest of mine into the box, I slip my bad arm from its sling and jump on top of Stella, pinning her arms above her head and trapping her thighs between my knees.

"What was that, baby?"

Her chest heaves as she stares up at me.

"Oh shit. We might have to leave. They've both got that look."

"What's *that* look?" Stella asks without ripping her eyes from mine.

"We're about to start a marathon fuck fest, and we don't care who watches," Emmie announces happily.

"How would you even know that? I haven't fucked her in front of you... yet."

Stella's eyes darken at my words. My little hellion is just as up for a little exhibitionism as I am.

"And you're not about to start now," Calli says, grabbing another doughnut and getting up. "Em, you coming, or did you want to watch? I know it's been a while, but surely you haven't forgotten how it works."

A laugh rumbles in my throat, but my eyes don't leave my girl.

It doesn't escape my attention that both Emmie and Theo seem to be in the same boat. Maybe they really could make use of each other. It's got to be better than them killing each other. Unless Emmie wasn't lying about the rat poison and he's already dead in his room, of course.

"See you later, cous," Calli calls through Theo's

door, but she doesn't get a response. "Idiot," she mutters, lacing her arm through Emmie's and leading her toward the door. "What? Did you want to go check on him?" Calli asks when Emmie doesn't immediately move to leave with her.

"What? No, of course not," she spits. "Have fun, kids. Try not to make a mess on Theodore's sofa." Hearing Theo's full name makes Stella's brows pinch.

"What?" I ask.

"I've never thought about his whole name."

Dropping my head, I nuzzle her neck. "I'm glad. Hopefully, that means you were thinking about me instead," I growl against her, damn near drowning in her sweet scent and the softness of her skin.

"Or Emmie's dad," she suggests bravely. "Oh my God, Seb," she squeals when I dig my fingers into her side, tickling her.

She thrashes about beneath me, allowing me to push my hoodie up, exposing her belly and sports bra.

"Seb," she cries when I don't let up.

My shoulder screams in pain, but seeing her smile beneath me makes it more than worth it.

Wrapping my fingers around the fabric covering her tits, I drag it up, exposing her and immediately dropping my lips to one of her nipples, sucking it deep into my mouth.

"Oh God," she moans loudly, her back arching, offering more of herself to me.

Her fingers thread into my hair, holding me in place. Not that I'd be going anywhere. I haven't had her since Sunday, and that's entirely too long.

My lips are still teasing her breasts, making her moan for more when I shift, dragging her shorts and knickers down her legs and throwing them over my shoulder.

"Need to taste you, baby."

Dropping to my knees, I drag her arse over the edge of the cushion.

"Yes," she cries, spreading her legs for me before I get a chance to do it myself. "Fucking knew you were just as desperate as me."

I growl, pressing my palms against her thighs and spreading her wider.

Her cunt glistens with arousal, and my mouth waters.

"Seb, please," she begs when all I do is stare at her.

"You've got such a pretty pussy, baby."

"I'm glad, but could you stop fucking looking at it and touch it instead?" she demands, making me laugh.

"Only because you asked so nicely."

CHAPTER FIVE

Stella

"Oh God, yes," I scream when he latches onto my clit and sucks until I don't know where the pain starts and the pleasure ends.

My nails scratch his scalp before my fingers twist in his messy hair in the hope of dragging him closer.

I shouldn't be letting him do it. He should be resting. But fuck.

"Shit," I cry when he pushes two fingers deep inside me, curling them in the way he does that drives me fucking crazy.

My orgasm races forward faster than I ever thought possible as he works with precision. I guess thinking he was fucking dead and then having to hold off for a few days will do that.

"Seb," I cry. "Yes. So close."

I forget about where we are, about who might be listening. All I care about is the pleasure that's right on the brink of exploding within me.

"Come for me, baby," he growls against me, his deep, rumbling voice doing things to me.

He ups his speed, pressing his tongue against my clit that little bit harder. I shatter.

"Seb," I scream as my body convulses and trembles, lighting up like a million fireworks.

He doesn't stop until the last tremors have left my body, and when I glance down at him sitting between my thighs, he's got the widest fucking smile on his face, his mouth and chin glistening with my pleasure.

"Fuck. I love you," he booms, wiping his hand across his mouth and diving for me.

His lips collide with mine in a bruising kiss. Being able to taste myself on him only spurs me on as I drag my feet up his body, tucking my toes under his waistband.

"Fuck, baby," he groans when I expose him and reach down to wrap my fingers around his hard length. "I need inside you, Hellion."

"I'm right here. Take me."

With his hands firmly on my hips, he climbs onto the couch and settles between my legs.

Reaching down, he rubs his cock through my wetness, teasing both of us if the way his abs tense and his jaw tics are anything to go by.

"Seb, just—fuck," I bark when he does exactly as I was about to demand and fills me in one quick thrust.

My pussy ripples around him, adjusting to his sudden invasion.

He stills for a beat as he folds over me, finding my lips. His tongue licks into my mouth, mimicking how his cock moves inside me when he starts rolling his hips.

"I've missed you so much, Hellion."

"I've been right here," I breathe when he tucks his face into my neck.

"I know but... I needed you. This. I was so fucking terrified when I answered your call. I—"

Twisting to the side, I grab his rough face in my hands and drag him so he has no choice but to look at me.

"I'm right here, baby. I'm fine."

"Thank fuck. I'm gonna kill that motherfucker over and over again when we finally get our hands on him."

"Get in line. That sick fuck is mine."

I didn't think it was possible, but at the thought of me killing someone, Seb only gets harder inside me.

"You're perfect." His lips claim mine again, stopping me from responding—not that I'm sure what I'd say even if I could.

"Need more," he groans into our kiss.

"Fuck me, Seb. Take what you need."

Lifting up, he rests his weight on his forearm against the arm rest while he tucks the other against his chest, making guilt slam into me, but when he rolls his hips once more, grazing over all my nerve endings, I forget everything.

"Yes, yes," I cry, encouraging him as he hits that spot over and over.

My second release surges forward.

"Clit, baby. Let me watch you."

Not missing a beat, I skim my hand down my stomach and do exactly what he says.

"Oh shit, yeah," he groans as I tighten down around him, my release hitting me in record time.

In only seconds, a growl rumbles low in his chest as his cock jerks inside me, filling me with hot jets of cum.

He collapses on top of me, both our chests heaving as we fight to catch our breath.

"I'll never get enough of you, Hellion." And as if to prove his point, his cock begins to harden inside me once more.

"You're meant to be resting," I say, finally remembering that I put him on a sex ban when we got back from the hospital.

"We can for a few minutes. Then we can go again."

"Not happening. I need you healed properly so we're ready to take that motherfucker on together."

"You know exactly what to say to make me hard," he murmurs against my throat, his hot breath making goose bumps erupt across my entire body.

I'm too lost to him to hear footsteps in the distance, but I sure as shit hear the door open and Alex announce, "Hey, what's up motherfuck—oh shit."

Both his and Nico's laughter ring out through the air as we both scramble to cover ourselves up.

"Looks like we were five minutes too late," Nico

says, falling down one of the other couches. "Shame. I could do with some excitement tonight."

"You consider watching us fuck as entertainment?"

"Live porn? Hell yeah. If I'm lucky, Seb might even get his knife out and cut you up a little."

"Jesus, Nico," Alex mutters.

"What? Nothing wrong with a little blood play, hey, Princess?"

"Uh... Seb shown you his brand yet?" I ask, turning this away from ever having to agree with Nico on anything remotely sexual.

"Fuck off," Alex barks. "He didn't let you?"

"Too fucking right he did. He owed me." I can't fight my smirk as I remember just how weirdly hot it was, watching that blade slice through his skin.

"Let's see then," Nico says, suddenly looking a little more interested.

They're both in their work suits, but clearly they haven't had a fun day.

"Fuck off, I'm not showing you," Seb grunts, dropping back to the couch beside me and pulling me into his body.

"Don't be a pussy. We want to see the evidence of you handing your balls over to Stella."

"I'm not wearing any underwear."

"Mate, we've seen your cock way more than I'm sure is healthy," Alex points out, making me more than a little curious about the shit the five of them have gotten up to in the past. But then I think about Nico's party—and I guess I have my answer.

"Go on." I nudge him gently, more than happy to be on the guys's side.

"For fuck's sake," he grumbles, shoving his sweats down once more and cupping his dick as he exposes his inner thigh for his friends.

"Fucking hell, I thought she was joking," Alex barks, clapping his hands in amusement.

"Nope," Seb says, almost smugly, as he covers himself back up again. "She owns my arse. Don't care who knows it."

Wrapping his arm around my shoulder, he pulls me close and drops a kiss to my head as Nico starts gagging.

"Fucking weirdo," he mutters, clearly having never met a woman who's really given him a run for his money and kept him on his toes. It'll happen one day, and it'll be amusing as fuck, I'm sure.

"Where the fuck is Theo?" Alex asks, dragging a joint from his wallet and putting it between his lips.

Seb sniggers beside me, I assume thinking the exact same thing I am.

"In his room. I'm guessing that since his music isn't up loud he's getting off to my girl screaming my name."

"Fucking hell," I mutter. I might have been thinking it, but it didn't need saying out loud. "I'm gonna go and clean up."

Dropping a kiss to Seb's lips, I slip from his hold, grab my discarded panties and head down the hallway.

"Have you two seen Toby today?" I ask before I turn into our room.

"Yeah," Nico says. "He's good. Just bored." I nod,

glad that he hasn't been alone, and slip into the bedroom, but not before Nico continues. "Should be out in a few days. Not that he's looking forward to that much, either."

"He can come here," Seb offers, happily giving away another of Theo's beds.

"And listen to you two fucking every ten minutes? Pretty sure he'd rather take his chances with his cunt of a father," Alex blurts out.

As I head for the bathroom, Seb's cell lights up on the dresser, and I can't help but laugh when I glance down at it and see the preview.

Theo: I fucking hate you.

"Are you really sure you want to do this?" Seb asks for the millionth time since we woke up.

We've barely moved since I opened my eyes and found him watching me sleep. It seems to be his new hobby, and I'm not sure if I love it or am completely freaked out by it.

"Yes," I assure him, tilting my head to look at him.

Reaching up, I run my fingers over his brow, trying to smooth the creases of worry away.

"It's going to be fine."

"I appreciate your positivity, but there's a very slim chance of that being the case."

"Your sisters are awesome, Seb. And I can't wait to meet Phoebe."

A smile curls at his lips at the mention of his niece.

It didn't take me long to figure out who the two beautiful dark-haired women were who turned up in my hospital room on Monday morning. They both shared the same mysterious eyes as the guy next to me.

Both of them were practically tripping over themselves with excitement to meet me, despite the reason both of us were lying in hospital beds.

I knew they were going to be awesome just from the fond way Seb talks about them, but nothing could have prepared me for just how lovely, supportive and protective they were of their little brother.

It warmed my heart to see the depth of their love for him, even in the short time we spent together. After all the loss he's suffered, and the ongoing pain with their mother... I couldn't help but love them both instantly.

And thankfully, they seemed to approve of me as well.

I've never met a guy's family before. Hell, I've never had a serious boyfriend. The day I called Seb that to freak him out, it hit me just as hard.

Moving in with him should have been the big step, but everything about that felt right. But giving him that title? It felt so official. So real. But so right at the same time.

"I want you to meet her too, but—" Seb says, dragging me from my thoughts.

"I know, Seb. But I'd never judge you, her, any of you because of how she's dealt—how she's dealing—

with all this. I want to be a part of your life, the good, the bad, and the ugly, if that's what you want too."

"It is. I've just never..."

"Trust me," I urge, staring up into his dark eyes. "Nothing will scare me off now. I've seen most of the bad already."

"Only most?"

A smile curls at my lips. "I'm sure there's plenty of other shit that you've done that you haven't told me about yet. Like, how many people you've killed and how you did it."

He chuckles lightly but isn't forthcoming with the answers I'm digging for. If he thinks a high body count is going to turn me off him, he clearly doesn't know me very well.

"Today isn't the day, baby," he breathes, dipping down and brushing his lips across mine in the most teasing, gentle kiss.

"You can't distract me with sex, Sebastian," I chastise, although as I say the words, my body automatically leans into his, molding into his side.

"Oh yeah? Would you want to bet on that?" He chuckles as he nuzzles my neck, causing goose bumps to erupt across my entire body.

"You're a bad influence," I breathe as he rolls me onto my back and stares down into my eyes.

"I do try. Now stop distracting me, I'm hungry." He winks before descending my body and making me groan.

My laughter is cut off when he pushes my legs wide and buries his face between them.

By the time we arrive—late—at Seb's family home, my legs are like jelly, and I swear I could nap for the rest of the day.

His hand squeezes mine as we step up to the front door. I don't need to look at him to know he's nervous.

"It's okay, Seb. You don't need to—"

"About freaking time," Zoe announces, swinging the door open wide and smiling right at me. "He actually brought you." She pulls me in for a hug as if we're long lost friends, and I startle at her friendliness. I'm not used to such obvious shows of affection, especially with someone I've just met.

"Come on, dinner is nearly ready."

"Yorkshires?" Seb asks as we step inside and kick our shoes off.

"You have no faith, Bro," Zoe says happily.

"There's a reason," Seb mutters.

I look between the two of them with a smile on my face. I love their banter, but even more, I love the look of pure adoration in both of their eyes as they give each other grief. It's such a relief to see that Seb does have this kind of love in his life, even if his parental situation is beyond fucked up.

The house is nice. It's smaller than Dad's, and certainly smaller than the two Cirillo estate houses, but it's still impressive. And I'm sure with a little TLC it could be an incredible home once again, but as it is, it's totally tired. I understand why; I can't imagine keeping up with maintenance on this place has exactly been top of everyone's priority list.

"Brace yourself," Seb whispers before we walk through to the kitchen.

"Look who finally graced us with his presence," Zoe announces, ensuring that all sets of eyes turn our way.

"Stella," Sophia breathes, putting down the oven gloves in her hand and coming over to hug me too.

"Hey, it's so good to see you again."

The second she releases me, her hands grip my upper arms, holding me in place as she studies me. My cheeks burn, knowing that she'll probably recognize the concealer on my neck that's doing a not-so-great job of hiding the marks Seb left behind on my body this morning.

"Sebastian," she growls, confirming my suspicions, "you're meant to be resting."

"Don't worry, Sis. Stella kept me on bed rest," he quips, walking over to the oven and shocking the fuck out of me when he starts checking on things.

"Does he always do that?" I ask, watching him with amusement as he pulls the milk from the fridge and sets it down by a jug and some eggs.

"Just wait," Sophia mutters, "you're probably about to learn something new about your boy."

I'm too enthralled watching Seb beat some batter that I don't even notice the dark-haired girl toddling her way over to us.

"Mama."

"Come here, baby girl. You need to meet Uncle Sebby's girlfriend."

Hearing someone else call me that fills my belly with butterflies.

Ripping my eyes away from Seb once more I glance back down at his niece.

"Hey, gorgeous girl," I coo at her, and she gives me a wide, toothy smile, immediately holding her arms out for me.

Sophia laughs at her daughter, who's wiggling in her arms to get free.

"I think she likes you. Seems like Seb's not the only one under your spell."

As I take Phoebe from Sophia's arms, I hear Seb mutter, "I knew this was a bad idea."

"Ignore your grumpy uncle," I say to Phoebe in a baby voice. "He's just angry that he's outnumbered by all these awesome women."

"Awesome?" Seb scoffs.

"You know she's talking sense, little brother," Zoe says, slapping him across the head with a spatula.

Pulling out one of the chairs around the table, I sit down with Phoebe still in my arms.

"Where's Mum?" Seb asks hesitantly.

"Putting her face on," Sophia says, pulling the oven open to check on what's inside.

Giving them some privacy, I look back down at Phoebe and start talking nonsense to her as the others continue to move around the kitchen like a well-oiled machine, chatting away and catching up with each other.

It's only a few minutes later that my skin prickles with awareness, and when I look up I find him resting his ass back on the counter, watching me with something like awe in his eyes.

'Hey,' I mouth, smiling at him.

"Hey." He smirks, his teeth biting into his bottom lip seductively. It's totally inappropriate for our current company, but I can't stop the ache of need—despite the number of orgasms he's already given me this morning —tugging at my lower stomach.

"You two need to stop eye fu—" Zoe's words falter when her older sister cuts her a scathing look. "Screwing each other."

"We making you uncomfortable, Zo?" Seb asks with a wicked glint in his eye as he pushes from the counter. "Maybe you should be less weird. Some guy might be interested then."

I'm just about to chastise him for winding up his sister, but I don't get a chance because he's already closed the space between us. Holding my chin in a tight grip, he slams his lips down on mine in a bruising kiss.

"Seriously?" Zoe mutters.

He doesn't pull back until I'm breathless and squirming in my seat. It's completely inappropriate while I have a toddler in my lap, but I can't really find it in myself to care. Especially when I look down and see that Phoebe is staring up at us with the widest goofy grin on her face.

"I think she approves of you, Hellion."

"I think she's utterly besotted by you," I point out as she stares at him like he literally just hung the moon for her.

"Well, yeah. That's because I'm f—" Another growl

rips through the air. "Freaking awesome," Seb finishes, pinning his sister with a death stare. "Come here, beautiful girl."

"No, you shouldn't—" Seb ignores my argument as he plucks Phoebe from my arms and sits with her in the chair beside me.

Her infectious giggles fill the kitchen as he tickles her. Both of them have wide smiles on their faces, and it completely melts my heart.

Feeling eyes on me, I look up to find Sophia and Zoe watching us with a similar soft look on their faces.

Until footsteps sound out from somewhere beyond the kitchen and everyone visibly tenses.

"It'll be okay," I whisper to Seb, reaching over to squeeze his hand.

CHAPTER SIX

Sebastian

My heart pounds throughout my body as Mum's footsteps get closer.

Sophia and I share a look, and I find the same apprehension in her eyes.

Her expression fills me with dread, because I know she's already seen what kind of mood Mum is in, and I really don't want this whole thing to be a disaster. I'd really like for her to meet Stella and just be normal. Just once.

But I fear it might be too much to ask.

The second Mum's feet hit the hallway, I stop breathing.

It seems to take her forever to get through to us, but when she does and I get a look at her, I breathe a huge sigh of relief.

She looks... good. Really good.

It's almost too good to be true.

"Seb, my boy," she says with a wide smile on her face.

I glance at Sophia, who shrugs in a 'just go with it' way, and I push to stand with Phoebe still in my arms.

"Hey, Mum." I close the space between us and drop a kiss to her sunken cheek.

She might look good, better than I've seen her in quite a while, but that's not to say that she looks healthy. Her eyes are still dark, her skin a weird grey colour and her lips thin and puckered. It's clear she's not well despite the effort she's clearly gone to in an attempt to cover it up.

"Where's your—" She scans the kitchen quickly before her eyes land on Stella tucked into the corner at the table. "Girl?" she sighs, her entire face lighting up.

I can't help but smile too, because Stella looks more awkward than I've ever seen her.

It seems that meeting my parents—or my mum, at least—is one thing that cracks her hard shell.

"Hi," she squeaks, looking between Mum and I nervously. "I'm Ste—"

"Stella, I know, sweetie. I've heard so much about you."

"O-oh?" I splutter. I've barely spoken to her since Stella got stabbed, so I know it hasn't come from me.

Mum glances over at Sophia, and I find my answer.

"H-hi, Helen. It's so good to meet you." Stella hops up from her chair and awkwardly moves toward Mum, who immediately wraps her frail arms around my girl and pulls her into her body.

55

I can't help but laugh at the look of shock on Stella's face.

I'm not entirely sure what she was expecting from meeting Mum, but I'd hardly painted her in a great light, so I'm not surprised by her reaction.

"I can't believe my boy has finally met someone. And someone as beautiful as you." Stella backs up again and falls into her chair once more while I lower a wriggling Phoebe to the floor. "You know, when the time comes, you're going to make me gorgeous grandbabies. Just like my little Phoebe, isn't that right, sweetie?" Mum says, bending down to my niece who wobbled straight over to her.

Glancing at Stella, I find a horrified look on her face.

"Don't worry, she's not expecting them anytime soon."

"Am I not?" Mum asks, still looking distracted by her granddaughter but clearly listening to everything happening around her.

"Ignore her," I tell Stella, going back to the oven to check on my Yorkies when the buzzer goes off.

"Have you had one of Seb's Yorkshire puddings before, Stella?" Mum asks, taking the seat I vacated when she came in.

"Uh... no. I actually had no idea he could cook."

"Sebastian," Mum chastises. "You need to cook for your girl. Look after her. Keep her happy."

"Too busy keeping her alive right now," I mutter, much to Sophia and Zoe's amusement and horror.

"I'll make sure he does. We've been kinda busy."

"So I see," Mum mutters, staring at Stella's neck before turning back to me. "I'm starting to wonder if you're secretly a vampire, my dear."

I snort a laugh. She has no idea how close to the truth she is.

"Dinner's ready," I announce happily, hoping to put an end to that line of conversation. The less my mum and sisters know about how Stella and I like to get our kicks, the better.

"I'm excited. It's my first proper English roast dinner."

Mum gives me a scathing look, but there's no malice behind it, just teasing.

"I promise I'll cook for her soon. We can send Theo out, he needs some fun."

"You know you're both always welcome here," Mum says, making my insides twist with guilt.

"I know, Mum," I say, placing down a steaming bowl of potatoes as Sophia brings her golden roast chicken over.

A loud bang from out in the hallway startles all of us. Stella's eyes go wide as she jumps up, her hand going for the gun I know she's got tucked into the back of her jeans almost as quickly as I go for mine.

It might be overkill for dinner with my family, but I'm taking no fucking chances.

Loud footsteps head our way as all the air seems to get sucked out of the room.

But the second a person emerges, I breathe a sigh of relief.

"Stand down, Sebby," Jason says, marching in and going straight for my sister.

"Ugh..."

"You made it,' Sophia gushes as Phoebe babbles at the sight of her daddy.

"Sure did. And I found this stray loitering in the driveway. You weren't going to feed him, were you?" Jason asks as Carl joins us.

"He's meant to be security," I point out.

"Come on, bro. We've got enough firepower in here to overpower any motherf—" My sister growls and all of us laugh. She's really fighting a losing battle here.

"Flicker, motherflicker," Jason points out, much to our amusement. "Just let the man eat, yeah?"

"Sure," I concede, pointing to a free chair. "Because that's any better. I'll grab you a plate."

"Appreciate it, man," he says, looking more grateful than I was expecting. Maybe it was a little mean, expecting him to stay outside on his own.

Jason and Carl are practically bouncing in their seats waiting to dish up when I get back.

"Ladies first," Sophia says, chastising the guys.

In only a few seconds, everyone—or the ladies at least—dive in.

I sit back watching as Stella fills her plate, her eyes wide as she focuses on the food. We didn't eat before coming here—well... I did, but not actual food—so I know she's got to be as hungry as me.

As if she can sense my attention, she lifts her head before she takes her first mouthful, her eyes finding mine immediately.

The smile that lights up her face melts my heart.

Seeing her here, having her in the middle of my fucked-up family... it makes my heart ache in the most incredible way.

'I love you,' I mouth across the table, making her smile widen before she returns the sentiment.

Running my eyes over everyone, contentment settles within me.

Mum even looks happy as she eats, and for the first time in... forever, I wonder if there really is a chance of her turning things around. If Stella's presence might have some weird healing powers for her, just like she did for me.

Easy conversation rumbles around the table, and Carl joins in as if he's always been here. I'm not overly happy about him getting too close and witnessing Mum if she has a meltdown, but as it is, she looks like she's holding it together. She's not even drinking. No one is, actually.

It's not until dessert is served that everything goes to shit.

A loud alarm blares from outside somewhere, and Stella immediately jumps up, clearly recognising the sound.

"My car," she blurts out in a panic, racing toward the front of the house.

Jason, Carl, and I are right on her tail.

"Stella, wait, it could be a... trap," I say, knowing it's too late because she's already standing in the middle of the driveway, screaming in frustration.

"You motherfucker," she wails, spinning around on the spot as if she's going to find the culprit.

It's pointless. I think we all know that he's already long gone.

"Fuck. This is my fault. I shouldn't—"

"You weren't to know," I say to Jason, although I have to force the words out through clenched teeth, because he's usually fucking smarter than this.

I guess it was naïve of all of us not to expect that something would happen here.

Stella silently fumes as she stares at her baby's slashed tires and shattered window.

Stepping up to her, I place my hand on her lower back.

"That sick fuck is watching us. Following us," she seethes.

"I know. Told you I should have driven."

She sucks in a breath, ready to snap, but the second she looks into my eyes, all the fight leaves her.

"I'm sorry, baby," I whisper, wrapping my arms around her and holding her tight.

"Why? It's not your fault."

"I haven't caught him yet," I mutter, unable to stop the feeling of failure washing through me. I should be protecting her, yet he just keeps getting in hit after hit, and none of us see it coming.

"This isn't on you, Seb. We'll find him together. Kill him together."

A groan rumbles in my throat at the image her words drag up.

"Now that's something I can get on board with."

Tucking my fingers under her chin, I brush my lips against hers for the briefest moment, more than aware that my entire family is watching us right now.

"Do you think Theo will let me drive his Ferrari while it's getting fixed?" Stella asks with a mischievous glint in her eyes.

Shaking my head, I laugh at her. "Nice try, baby."

She shrugs, looking back over at her beloved Porsche once more.

"Carl, can you get this sorted?" I ask, taking Stella's hand and leading her away. Her poor baby has been through a hell of a time the past few weeks.

"Sure thing."

"What's going on?" Mum asks the second we step back inside the house. Both Sophia and Zoe are well aware of everything that's been happening, but clearly, they decided to keep Mum out of it. Wise.

With her seemingly doing so well, the last thing we want to do is send her back down again quite so soon.

"Just some guy who's trying to intimidate us. Nothing we can't handle."

"Sebastian," Sophia screams from the kitchen, forcing us all to move.

"What's—fuck."

I study Phoebe's ruined teddy in her hand.

It's had the eyes ripped out, and there's a giant slash through its belly, all the stuffing bursting out.

"The back door was open," Zoe says, not really needing to give us any more evidence that he was fucking here. Inside our house.

A violent shudder runs down my spine.

"Sebastian, what's really going on?"

"Fucking hell," I mutter, scrubbing my hand down my face.

This time, Sophia doesn't complain about my language. Instead, a concerned expression washes over her face.

I get it. I feel it too.

"You should probably take Phoebe home. We don't want her around this." *We don't want to make her a target.* I keep that final thought to myself. It doesn't need saying.

We all know what's at stake here.

It would just fucking help if we knew what this motherfucker actually wanted.

I thought it was Stella.

But then he threw me for a loop when he sent me that photo of her, allowing me to find her.

Did he want her dead, or was I meant to find her still breathing?

Was it a test? Was he trying to find out where my loyalties really were with her?

Exhaustion weighs heavily on me as I stare at my sister.

"Yeah," she agrees. "Are you going to be okay? What about Mum? Should I take her with me?"

I glance back at where she's sitting at the table beside Stella.

I want to say yes, but I already know it's not worth the fight.

"She won't go with you, and we both know it."

"I know," my sister sighs sadly.

"Jase, Carl, and I will check the house before you go. Test the alarm and make sure she sets it. But it's not her this sick fuck wants. It's Stella." *I think.* If he's as clever as he's turning out to be, then he should know that hurting Mum isn't going to get him all that far. Especially when we're all pretty much expecting to wake up one morning and discover she's OD'd as it is.

She nods. "Okay. I'll start on this lot."

Leaving her to dispose of the ruined teddy and start cleaning the kitchen, I turn to Mum and Stella.

Letting out a sigh, I drag a chair over.

"Are you both okay?"

By the time we'd cleaned up the mess we'd made in the kitchen and made sure that the house was secure, my shoulder was aching—not that I was going to openly admit that—and I was more than ready to take my girl home.

Confident that Mum was safe and that she wasn't going to do anything stupid, Carl drove us both home, promising to have Stella's baby delivered back as good as new.

Theo was out, so after instructing me to sit my arse down on the sofa, Stella made us both a seriously impressive hot chocolate with all the trimmings, sat down beside me, and stared at whatever I'd thoughtlessly put on the TV.

Melancholy ripples through the room, the TV

barely even loud enough to hear as we lose ourselves in our thoughts.

"This isn't going to end, is it?" Stella says sadly after the longest time of just hugging her mug in her hands.

"Of course it is. We're smarter than him." Although, the words taste bitter on my tongue as I even say them. He's proving that he is, in fact, smarter than us time and time again.

"It doesn't seem to be getting us very far right now, Seb."

"I know. I just..." I trail off, not really having anything to say. "Evan is running the security footage at Mum's place, see if we can see anything. If not, we just need to trust that we can outsmart him at some point."

Stella swallows nervously. "We need to get out and give him opportunities to strike. We can't allow him to follow us to school with this shit. We can't put all those lives at risk."

"Agreed. But I don't think he'd be stupid enough to try something at school. The security in that place is insane."

"So you're saying maybe that's the place to catch him?"

"Maybe. But you're right about everyone else. He's already caused enough damage."

She lets out a sigh and settles back into the cushions once more, resting her feet in my lap.

"I hate this," she says, sounding exhausted.

"It'll get better. I fucking promise you."

CHAPTER SEVEN

Stella

By Friday evening, everything was beginning to get to be too much. Toby was still in the hospital despite being told he should be able to be discharged soon. Seb and I have spent all week out of the house, wandering aimlessly around London in the hope of dragging this fuck out of hiding, forcing something to happen.

Nothing has.

And I'm going out of my mind.

I know he's doing it on purpose to freak me out. It's how it's worked in the past. He leaves it long enough for me to think he's got bored and found someone else to torment, and then boom, there he is, blowing shit up right in front of my face. I mean, not literally. Not yet, anyway.

I think everyone else is feeling a little the same, because it's the beginning of the weekend and we're all just lounging around at Theo's, drinking beer. I can't imagine it's the guys' usual way to spend a Friday night —Nico and Alex especially, as they seem to be the biggest party animals of the group.

I'm just about to suggest we do something when all of their cells ping simultaneously.

Glancing over at Seb, I watch as he pulls his cell from his sweats and stares at the screen at the same time everyone else does.

"We should go," Nico says.

"Go where?" I ask, feeling left out.

Seb passes his cell over for all the fucking good that does, because all I find is an address staring back at me from an unknown number.

"Helpful," I mutter, passing it back.

"It's for a fight," Theo says, filling in some of the blanks.

"Like, an underground fight?" I ask, my interest more than piqued.

"Yeah. It's in an hour in an old hotel across town."

"So... what are we waiting for? Nico is right, we should go."

"I'm not sure it's—"

"Seb," I say, scooting to the edge of the couch. "We need to be out. We need to lure this fuck from his hiding place. And I can't imagine a better way to spend our Friday night than to watch a couple of guys beat the shit out of each other."

His brow quirks. "Really?" he asks, his eyes

darkening as other ideas for how we could spend the night.

"Do you know who's fighting?" Theo asks Alex.

"No. Xander has been gunning for another shot in the ring, though, so maybe him."

"We're going," I announce, jumping to my feet and placing my hands on my hips, waiting for one of them— Seb mainly—to argue.

But to my surprise, when he speaks there is no argument.

"You heard the princess. Get your shit together."

"Give me thirty, I need to change."

I glance down at my sweats and oversized hoodie and cringe. Yeah, I definitely need to change.

Theo catches my eye as I spin around, and an idea hits me.

Grabbing my cell the second I'm in the bedroom, I shoot Emmie a message.

This kind of thing has her name all over it.

Stella: Wanna go out?

Emmie: YES! I'm bored AF. Where we going?

I consider her question for a moment, my finger tapping on the side of my cell.

Stella: It's a secret, but I think you'll love it.

Emmie: Oh, mysterious. What am I wearing?

Stella: Your normal shit. We'll pick you up. 45 mins.

She sends me a thumbs up and I put my cell down to get ready.

Racing to the bathroom, I have the quickest shower of my life before pulling on an old band tee, fishnets, and a pair of hot pants that barely cover my ass.

After curling my hair, which is in desperate need of a freshening up—the silver is fading and exposing the warmer tones beneath that I banished a few years ago—I pile on the black eye makeup and add the darkest red I've got to my lips.

I'm spraying myself with my favorite perfume when Seb slips into the room.

"Whoa, you borrowing Emmie's clothes now?"

Spinning around to look at him, I narrow my eyes. "Funny. You going like that?" I ask, glancing down at his grey sweats that give me a nice tease as to what he's rocking beneath.

"Looking at me like that, you're making me not want to go anywhere but this room, Hellion."

"Rein it in, Sebastian. We're going out. I wanna see some big bad gangsters lose some blood."

Dragging his shirt over his head and dropping his sweats, showing me everything he's got seeing as he's commando beneath, he pulls on a pair of boxer briefs and reaches for some clean clothes.

"There's something wrong with you, you know that, right?" he asks, his voice teasing.

"Takes one to know one."

Sitting on the edge of the bed, I pull on my heeled biker boots and do up the buckles.

"You ever been in the ring?"

"Not for a proper fight. I've only trained with the guys. Alex, Daemon and Nico fight, though."

"Oh yeah?" I knew they had skills from the day we all sparred down in the gym, but it never occurred to me that they might actually fight, like, for real.

"They don't really agree to fights during the football season because Coach hands them their arses when they turn up half dead after."

"So they're not very good then?" I deadpan.

He chuckles. "Yeah, actually they are."

I nod, pushing to my feet once more, grabbing my purse and throwing it over my shoulder.

Walking up behind Seb, I wrap my arms around his waist, resting my chin on his shoulder, thanks to the extra inches my boots provide.

"Hey," I say, capturing his eyes in the mirror in front of him.

"Why do I get the feeling you're about to ask me for something that I'm not going to like?"

"Because I am," I respond with a smile.

"Go on."

"We're picking up Emmie on the way."

He lets out a sigh. "Really?"

"Yep. It's totally her thing, don't you think?"

"Probably," he admits. "The guys won't be happy."

"Fuck the guys. It's my night too, and I want one of my girls there."

"You couldn't have just invited Calli?"

"You think she'd have any interest in watching a couple of guys beat the shit out of each other?"

"Not for a second, but at least we wouldn't have to put up with her and Theo eye-fucking each other all night."

I can't help but laugh.

"Maybe we should send them in the ring. Make them hash out whatever it is that's going on between them."

"It's fight night, baby. Not live porn night."

Releasing his waist, I swat his shoulder playfully.

"You're a nightmare."

"You can break the news to Theo."

"Or we can send him with the others and we'll turn up with his little surprise in tow."

Seb shakes his head in amusement. "You're playing with fire," he warns.

"Yep, it's fun. Now let's go." Yanking the door open, I march through it to where the guys are still waiting.

"Holy shit," Alex blurts out before damn near choking on his beer.

Nico slaps him on the back, way too hard, in order to help him out.

"Yeah, I think you fucking got it," he complains, punching Nico in the shoulder.

"You look banging, Princess," Nico says, lazily running his eyes down my body.

"Do you want to make it to the fucking fight?" Seb growls from behind me.

"All right, chill the fuck out, man. I've hardly bent her over the sofa and fucked her."

"The fact that you're thinking about it is bad enough," Seb mutters.

"Fuck's sake," Theo says, collecting up the bottles and dumping them in the kitchen. "Let's go before fight night ends up being here."

Grabbing a jacket, he pushes his arms through it before dragging his gun from the drawer and tucking it into the back of his pants.

"You got yours?" Seb asks me, and I pat my purse.

"Good to go. My knife is in my pocket, too."

"Good. Stella and I are driving separately. We'll meet you there," he tells the others as they make their way down the stairs toward the garage.

"Why?" Alex calls back. "Need to make a pit stop for a little alone time?"

"Nope. We'd have happily done it just now with you all listening."

"Yeah, don't we fucking know it," Theo shouts back.

"Jealousy isn't a good look, bro. Maybe we can find you a girl tonight."

"At a fight? Un-fucking-likely."

"We'll see," I whisper, quiet enough so that only Seb can hear me.

He shrugs, and I laugh in accomplishment.

Alex and Nico pile into Theo's Maserati, and Seb opens his passenger door for me as I stare at Theo's Ferrari with longing.

"Why thank you, kind sir," I mock when I turn my attention back to him.

My ass is only seconds away from hitting the leather when he reaches out and grasps my throat.

His eyes flick between mine and my dark lips as my heart rate picks up.

"You want kind, Hellion, you're with the wrong guy."

I smirk at him, daring him to prove it.

"Later," he breathes, reading my silent words.

He releases me, and I fall into the seat in a heap and let out a groan of frustration.

"You okay?" He shoots me a wicked look as he drops into the seat beside me and starts the car, his sexy hands wrapping around the wheel and doing crazy things to my insides.

I bite down on my bottom lip as I imagine what those fingers would feel like, stretching me open and—

"Hellion," Seb growls.

Schooling my features, I drag my eyes away from him and look out of the windshield.

"We're going to be late."

I don't need to look over to know he's smiling at me. I can sense it.

After a beat, he pulls out of the garage and guns it from the driveway toward Emmie's part of the city.

She lives on the other side of Knight's Ridge College. Since doing a little bit of Googling after she confessed to who her grandfather is, I've discovered that she lives right on the edge of the Royal Reapers' territory, whereas we're obviously right in the middle of the Cirillo Family's.

My need to know if Seb is aware of who Emmie is related to is almost too much to contain as we get closer to her house, but I just about manage to swallow the question down. Something tells me that if he knew, he'd say something about it. Guilt twists my insides that I haven't told him, but then I figure that it's not my secret to tell. It's Emmie's life, and I respect her need to keep it away from the guys.

I found some old newspaper articles from a few years ago that alluded to the fact the Reapers and the Cirillos have some bad blood in their past, and I'd hate to be the reason the guys—Theo—had any more issue with Emmie. Assuming *he* doesn't already know exactly who she is.

The back door to the car opening startles me.

"Hey bitches," Emmie says happily, dropping into the back seat.

"You okay?" Seb whispers, noticing that I got lost in my own head for a bit there.

"Yeah, I'm good." I smile at him before turning toward the heavily made-up girl in the back seat. "Whoa, your makeup is on point, Em."

"Thanks. I was bored and actually did it before you even messaged. It was just meant to be. So, where are we going?"

"You wanna watch some dudes beat the shit out of each other?"

"Depends on whether Theo is the one getting his head kicked in," she deadpans, making Seb snigger beside me.

"Probably not, but I can offer you two randomers going at it."

"I guess I'll have to take that, then. So what is this, some underground mafia shit?"

"No," Seb answers. "You ever heard of The Circuit?"

"Holy shit, we're going to a Circuit fight?" she asks, suddenly sounding more excited than I've ever heard her. "You guys get invites?"

"Sure do."

"Lucky arseholes. I've been trying to get on the list for-fucking-ever."

"Clearly you have the wrong contacts."

Emmie's eyes meet mine in the mirror. Her gratitude for me not telling Seb who she is is clear in her eyes.

The ride to the venue is short, and seconds after parking in the makeshift lot out the back of the derelict hotel, the three of us climb out of the car.

"Are you okay leaving it out here?" I ask, looking around at the beat-up cars and bikes around us.

"Yeah, no one would dare touch it." *Other than him.* Seb doesn't need to say those words. I hear them loud and clear.

"There are a lot of bikes here," Emmie comments, her eyes scanning the array of models.

"The Circuit pulls in fighters from the local MC as well as us and a few other organizations."

"Organizations?" Emmie asks with a raised brow.

"Fine. Gangs. Better?"

"Much. Let's just call it as it is, yeah? So, a room full of bloodthirsty bikers and mafia. What could possibly go wrong tonight?" she asks lightly as we make our way to a door that's being guarded by a couple of leather-cut-wearing scary dudes.

Seb goes on ahead, clearly recognizing them, and Emmie steps into my side.

"This might have been a really bad idea," she whispers, pulling the hood up as if she feels the need to hide.

"How many members of the club do you know?"

"Not many, but a lot know me."

"Shit," I hiss, realizing that I might not have thoroughly thought this through. "You want to be here though, right?"

"Hell yes! I've been begging my uncle to come for ages, but apparently, I'm too young and innocent or some bullshit."

I can't help but snort a laugh. "Does your uncle know you at all?"

"I think it's more that he's scared of my dad's reaction, to be honest. Dad doesn't know I've been hanging out with Cruz, and he'll kill me if he finds out."

"If?" I ask.

"Okay, when. I just... ugh... I want to know who I am. My history."

"Trust me, I get that. So we spend the night in the shadows."

"Or I just man up and tell the guys who I really am. Do you really think they don't know?"

"Seb clearly doesn't," I whisper.

"No, but does Theo?"

"Probably. I get the impression that fuckwit knows everything."

"Yeah, he is a bit like that, huh. Fuck it," she says, throwing her hood back off. "Who gives a fuck if they know. I'm sure no one will even recognise me."

"Come on then, Princess Emmie," I quip, earning me a death glare which I'm sure would make many others cower.

Standing a little taller, she links her arm through mine and we finally join Seb, who introduces me but thankfully ignores Emmie.

"So who's fighting tonight?" Emmie asks as we descend the stairs toward the basement.

With each step we take, the temperature increases and the excitement gets louder. The scent of the old, forgotten building mixes with male sweat and makes my nose wrinkle.

"Xander and Joker."

"Oh sweet, it should be a good night then," she shouts over the increasingly loud music that booms from beneath us. The confidence in her voice shows that she really does know what she's talking about, and Seb shoots me a confused look.

I just shrug it off, but I don't think for a second that Emmie is going to get out of tonight without being discovered.

I'm just not sure if that's going to be a good thing or

not. Hopefully the former. Maybe if Theo doesn't already know, finding out might make him look at her a little differently.

I shake my head at my own thoughts. They're bullshit. Of course he knows.

We're engulfed by the darkness at the bottom of the stairs and surrounded by a thick cloud of smoke, both cigarette and weed.

"Jesus," I cough as my eyes water.

"You'll soon get used to it. Come on, let's go find the guys and deliver Theo's gift."

I laugh, threading my arm through Emmie's and allowing Seb to drag us toward a makeshift bar built of old crates.

With three warm beers in hand, Seb continues fighting through the crowd, most of which are already drunk and more than ready for a little bloodshed.

We're pushed and jostled as we make our way through the bodies who are standing in front of the ring. Once we're almost through, I spot Theo, Alex, Daemon and Nico standing in what looks like some kind of VIP area.

Of course. I can barely control the need to roll my eyes as I stare at the four of them standing there like they fucking own the place.

"Is this a Cirillo event?" I ask in Seb's ear as we finally break free of the crowd.

"No. The Circuit is neutral. Mickey uses fighters from all the London organizations. Anyone who will bring him the money. But this fight is on our territory, so we get a cut of the profits and take control of security, that kind of thing."

"So you all knew this was happening before the message came through?" I ask with my brows pulled tight.

"No. Evan and Jonas work with Mickey. They'll have sorted everything. We don't automatically find out unless we ask, Alex, Daemon or Nico are fighting, or we're needed for security."

I nod as we step up to the others, and I can't help smiling when Theo's face morphs into one of pure fury at the sight of the girl behind me.

What the fuck is his actual problem?

"Stella," he growls.

"What? I brought a friend. Suck it up, Cirillo."

His eyes flick between mine and Seb's as if he's waiting for Seb to what... tell me off for asking him to pick up Emmie?

Ugh. Conceited asshole.

"Whatever," he mutters, waving us off and disappearing through the crowd.

"Uh oh... looks like you poked the already angry bear, Princess," Alex mutters lightly.

"He needs to get over himself," I mutter, watching him get swallowed up into the crowd.

Alex shrugs. "Your friend gets him all kinds of crazy."

"He's a dick, and we're better off without him," Emmie announces, tipping her bottle to her lips. "What time is the main event?" she asks, forgetting all about Theo's reaction to her.

"Thirty minutes. Just a few warm-up fights first." Nico cracks his knuckles as if imagining stepping inside the ring himself.

"Boys!" a deep voice booms as an older, tattooed, rough-looking guy steps up to us. He's got scars on his face and a nose that looks like it's been broken one too many times. Mickey, I assume.

"Mickey, how's it going, man?" Alex asks. "Long time no see."

"Had to keep our heads down after the bust on the last fight."

My brows lift as I listen, intrigued.

"That was a fucking crazy night."

"Well, fingers crossed tonight runs a little more smoothly."

"Fucking better, I need the money after that shit show. So who are you betting on, boys?"

I drift off when they start talking about fighters' stats and turn to Emmie, who's got an unusual smile on her face.

"What's got you so happy?" I ask with a smile of my own. Hers is infectious.

"This. I've wanted this for as long as I've known it's existed. But Dad keeps everything about this side of our lives locked up tight. Cruz is helping me discover it all, but he's not exactly happy about it. Something tells me he's actually scared of my father. Not that he'd ever admit it."

"Your dad's in the club though, right?"

She shakes her head. "No. He got out when my

mum was pregnant with me. He didn't want this life for me."

"How's that going for him?"

"Well, right now, he's too busy with Piper to notice what I'm up to. So I'd say good."

"Piper?" I ask.

"Miss Hill."

"Ooooh. He's gonna lose his shit when he finds out. I bet he's hella hot when he's mad."

"Shut up, you idiot." She slaps me on the shoulder lightly, laughing at my comment. "He's actually scary as fuck, but I'm sure I can handle it." She winks, and the innocent face she puts on makes me laugh.

"Who's scary as fuck?" Seb asks, wrapping his arms around my waist, pressing his front to my back.

"Emmie's dad."

"Should I start getting worried that I don't ride a motorcycle?"

"There's always time to learn." I pat his arm patronizingly. "You've got the ink down. Although a little more wouldn't go amiss."

"Oh?" he asks, his voice deep in my ear, sending a wave of need through me. "You ready for a fight, baby?" he breathes.

"Uh... I wasn't trying to— Oh," I say with a laugh as he turns me to see two fighters, both wearing nothing but shorts and taped-up hands stepping into the ring. "The warm-up?"

"Yeah, although they've been known to be pretty brutal. Consider it an audition for the main event.

And as if the fighter closest to us hears Seb's words,

he flies at the slightly smaller man, throwing punch after punch until he taps out only moments later. The crowd goes wild, making me wince as the winner celebrates with his taped fists high up in the air. Smug fuck has barely even broken a sweat.

"Okay, that was..."

"Brutal."

CHAPTER EIGHT

Stella

After the bloody and beaten man was dragged away from the ring, two new guys stepped up who were much more evenly matched.

They were the perfect warm-up for the crowd who were eagerly waiting for the main fight.

I hop up on a large crate behind me, Emmie following, giving us both a much better view seeing as almost everyone inside this old, dilapidated building is taller than us and blocking our view.

The building itself isn't all that different from the one we had the Halloween party in, and that makes a trickle of unease race through me.

I should feel safe knowing that most of this place is full of men who'd happily protect both me and Emmie —assuming she gets recognized—but that's exactly how

Halloween was meant to be as well, and look how that turned out.

"This is fucking awesome," Emmie shouts as the fighter who's beginning to come out on top lands a particularly painful-looking punch to the other guy's face, seeing blood spraying across the already disgusting floor.

Ripping my eyes from the fighters as they dance around each other, I find her bouncing in her seat right along with them.

"Yeah," I agree. "It is."

Scanning the crowd for the guys, I spot Seb talking to Theo over by the bar. Every few seconds, he looks over to make sure I'm exactly where he told me to stay.

Theo still looks pissed. Actually, he looks more than pissed. Even from here, through the darkened room and the smoke, I can see that his jaw is clenched tight as he listens to whatever Seb is saying.

"Hey," a familiar voice says, passing me up two new bottles of beer.

"Hey," I say, smiling down at Daemon. "I haven't seen you for a while."

"Been busy trying to catch your stalker, Princess."

"Well, I appreciate that. How's it going? The guys haven't said much."

"That's because there's not much to tell. The security footage from Seb's house just showed a dark figure. Nothing to pin on anyone," he says, repeating what I already know. "We're still keeping tabs on people." I assume he means the Italians but doesn't want to say it when we're inevitably surrounded by a few of them.

"If you need any help, I'm more than willing to—"

"You really think he'd let you do anything stupid?" Daemon asks, nodding his head in Seb's direction.

"He doesn't have the control to *let* me do anything."

Daemon stares at me with an unreadable expression on his face as if to say 'really.'

"Look, I want this motherfucker caught. He's hurt too many people I care about."

He nods once before the roar of the crowd cuts off anything he might have been about to say.

Looking toward the ring, I find the guy who was winning now celebrating while the loser limps off, looking rather worse for wear.

The excitement around me kicks up a few notches with the knowledge that the next two fighters in the ring are the ones everyone has been waiting for.

I have no idea who either of the guys are, or which gangs they belong to, but it seems none of that really matters here tonight. Everyone is here for the same reason, and they appear to have left any rivalry at the door.

The music gets louder as people start to chant, the alcohol and fuck knows what else in their systems making them start to lose control.

It's quite a sight sitting up here, watching all the big bad gangsters lose their shit. They're like a bunch of kids in a candy shop.

A little voice within wants to tell me that I should be scared. Emmie and I are only two of a handful of women in here that I've seen, but it doesn't bother me in the slightest. I know how to look after myself, and I know those who are looking out for me are more than capable.

Seb reaches us just in time for the crowd on the far side of us to part, and two dark, hooded figures appear in the darkness through a heavy cloud of smoke.

Fear takes hold, making my entire body tense.

Memories from Halloween slam into me—me racing through the grounds with a hooded figure following.

I have no idea if he senses it or if he sees my reaction, but Seb's warm hand lands on my thigh before he hauls himself up in the small bit of space beside me. Wrapping his arm around my waist, he holds me tight.

Forcing myself back to the here and now, I drag in a deep breath through my nose, slightly regretting it when the heavy smoke in the room hits the back of my throat.

"You okay?"

"Yeah, of course," I lie, not wanting him to know that just a dark hooded man freaks me the hell out.

I should be stronger than this.

If I allow my fear to get the better of me, then *he* will win.

Both of the fighters enter the ring and they're announced, although I can barely hear anything over the shouts and screams of the crowd.

"They're both Reapers," Emmie shouts in my ear.

"How do you know that?"

"Look at their tats."

I scan their torsos until my eyes land on two identical markings.

"You know them?"

"Xander, yeah. He's hot."

I look between the two of them, trying to work out which one she might be talking about. To be fair, in just a pair of shorts with their ink on display, they're both looking pretty fine.

"The lighter haired one," she says, clearly sensing my confusion.

"Yeah, he is."

A bell rings for the start of the fight, and a ripple of silence goes around the room as everyone waits with bated breath to see who's going to get the first punch in.

Emmie screams in excitement beside me when Xander is the one to make the first move.

"Fucking hell, Em. I nearly pissed my pants," I shout at her.

"Sorry. Sorry. It's just exciting. Isn't it?"

It is, but I don't tell her that. Instead I just laugh, focusing back on the fighters.

By the end of the third round, they're both looking pretty battered as their trainers pass them each a bottle and they wipe the sweat and blood from their bodies.

Seb leans into my ear. "Joker's going to go down in the next round."

I rear back, looking at him. "How do you know that?"

"Just call it a sixth sense." He winks.

"Sebastian, is there something fishy going on?" I ask with a raised brow.

"You're in a room full of ruthless, immoral bastards, baby. Of course there's something going on."

"Right, of course." How naïve of me to think this could be a legit fight.

And sure as shit, not two minutes into the fourth round, Joker goes down and taps out.

The entire room goes crazy as Xander is announced as the winner, including Emmie, who screams bloody murder in my ear.

Although the shrieks of excitement soon turn to those of fear when a series of shots ring out before a loud explosion on the other side of the room makes the entire building shake around us.

My heart jumps into my throat as chaos ensues.

I've never seen people move so fast in my entire life as those not used to this kind of violence run full-speed to the only staircase to escape.

"Come on, let's go," Seb shouts, dragging me from the crate.

My heart is pounding in my ears as I reach for Emmie, but she's already moving.

"Window," Seb booms, taking my trembling hand and running in the opposite direction to everyone else.

Smoke fills the room faster than I thought possible as Seb drags us straight into the thick of it.

"I fucking hope you know where you're going," I scream at him, my eyes stinging and my lungs burning as I fight not to breathe it in.

"Don't I always?"

Gunshots somewhere dangerously close behind us cut off any kind of response I might have had.

I look back, but we've been engulfed by smoke. The only thing I can make out in the distance is the bone-chilling sight of huge orange flames.

"Emmie?" I scream, realizing that she's no longer beside me. "Seb, we've lost Emmie."

He comes to a stop and places his hands on my waist.

"I'm getting you out, baby," he says firmly, his voice rough from the effects of the smoke on his throat.

"No, we need to—"

"No," he barks in a tone that stops me from arguing. "I'm going to lift you. There's a window, crawl through it, take my car and go home. Lock yourself in."

"I'm not leaving you here."

"Do as you're told, Hellion."

His eyes hold mine, and I know I've got no choice but to comply—if for no other reason than we're going to suffocate if we stay here any longer.

Shoving his keys into my purse, he lifts me until I can place my feet on his shoulders and locate the window he mentioned.

It's fucking tiny, to the point that I have no idea if I'll actually be able to squeeze through it or not.

Reaching for the latch, I try to wiggle it free but it doesn't budge.

"Fuck. It won't open," I shout.

"Smash it. Do anything."

My hands tremble and my head begins to spin from the smoke inhalation, and it's only getting worse being higher up.

Black spots appear in my vision as I fumble with my purse, trying to grab my gun.

I can barely grip it hard enough, but I aim in the right direction and shoot, the glass instantly shattering before me.

"What the fuck?"

"Doing as I'm told," I shout, sucking in a deep breath of air as it rushes inside the basement.

"Fuck," he grunts as more shots sound out around us.

I use my gun to knock out the glass from the frame before shouting for him to lift me higher.

"You need to come too," I plead as I haul myself up with my forearms and begin crawling through the hole, hoping like hell I don't slice myself up too badly in the process.

"No, I need to find the boys. Get straight in the car and drive home. Promise me," he calls, his voice pleading with me to do the right thing. To get myself safe so he doesn't have to worry about me.

"I promise," I say, dragging my legs through and rolling away from the window on the cold and hard ground beneath me.

"Run, Stella," I hear him say as more shots and a loud crash ring out.

I stumble to my feet, my lungs and throat burning as I scan my surroundings.

I'm in the parking lot, but I can barely see anything. There are people everywhere as they try to flee the scene.

Racing forward, my legs barely keep up with my

body as I move toward the cars, pulling Seb's keys from my purse.

The last thing I want to do is leave, but I know he's right. If this is about me—if—then I need to get the hell away.

"Emmie?" I scream, pain ripping through my throat as I do so in the hope of finding my friend, but my voice gets lost in the chaos.

I search for her in the crowd, but I don't see anyone I recognize.

I'm still looking in the opposite direction when I run straight into another person.

"Shit, I'm sor—" I gasp when hands capture my upper arms, holding me up. Turning my head, I immediately lock onto a pair of black eyes. Although it's not those that catch my attention but the injuries littered across his face.

He's the fighter.

The one who just lost.

More gunshots come from the building before the sound of sirens in the distance pierce the air, and I remember that I need to be doing something that's not standing here staring at this guy as if I know him.

Ripping myself from his hold, I run, weaving through the people in front of me until I press the unlock button for Seb's car and see the lights ahead.

I want to sigh in relief, but I can't. Not while they're still inside and Emmie is gone.

"Fuck. Fuck," I bark, slamming my palms down on the wheel.

As I look back at the building, my heart jumps into

my throat at the sight of the flames now licking up the outside walls.

"Please. Please," I whisper, begging anyone who will listen.

I need all of them out safe.

By the time I pull out of the parking lot, the crowd has thinned a little, which ensures I don't flatten anyone as I make my escape.

Still, I search the crowd for Emmie's face, praying that I'll be able to find her. But all the faces, most of which are darkened with soot, many holding painful, possibly life-threatening wounds and gunshots, are unrecognizable.

Forcing down the giant lump in my throat when I don't see anyone I know, I press my foot to the gas and leave the destruction behind.

A sob rips from my chest knowing that I'm leaving Seb. Leaving all of them. But what else can I do?

Theo's car isn't back when I pull up into Seb's space, and I let out a pained breath when I kill the engine.

Thoughts of them dying down in that inferno won't leave my head while my paranoia starts to take its hold on me.

Staring into the rearview mirror, I search for movement, anything.

Was this all part of some big plan to get me alone?

I shake my head, feeling ridiculous.

How would anyone have known I'd be forced to leave alone? If this was about me, surely someone could have just taken a clean shot at me while I was sitting up on that crate.

This isn't about you, Stella.

But still, when I finally climb from the car, it's with my gun in my hand ready to fire should I need to. My blood rushes past my ears as my chest continues to heave, and it's not until I slam and lock the door behind me that I finally force myself to relax.

I'm safe here.

Now I just need to wait to see if anyone else is.

CHAPTER NINE

Sebastian

"**S**eb," a familiar voice booms through the smoke-filled space. "Fuck, are you okay?" Theo asks when I approach him after fighting my way through broken furniture and dead bodies.

He's crouched down behind an overturned table with his hoodie covering his mouth to help him breathe.

"Yeah. Stella's gone home. What are we dealing with?"

He shakes his head. "I dunno. We've taken out four of them. The others have vanished."

"We'll get them. Those fucks aren't leaving here without us."

"Where are the others?"

"Hunting. You packing?"

"Of course," I say, lifting my gun.

A loud crash cuts off whatever Theo was about to say as a part of the building collapses around us.

"We need to find those motherfuckers and get the hell out of here while we can."

Another round of shots pierces the air before Daemon's cold, hollow voice booms.

"A little fucking help would be nice."

"Let's go," Theo instructs.

We make our way through the room, keeping low in the hope of finding a little air as we move closer to the flames.

The heat begins to singe the hairs on my forearms, but it's not enough to stop me. Not when I know that my brothers are down here.

We find Alex and Nico with two guys pinned to the ground, both with blood oozing from them. Daemon has another pinned to the wall with his forearm pressed into his throat.

Reaching out, he rips the guy's balaclava off, giving us a look at his face.

"Fucking lying cunts," Daemon spits in the guy's face.

I have no fucking clue who he is, but clearly, Daemon is well aware.

Something else collapses behind us, the flames beginning to engulf the space.

"We need to fucking move," Theo says as Alex and Nico haul the guys from the floor.

Thankfully, almost everyone else who's able to has left.

"Where the fuck did the Reapers go?" I ask.

"This was a fucking setup," Daemon barks, confirming my suspicions.

Silently, we make our way up the stairs and burst out of the burning building right before the ceiling falls in behind us.

"Fuck, that was close," Alex mutters, looking back at the devastation.

A black van pulls up in front of us, and the second I look up, I find Evan in the driver's seat, Galen right beside him.

"Get them in, tie them up," Daemon instructs as if he's the fucking boss.

His tone of voice clearly ticks Theo off as well, because he sidesteps Alex and gets right in Daemon's face.

"Do you want to fucking remember who you're bossing around?"

Daemon's jaw tics, his eyes darkening with anger.

"Remember your fucking place, soldier," Theo scoffs, highlighting, and not for the first time, that he's always going to be higher up the Family than all of us. No matter how many years or kills we might have under our belts.

"Enough with the dick measuring," Alex mutters. "How about we just get the fuck out of here before the cops show up?"

The bright blue flashing lights in the distance hint at the fact that they're not far away.

"Get the fuck in," Evan booms, overriding any

authority Theo might have, and all of us immediately follow orders.

I just swing the back door closed as the first cop car races around the corner of the burning building. Without waiting for us to even sit down, Evan floors the accelerator, taking off across the city.

We can't see anything back here, but we don't need to to know where we're going.

All of us might be young and relatively new to this, but we all know what's coming next.

So do the stupid fucks we've now bound and gagged beside us.

If they weren't already regretting going up against us, then they're certainly going to by the time the night is out.

It only takes us ten minutes to get the men inside the old warehouse and strapped to chairs while both Evan and Galen watch, more than happy to let us be the ones to get our hands dirty.

"So," Evan starts once they've been sitting there waiting for something to happen for long enough. Part of me wants them to squeal like fucking pigs just so I can get back to Stella. But the other part, the part that remembers everything from the past hour, wondering how she looks after climbing through a window full of broken fucking glass, wants them to keep their secrets, to make us work for it.

I crack my knuckles, ignoring the ache in my shoulder.

I was already gunning for some action after

watching the fights. But now? Now I'm fucking desperate for it.

"Care to tell us why you decided to blow up a Circuit fight on fucking neutral ground, you Italian fucks?" Evan barks. Although anger laces through his voice, his face is a stone mask, giving absolutely nothing away.

Each of them holds his eyes firm, no words falling from their lips.

Fucking fine by me.

Evan doesn't even get a chance to glance back at me. I surge forward, slamming my fist into one of the stupid fuck's faces.

The sound of his jaw crunching under the force of the hit fills the room, sending a rush of adrenaline through me.

He doesn't react, though, just flexes his jaw when the immediate pain from the hit fades.

"Need more?" I mutter. "I can go all fucking night, motherfucker."

My second blow lands on his nose. Blood explodes, soaking into his white shirt and spraying my arms.

"Dirty cunt," I spit, shaking the warm splatters from my skin.

"Anyone want to talk yet?" Evan booms.

They're still silent.

"Nico, Alex. Care to join the party?"

They don't need to be asked twice. Both step forward to land a few painful blows on the other guys while Theo and Daemon stand back, watching us get our prisoners warmed up.

"O-orders came from above," one of them finally gurgles, spitting a mouthful of blood by Nico's feet. His face is swollen and bleeding from Nico's steel knuckle dusters.

"No fucking shit, arsehole," Alex growls.

"We're going to need more than that if you think you've got even a small chance of getting out of this alive."

Evan is lying. We all know that.

None of these fucks are getting out of here tonight for the fucking stunt they pulled, no matter where the orders came from.

We have neutral ground for a fucking reason.

The three of us continue until the guys strapped to the chairs are barely conscious, all six of us covered in blood.

My chest heaves, sweat trickles down my spine, and my muscles ache, but it's so fucking sweet.

The only thing better would be if my girl was here.

Fuck yeah.

A smirk pulls at my lips as I think about her covered in blood, fucking her up against one of the walls as we celebrated getting what we need out of these cunts.

Maybe I shouldn't have sent her away.

"We don't know where the order came from, okay? Boss wouldn't tell us."

I stare at the man before me, his eyes almost completely swollen shut.

"You're lying," I hiss.

"H-he's not," another confirms. "We were told to come and make a scene."

"Why?" Evan booms.

"We don't know."

"P-please," the first man whimpers, clearly in agony. "We were just following orders."

I glance over at Evan, trying to get a read on what he thinks.

I don't believe a fucking word of it, but he's the body language expert here, so we'll see if I'm onto something or not.

"Theo, Daemon." He nods at both of them, and the three of us instinctively take a step back, knowing that's what the boss wants.

The smirk on Daemon's face is downright deadly as he takes a step forward, pulling his knife from his pocket.

Oh fuck. This is going to hurt.

Theo follows his move and they both select their victims. The ones who squealed first. They both press the tips of their knives to their throats.

"The truth," Evan demands.

Theo is the first to push his knife into the guy's throat, and the one in the middle panics.

"You've got a snake."

"Who?" Evan asks, showing zero reaction or shock.

"Honestly, we don't know. But this order... it came from within your family."

"You're lying," Galen states, speaking for the first time.

"No. I'm not. We know you've been looking for someone to blame all your shit on recently, and we know you can't find anyone. It's because you're looking in the wrong place."

I glance at Galen, and his eyes meet mine, both of us thinking the same thing.

Stella.

"Go," he says to me. "Alex, Nico. You too."

"Sir," Alex mutters to Galen.

The three of us turn our backs on our captives as one of them screams bloody murder. But I don't look back to see what either Theo or Daemon has done.

My only concern is Stella.

If this is a setup, if *he,* whoever he is, has planned this, then he could have been waiting for her.

"Fuck. We need to find her," I say, running out of the warehouse.

To my amazement, Carl is waiting for us with the engine already running.

"We need to get home."

"You got it," he agrees as we all pile in. "Have fun?" he asks with a smirk, glancing over at the state of me.

"Something like that," I mutter, looking down at my busted knuckles.

My fists curl. It's nothing compared to what's going to happen when we get to the bottom of this.

CHAPTER TEN

Stella

With my arms locked around my legs that are pressed to my chest, I rock back on the couch.

"Come on," I beg quietly. "Come home. Please."

I'm sitting in the dark, just in case anyone does come looking for me and sees the lights on. I promised Seb that I'd get home safely, and I fully intend on keeping that promise.

I fight to keep my fear down, but as the seconds pass, it's becoming harder and harder to convince myself that everything is okay. That Seb—all of them— got out safe.

My entire body trembles, and my blood feels like ice racing through my veins as I wait for something, anything, from them.

My cell sits silently beside me and I will it to light up with Seb's name, for him to tell me that he's coming for me.

But it never does.

The need to call Calli, my dad, Toby, rushes through me but I can't. I don't want to scare Calli or make Toby feel useless. And I have a suspicion that Dad will already be involved in what's going on, so the last thing he needs is me calling like a needy little kid.

I blow out a shaky breath.

They'll be okay. They're just helping people or something.

A loud crash outside makes me scream like a little bitch, and I jump from the couch on weak legs.

The thought of this being about separating me from the guys so that he can get to me is still raging in my mind.

I shake my arms out at my sides as I walk toward the window and look out.

I can't see anyone, or anything of concern, but someone is down there.

There's another bang, and then a rattling of the door from the garage, explaining why I can't see anyone.

It's not the guys though, I know that much. That lock is weird, but they all know how to work it with ease —unlike me, who's given up a few times in favor of the front door.

I bite down on the insides of my cheeks to stop me calling out to see who it is.

The rattling continues for a few seconds, my

stomach churning and my heart threatening to pound right out of my chest.

The next time I hear anything, it's the front door.

"Oh my God," I gasp, grabbing my gun and racing down the stairs with it raised and ready to defend myself.

Fuck. Fuck. Fuck.

Am I about to get my first kill?

My foot hits the bottom step as the door swings open. I pull the safety down and have my finger on the trigger when... Emmie looks up at me with wide, horrified eyes.

"Fuck. That was you?" I bark, lowering my gun. "Jesus. Fuck. Em."

She swings the door closed and I damn near throw myself at her, wrapping my arms around her and squeezing tightly as I try to calm down.

I already know that Emmie's not really a hugger, but with me pinning her arms to her sides, she doesn't even get a chance to attempt it.

"I'm so glad you're okay," I breathe.

"Okay, Stel. You're scaring me a bit," she confesses.

"I'm sorry. I'm just... I'm freaking out."

"You think?" she asks as if we didn't both just escape from a fucking burning building.

"Where are the guys?"

She shakes her head, her brows pinching.

"I-I don't know. Aren't any of them here with you?"

Taking her hand in mine, I double-check she locked the door properly and then drag her up the stairs.

"Seb pushed me through a window, gave me his car

keys and told me to get my ass back here. I left him in the building," I confess, my voice cracking with fear.

"He'll be okay," she assures me from behind, although her own voice conveys her true feelings. "They all will be," she adds, as if just hearing the words out loud will make them true.

On any other day, I'd tease her for showing that she cared. But right now, that's the furthest thing from my mind.

"You want a drink?" I ask when we get to the top of the stairs.

"Uh..." Emmie hesitates. "S-sure."

I leave her to take a seat, pulling the freezer open and grabbing the bottle of vodka that I'd stashed in there a few days ago.

Twisting the top off, I bring the bottle to my lips and swallow down a couple of shots. Not enough to get wasted, just enough to hopefully take the edge off my fear.

Dropping onto the opposite couch to Emmie—the one I was sitting in when she scared the shit out of me —I curl up and wrap my arms around my legs once again.

"Anything?" I ask when Emmie checks her cell.

She shakes her head before silence falls around us.

"You should go and clean up." She nods toward my arms.

When I look down, my eyes widen at the blood covering them.

"Shit, I—" Now I see them, I can admit that they do actually hurt.

"Your legs, too. Come on, do you have a first aid kit here?"

"No," I bark, staying put. "I'm not moving until they're back."

"You're dripping," she says, glancing at the floor. "Theo will kill you for getting blood on—"

I raise a brow at her.

"What?" she snaps. "You know I'm right."

"I know," I grit out through clenched teeth. "I just... I need to know they're okay."

"I get that, Stella. But sitting here bleeding out in the process isn't going to help."

She pushes from the couch and comes over. Prying the bottle from my lap, she takes a swig before placing it down and reaching for my hand.

"Come on." She tugs hard enough that I have little choice but to climb back to my feet and follow her down to our bedroom.

The second we step inside, Seb's lingering scent hits me and I have to fight not to let a sob erupt.

The longer this goes on, the less I'm able to ignore the panic growing inside me.

"Have faith," Emmie says, sounding much more confident about the guys' skills than she usually would. Extenuating circumstances, I guess.

"I know. But..." I trail off, not wanting to lose my shit until I know for sure. "Maybe we should go back. Help or..."

"No. You need to be here. If this is something to do with that sicko that's been following you, then he's probably waiting somewhere for you to do exactly that."

Emmie pushes me toward the closed toilet seat, and I lower my ass down as she rummages in the bathroom cupboard for some supplies.

She sets about cleaning up the cuts that mar my legs from dragging them through that window.

"This one is deep. It might need stitches."

"Just cover it up, it'll be fine."

"Stella, I really think—"

"You said we need to stay here. I'm not going to a fucking hospital for a fancy Band-Aid."

She glances up at me, an argument playing on her lips, but she swallows it down.

"Okay. But when they're back, you might want to reconsider."

"Yeah, we'll see."

She gives me a look that says it all. *Seb will make you go.*

Yeah, if he's alive.

"Come on, I need more of that vodka."

"Em?" I ask as I follow her back down to the living room.

"Yeah."

"How did you get back here so fast?"

Her face is a little pale when I turn back around to her.

"Umm... I... uh... drove Theo's car."

"Uh..." I start, a smirk pulling at my lips. "He let you drive his baby?"

"Let me..." she says, her nose wrinkling.

"Oh my God. He is going to kill you." I spin around to grab the bottle, a thought hitting me. "Wait," I say, quickly swallowing a shot, "you don't have a fucking license."

"I figured it out... kinda..."

"Kinda? What did you do, Em?" I ask, my eyes wide.

"Well, what did he expect? He gave me his keys, told me to fuck off as fast as I could. I thought he was telling me to use it."

She's got a point—he might have been, but something tells me he wasn't. He barely even lets us touch his car, let alone any of us near the wheel. And we have licenses.

I'm about to ask what she did again when voices downstairs hit my ears.

"They're here," I shout, dropping the bottle and running for the stairs.

I'm halfway down, the top half of my body going faster than my legs in my need to see that he's okay, when the front door opens.

"Seb," I cry, launching myself from the stairs.

Thank fuck he's paying attention, because he manages to catch me midair without stumbling back too far.

"Fuck, baby," he grunts as I wrap my arms around him, holding him as tight as physically possible.

"I was so scared you didn't get out."

"Shh," he soothes in my ear, holding me equally as tight as he begins to climb the stairs.

Voices follow us, but I don't lift my face from the crook of Seb's neck to see who's with him. I'm just too fucking relieved that he's here and in one piece.

He lowers us to the couch once we're upstairs and wraps his hands around my upper arms, dragging me back from his body.

Reluctantly, I let go, but my heart drops into my throat when I get a proper look at him.

"Holy shit," I gasp, my eyes flicking over all the blood covering him. "Fuck, are you—"

"It's not mine, baby. It's okay. I'm okay."

My eyes fill with water, the burn behind them too much to deny, and a tear falls free.

His entire face softens at my reaction, and he reaches up with one dirty hand and wipes the tear away, probably smearing my cheek with whoever's blood that is.

"Uh... as heartwarming as this is," Alex starts, making me turn around to look at who arrived with Seb, "is anyone gonna tell us what happened to Theo's car?"

Just like Seb, both Alex and Nico are covered in blood, and the places that aren't covered are black from the fire.

Emmie groans, throwing herself down on the couch. "I had a teeny accident on the way here."

"Teeny?" Nico scoffs.

"What did you do?" I ask again. I knew she was hiding something.

She visibly winces. "I got a little friendly with a wall."

"A little friendly?" Nico asks, his brows damn near hitting his hairline.

"Shit was intense. I wasn't concentrating."

"No shit," Seb rumbles. "He's going to fucking

slaughter you when he sees it. You'd better be ready to get your tits out to distract him or something."

The guys snort a laugh at his comment while I lightly slap him on the shoulder.

"I'm not... ew, no. I should probably just leave before he—"

"Hell no, you're not running away from this," Alex states, folding his arms across his chest and taking a step forward as if he's getting ready to physically keep her inside the apartment.

"Fine. But only because I want to see if he's alive."

"And you pretend not to care," I mutter, earning me a death glare.

"He's alive," Seb says confidently. "We left him and Daemon torturing the fucks who started all that."

"You caught them?" I ask, shocked.

"Of course we did. What do you take us for?" he asks with a dramatic eye roll.

"Where are they?" I ask, curious about their torture chamber.

Seb glances back at Emmie.

"What? I'm not going to say anything," she says, throwing her hands up in defense.

"They're where no one will find them."

I let out a frustrated sigh. I guess that's all I'm getting right now.

"Baby, you're bleeding," Seb says, running his finger down my arm.

"I'm fine."

"You're not. It's coming through the plaster."

"It'll stop."

He pulls his head back and stares me dead in the eye.

"I told her she needed stitches on some, but she refused to go to the hospital." Emmie helpfully adds.

"Good. I need you safe," Seb says, confirming that I did the right thing. "But they need looking at," he says as he inspects the deeper cuts on my thigh.

"I've got it covered," Alex says, dragging his cell from his pocket and walking to the kitchen. "Hey, you free to come and patch someone up for us?" he asks.

"Who's that?"

"His mum. She's a nurse."

"Oh."

"I'm gonna go shower," Nico says, backing toward the door. "But I'll be back. I'm not missing Theo's reaction."

"You're all overreacting. He gave me his keys. It's not my fault I can't fucking drive," Emmie snaps.

"He actually told you to drive his car back here?" Seb asks, sounding about as shocked as I was.

"Well... not in so many words. He threw his keys at me and told me to get here ASAP. His car key was there so I just thought... Whatever. It's not like he hasn't got enough money to get it fixed. You lot are all so fucking loaded it's sickening," she huffs, folding her arms across her chest. "I can take him," she mutters. "He's just a jumped-up son of a bitch who needs teaching a lesson," she mutters under her breath.

"Oh yeah, I'm not missing this for anything."

Nico disappears down the stairs again and Alex comes over with beer.

"I'll be ten. I'm going to shower too. Order some food, I'm fucking starving." He throws a takeout menu down on Emmie's lap and her entire body tenses.

"What am I, your fucking slave?"

"You can be whatever you want to be, babe." He winks seductively. "You might be more Theo's type, but I'm not one to turn down a hot little body when it's on offer."

"It's not, wanker," she snaps.

"You were only saying the other day that you needed some good dick, Em. Maybe you should take him up on the offer," I suggest. "I mean, I can only vouch for his kissing skills but—ouch," I complain when Seb digs his fingers into my ribs.

"Enough, Hellion," he growls in my ear.

Taking his dirty cheeks in my hands, I hold his eyes.

"Jealousy looks good on you, baby," I purr.

Leaning forward, I nip his bottom lip, making his eyes darken with desire.

"Do not fuck right there on the couch," Emmie whines behind me.

His hands tighten on my hips, forcing me to grind down on his already hard cock.

A moan rips from my lips as the seam of my hot pants grazes my clit just so.

"Nah, not until she's stitched up and not bleeding all over Theo's sofa. He doesn't need any more reason to go psycho when he gets home."

Having said that, he doesn't stop moving me against him, and I certainly don't make any moves to stop him.

"So you want pizza then," Emmie mutters, clearly ignoring us. "I assume the other bellends will want feeding."

"Yeah. Torturing people makes guys hungry," Seb confirms, his voice like pure fucking sex.

Reaching up, he grips my chin tightly, his fingertips digging into my skin in the most delicious way as he drags me down to meet his lips, his hips continuing to roll.

My release surges forward, and my surroundings vanish.

"Shatter for me, Hellion," he growls into our kiss.

One more graze of my clit and I fall.

He swallows my moans of pleasure as they rip through my body.

"So, flaming hot for you then," I hear Emmie announce once the blood stops rushing past my ears.

"Excuse me, I need to—"

"Go and knock one out in your bedroom?" Emmie offers.

"No," Seb scolds, lifting me from his lap and making no attempt to hide the fact that he has to rearrange himself in his pants as he stands, "a car just pulled up. I'm going to let Alex's mum in."

"Oh," she replies a little sheepishly while I snigger in amusement.

"Was that necessary?" she sulks once Seb's disappeared downstairs.

"After the stress of the past hour? Hell yes."

"Chance would be a fine thing."

"Alex has already offered. I'm sure you could still

—" She cuts me a look that stops me. "Oh come on, you know you'd love it."

"Yeah, probably," she agrees. "But what I wouldn't enjoy is their smug-as-fuck bragging after."

My lips part to argue, but to be fair, she's got a point.

"Stella, Emmie, this is Gianna, Alex and Daemon's mum."

"Hi, it's nice to meet you," I say, forcing a happy smile onto my lips while Emmie barely even glances at her.

"Pizza will be forty-five minutes," she mutters. "I'm going to pee."

"Right, let's see what we've got here," Gianna says, lowering a bag to the coffee table and dropping down beside it as she inspects my wounds. "We'll have you patched up in no time, sweetie."

CHAPTER ELEVEN

Sebastian

The pizza guy pulls into the Cirillos' driveway as I'm seeing Gianna out and thanking her for coming at the last minute.

"You've got yourself a little firecracker there, Seb," she says just before dropping into her car.

"Yeah, you've got that right," I say, rubbing the back of my neck as I think of my girl.

"Keep her close, yeah?" she says, a knowing glint in her eye.

Gianna might have taken a giant step away from this life when she left Alex and Daemon's dad a few years ago, but that doesn't mean she's forgotten what it's like. How the men behave. How the women get treated.

She wanted Alex and Daemon away from it all, but she was too late by the time she made her move. The

114

Family flowed through their veins from a young age, just like it did mine. There was no way they were going to leave with her.

"I have every intention to," I assure her. "She'd probably kill me herself if I didn't."

She chuckles. "It was nice to meet her."

"Thank you, G. We really appreciate you coming over at short notice."

"Anything for my boys," she says softly before dropping into her car. "Take care."

Her door slams closed as another car turns into the driveway.

The windows are blacked out, but that doesn't mean I don't know who's about to climb out.

I don't see Gianna leave. I'm too focused on Theo as he emerges head to toe in blood and looking fucking lethal.

A bolt of twisted excitement races through me.

This is not going to end well for Emmie.

"Hey, how'd it... go?" I whisper the end of the question as he storms past me.

I can't help but smirk as he marches toward his car and walks around the side.

The car that delivered him home disappears about two seconds before he booms, "Motherfucking cunt. I'm going to fucking kill her."

Part of me wants to talk him down. The other slightly more wicked part wants to watch how this is going to play out.

The pair of them need whatever's about to happen. I know that for a fact.

Without looking back, he rips open the garage door and heads for the stairs. I quickly turn and do the same.

I fly through into the living room only a beat after him, finding Stella's eyes wide as she watches my deranged friend shoot toward hers.

A growl rips from his chest as he intercepts her coming back from the toilet and slams her against the wall with his hand around her throat.

"What. The. Fuck. Did. You. Do?" he rumbles, his voice low and deadly.

But unlike most other people on the planet, Emmie looks totally unaffected by his temper, by the way his pulse thunders so hard it makes his eyebrow tic.

"Theo, it was an accident. Leave her alone," Stella tries, albeit weakly. She wants them to have at this as much as I do.

Theo sure fucking needs it.

Emmie tilts her chin up in defiance, causing some kind of angry groan to rumble inside Theo as he waits for an answer.

"You gave me your keys. You told me to, and I quote, 'get the fuck away as fast as you can.' So I did."

"Straight into a fucking brick wall?" He closes the space between them, his fingers tightening on her throat. "I never told you to drive my car, Ramsey." Her eyes flash with something as he says her surname. "You don't have a fucking license."

She shrugs. "Too late now. Better pull out Daddy's credit card and book it into a garage. I'm sure it'll buff out."

I try really hard not to, but I can't contain the laugh

that rumbles up my throat at her comment. She totalled the front of his beloved Maserati. It certainly isn't going to buff out.

Silence falls around us, save for Theo's heaving breaths as he stares down at a much smaller Emmie, who still refuses to cower.

He closes the space between them, his other bloodied hand clenching and unclenching at his side as if he's physically holding himself back from snapping her neck.

I know that fucking feeling, man.

I glance at Stella to see if she's thinking the same as me as a door opens deeper in the flat, and not a second later does Alex come strolling into the room, fresh from the shower.

He takes one look at Theo and Emmie and mutters, "So he's not happy about it then? Did anyone think to grab popcorn?"

"Take her home," Theo booms, dragging Emmie from the wall and throwing her at an unsuspecting Alex, who barely catches her.

"Fuck you, Cirillo. I didn't mean to fucking crash your car," she spits.

"What even fucking possessed you to... no. No. Don't fucking answer that. Why were you there tonight, Ramsey?"

"Because I invited her, asshole," Stella pipes up, although Theo doesn't register her words.

"Fuck you," Emmie hisses, her lips curled in disgust as she stares at my friend.

Just fucking kiss her, I want to scream. The tension between them is fucking insane.

Reaching out once more, as if he can't stop himself from touching her, he grabs her jaw.

"I'm fucking watching you." He leans in, his lips brushing her ear as he whispers something else, and damn if her legs don't fucking give out. If Alex weren't holding her, I swear she'd have dropped to the floor like a sack of shit.

Releasing her, he storms to the kitchen and drags out a fresh bottle of vodka from the cupboard before storming to his room and slamming the door behind him.

"Well..." Alex starts, his hands still gripping Emmie's upper arms. "That was intense."

She lets out a resigned sigh. "Just do what he said and take me home."

"You want to do as he says?" I ask in disbelief.

"Do I have a choice?"

"Always," Stella says before I continue with, "you could go in there and fuck his brains out instead."

"Yeah, that's a hard pass from me."

"Huh," I mutter. "That explains a lot."

"That explains what?" Emmie hisses, ripping herself from Alex's hold, finally able to stand on her own two legs again.

"You're both as pig-headed as each other. I hope you know that all this stubborn refusal is just wasting good sexy times. You could be in there tonight with his head between your—"

Crack.

Pain blooms in my cheek, my eyes narrowing on Emmie as she glares up at me.

I shake my head, an evil smirk appearing on my lips.

"You're playing with fire, Emmie."

"Yeah?" she shouts, the sudden volume making me wince a little. "Then watch me burn, motherfuckers."

Before I get to form a response, she's across the room and running down the stairs.

"I'll call an Uber. You can all fuck off."

"Em, no. I'll take—" I cut Stella with a look that stops her words mid flow.

"Alex," I hiss, giving him little choice but to take off after her.

"Fucking hell," he mutters, although he follows where she just disappeared and closes the door behind him.

"I can't believe she hit me," I say, touching my still burning cheek.

"I can't believe she didn't hit Theo."

"I'm pretty sure that's coming."

"They need to fuck."

"You fucking think?" I ask with a laugh.

Stepping up to where she's still sitting on the sofa where Gianna cleaned up her cuts, I stand between her feet and reach for her, pulling her against me.

"Hey," I breathe, brushing my lips over hers.

She lets me kiss her gently for a few seconds before she presses her hands to my chest and forces me to back up.

119

"You're not getting away with this that easily, Sebastian."

The way my full name rolls off her tongue makes a shiver race down my spine that comes to a stop at my cock.

I've always hated it, but there's something about the way it sounds falling from her lips that makes me hard in a fucking heartbeat.

"Getting away with what? Correct me if I'm wrong, but I'm pretty sure I saved you tonight, baby."

"That may be so, but correct *me* if I'm wrong... you got fucking shot last week and you've been what?" she asks, lifting my hand to inspect my knuckles. "Beating the shit out of some guy? You should be resting."

"I'm fine. My shoulder is fine," I assure her, telling her almost the truth.

It aches like fuck after both lifting her through that window and then unleashing fury on that Italian fuck. But it's all worth it.

"You're a bad fucking liar," she huffs, twisting away from me and storming toward our bedroom.

"Okay, so it aches a little, but I'd do it all again in a heartbeat if it meant I kept you safe."

I trail her into our room like a sad puppy, and I don't even care.

"What happened, Seb?"

"It was the Italians," I confess on a sigh.

"The Ita— I thought it was neutral ground, no risk of any attacks or fucking gang wars."

"Yeah, well. Someone seriously fucked up."

"Why'd they do it?"

"According to them, one of us tasked them to do it."

"One of *us*? Fuck off."

"I dunno. Maybe Theo and Daemon got more out of them." I throw my hands up in frustration.

"So this wasn't him?"

"Who the fuck knows?" Swinging the bathroom door open, I start stripping down on my way to the shower, more than ready to wash that arsehole's blood off me.

Stella follows me, her eyes burning into my back—or more so my arse—as I step into the stall and turn the water on. I'm blasted with something resembling ice before it starts to warm.

Staring down at my feet, I watch the water run red for a few seconds, feeling the anger and frustration start to bleed out of me.

Glancing over my shoulder, I watch her hop up on the counter to watch me.

My fists curl with my need to back her up against the wall and impale her on my cock, but even without her body being littered with cuts, I already know she wouldn't let me.

I make quick work of scrubbing my skin clean before I turn the water off and spin toward her, my cock hard and aching as it bobs between my legs.

Her eyes hold mine for a beat before they drop down to my shoulder, concern etching into her heated gaze, but I push it aside.

After a second, she drags them away in favour of running them down from my chest, to my abs, and finally my dick.

She sucks her bottom lip into her mouth as she stares at me.

Wrapping my fingers around my shaft, I stroke slowly as she begins to squirm.

"Seb," she warns.

"What, baby?" I ask innocently.

"You need to rest."

A chuckle falls from my lips.

"After the night I've had, that's the last thing I want right now. Didn't you know," I say, closing the space between us and brushing my lips across her jaw, "that violence makes me horny?"

A pained laugh comes from her.

"Everything makes you horny, Sebastian." Her voice is low, rough, and oozes sex. It does not help.

"Wrong, baby. *You* make me horny. And only you."

She shudders as I lick up the length of her throat before biting on her soft skin.

"You gonna be a good girl and give me what I need?"

"I should say no and force you to rest."

"You should," I murmur, wrapping my hands around the hem of her shirt and carefully dragging it up her body, careful of the plasters Gianna applied to her arms. "But you're not going to."

"No?" she asks, tilting her head to the side in curiosity. It's all an act, though. She knows as well as I do that she's not going to stop me. She needs me just as badly as I do her. And I'm about to prove it.

"No. You're wet for me, and you know it."

I pop the button on her shorts and tap her hips for her to lift her arse for me.

As carefully as I can, I peel both her hot pants and ruined fishnets down her legs. Dropping to my knees before her, I press a light kiss to every one of her cuts that Gianna covered.

"Seb," she whimpers when I spread her thighs wide and kiss up the soft, undamaged skin, licking the lingering scars I left on her thigh.

"Tell me you're not aching for me right now, Princess."

I look up at her through my lashes.

"Because I know you are."

Reaching forward, I press one finger against her soaked knickers hard enough to graze her clit.

"Oh God," she whimpers, sliding forward on the counter to give me better access.

"Such a filthy whore, Hellion."

"Seb, please," she begs, her fingers threading into my hair as she tries to drag me forward.

"Fuck, baby."

Unable to deny her, I hook my fingers into her knickers and drag them aside, exposing her slick, swollen cunt for me.

Dipping my head between her thighs, I lick up the length of her pussy, savouring her sweet taste.

"Fucking addicted to you, Hellion," I confess before spearing her with my tongue and making her cry out.

I eat her until she's screaming my name and my balls are aching for release.

Standing, I lift her from the counter and gently

lower her to the floor before running the tip of my cock over her lips.

"Open up for me, baby. I wanna come with my cock buried in your throat."

She does as she's told and immediately sucks me as far back as she can take me, humming in approval, making my release surge forward faster than I thought possible.

"Fuck. Fuck," I bark, my hips thrusting, my cock filling her throat.

My grip on her hair must be painful as my cock jerks and my cum slides down her throat.

She doesn't release me until I'm done, and then she just sits back on her heels and looks up at me with tear tracks down her cheeks and her lips swollen from my cock.

"Fuck, I love you," I say, reaching down to pull her up from the floor.

Lifting her into my arms, I carry her to the bed, pull the covers back and lay her down.

"I need to clean up," she argues.

"Later," I whisper, slipping into bed with her.

She doesn't even flinch at the fact that I'm still wet when I pull her into my body and hold her tight.

"It's okay, Seb," she breathes, correctly guessing why I'm clinging to her like she's my lifeline. "I'm okay. You got me out."

"I'm gonna start locking you in the flat to keep you safe, baby."

"And you know I'll just find a way to break out."

I can't help but laugh at her confession. Ain't that the fucking truth.

There's a crash somewhere on the other side of the door which makes both of us jump before a familiar voice booms, "Fuck. Did I miss all the excitement?"

Stella sniggers in my arms.

"Theo looked like he'd taken a blood bath," Stella says when everything falls silent once more.

"Yeah. I'm hardly surprised, though. He and Daemon can be quite... creative when they want to be."

"Oh?" she asks, her brows lifting.

"Just because he's not as quick with his fists as Nico, Alex and me, don't think that means he's not fucking lethal, baby. Theo's just... calmer, more thoughtful when it comes to hurting someone."

"Not sure if I should be terrified or turned on by that."

A growl rumbles in my throat at her confession, but all she does is laugh.

"Yeah, so fucking funny, Hellion."

Rolling onto my back, I pull her with me, letting her take the reins so I know I'm not hurting her as I thread my fingers into her messy hair and drag her lips down to mine.

CHAPTER TWELVE

Stella

The events of the night clearly didn't have any kind of real impact on Seb, because after making out for hours and getting tangled up in his sheets, he fell fast asleep. I guess that's what happens when nights like tonight are something akin to normal life.

I, on the other hand, am totally unable to switch off, so I lie there for hours, staring at the ceiling.

Hearing movement outside of our door, I slide from the bed as carefully as I can so I don't wake Seb, drag on one of his abandoned hoodies, and slip out of the room.

The apartment is in darkness aside from a glow coming from the kitchen, and when I round the corner I find Theo sitting at the counter, staring at his cell with a bottle of vodka in hand.

"Hey," I whisper, not wanting to startle him.

It takes him a few seconds to look up, but when he does, his expression is completely blank, giving nothing away about how he's feeling after everything that went down tonight.

"A-are you okay?" I ask, edging closer despite the fact that he's giving off serious 'don't come anywhere near me' vibes.

"Perfect. You?"

"Umm..." I hesitate, flicking the kettle on so I can make myself a hot chocolate in the hope that the warmth will help me sleep. "Y-yes. Tonight was—"

"You know who she is, don't you?" His question makes me turn back to him.

"Does it matter?" I ask.

"Of course it fucking matters," he spits.

"Why? Her dad is no longer involved, and it's not like she is."

"Isn't she?" he asks, shocking the shit out of me.

"No," I confirm with confidence. "Is that what your problem is? Why you won't give in to what you clearly want?"

His eyes widen in shock and I almost expect him to blow out of the room in frustration, refusing to answer my question. But he stays put.

"What makes you think she's what I want?"

I can't help but laugh. "Oh come off it. You really don't think we see it?"

"You don't know me, Princess. Not really." I think of Seb's words from before he passed out, and I know that Theo is right. I might have spent quite a bit of time

127

with him, with all the guys, since Seb and I sorted our shit out, but I don't know him. Not really. Although that doesn't mean I can't see the longing in his eyes every time he looks at Emmie.

He wants her. End of.

"Yeah, I'm starting to see that," I say, walking over and resting my forearms on the counter, staring him dead in the eyes. "Didn't have you down as a psychopath, Cirillo."

A dark chuckle rumbles in the back of his throat as an evil smirk curls at his lips.

"Didn't you get the memo, Princess? You're fucking surrounded by them. We've been trained from the day we were born. There isn't much the six of us—all the men around us—aren't capable of."

"And what about the women?" I ask, genuinely curious about his opinion on where we stand while they're out there killing and torturing their enemies.

"What about them?"

"Only good for keeping your house tidy and raising more little boys to continue your empire?" I ask, taking a punt.

I've experienced how they treat Calli. It's not hard to believe that the guys have similar opinions of what they want from their women.

"Depends on the woman," he confesses, taking a swig from his bottle.

One side of my mouth twitches in realization.

"Okay, yeah. I get it now."

"Oh? Care to enlighten me, Princess?"

"You think you want a girl like Calli."

"I don't want my cousin, Princess."

"Did I say you did? I said *like* your cousin. Like your mother, I'm assuming. You didn't fucking see Emmie coming, did you?"

"I have no idea what you're talking about."

"She scares you. She intimidates you. Big bad mafia prince Theo Cirillo is fucking terrified of a bike riding, leather-wearing girl."

He sits back and laughs like it's the most insane thing he's ever heard. The problem with that though is that all I hear is his nerves.

I'm fucking right, and he knows it.

Emmie is like no other woman he's experienced before. She doesn't cower down to him or do as she's told. She's the total fucking opposite, and he has no idea how to deal with that.

"We can keep this between us if you want," I say, cutting off his fake amusement. "But I need to warn you."

"Oh yeah?" he asks, his brows pinching with curiosity.

"You fucking hurt her, and she won't be the only woman you need to be scared of."

I turn my back on him the second I've delivered my threat and pour some boiling water into my mug.

"Nice try, Princess. I'm already fucking terrified of you."

Amusement flows through me, but I don't let it show.

"Good to know you're not totally stupid, Cirillo."

"Surely you've already figured this out," he says, his

voice getting closer with every word. His body heat burns through Seb's hoodie when he steps right up behind me. My head gets ripped back, my scalp burning. He grips my hair and twists so I have no choice but to look at him. "You're more dangerous than any of us. On top of your training, you've got this innocent pretty face and this sinful body. You'd have any man on his knees long before we could. The cunt who's after you clearly has no clue who he's dealing with."

I stand immobile, staring back into Theo's haunting green eyes, just waiting to see what he's going to do next.

My heart thunders in my chest as I consider the fact that he might be about to do something really fucking stupid, but although his eyes might flicker down to my lips briefly, he never closes the distance between us.

Thank fuck.

I'd really hate to have to watch Seb kill his best friend.

"Just so you know," he finally breathes, his voice deep and terrifying, "if you hurt him, I'll rip your heart out with my bare hands."

My breath catches at his deadly threat.

Part of me wants to laugh, but then I see it, the monster lurking deep behind the façade he wears, and my body trembles in his hold.

Before my brain manages to come up with anything resembling a response, he releases me and marches to his room, slamming the door harshly behind him.

"Holy fuck," I breathe, sagging back against the

counter, my trembling hand lifting to cover my racing heart.

By the time I've drank my hot chocolate and calmed my nerves after witnessing a side to Theo that I'm not sure very many get to see, I slip back into bed.

My body aches, my cuts sting, and all I want to do is drift off into a peaceful sleep and forget about the events of the night.

Pulling the covers back, I slip back into place with Seb's front to my back.

His arm immediately wraps around my waist and he tugs me back against him.

"Love you, baby," he mumbles in his sleep.

"I love you too, Seb."

With his soft snores filling my ears, I finally succumb to my exhaustion and let the darkness claim me.

The sound of Seb's cell ringing finally drags me from my peace, but even as I turn over to grab it, he still doesn't even stir.

"Shit," I hiss seeing multiple missed calls from Sophia. "Seb," I say louder, gently shaking his shoulder to bring him to.

"Yeah, baby. What's up?" he says, his voice rough with sleep.

"You've got a load of missed calls from your sister."

"Shit." His eyes spring open and he sits bolt upright faster than I thought possible.

Swiping his screen, he immediately calls her back.

"What's wrong?" he barks the second the call connects.

Sophia says something. It's too quiet for me to make out, even only inches away, but whatever it is makes Seb's eyes lock onto mine, allowing me to see the fear he's hiding from almost everyone else.

"Yeah, we're coming now. We'll be thirty minutes."

He's out of bed before he even kills the call.

"What's wrong?" I ask, although my stomach is already in knots with a good idea.

"It's Mum. She's in the hospital."

"Shit. What—"

"Overdose."

"Jesus. What are you waiting for?" I ask when he stands in the middle of the room, looking completely lost.

Stepping up to me, he takes my face in his warm palms.

"You should stay here," he whispers, concern pushing his previous fear away.

"Fuck that, Seb. You need me. Your family needs me. I wouldn't be anywhere else."

"But—" He looks down at my dirty skin from last night's fire mixed with the dried blood that I haven't been able to wash off yet.

"They're a few scratches. I'm fine. Get dressed," I demand before he really tries putting his foot down.

I physically push him away from me and toward his closet in the hope that he lets it go, because I'm not allowing him out of this house without me.

In only five minutes, both of us are dressed and heading out the door.

Theo is once again sitting at the breakfast bar, only this time he's on his laptop.

"What's wrong?" he asks the second he looks up and reads the fear that's written all over Seb's face.

"Helen's in the hospital," I offer.

"Fuck. I'll dri—" His face drops when he remembers the state of his beloved car, and his fists curl on the counter.

"We've got it. Thanks, though. I'll call you when I know anything," Seb promises, steering me from the apartment as Theo's eyes hold mine.

He's one hard motherfucker to read, but I'm pretty sure there's an apology in his mysterious depths somewhere.

It's totally unnecessary. His threat might have been a little more detailed than required, but I got it. He was only doing exactly the same as I did to him a few minutes before.

I wouldn't expect anything less from any of them if something were to go wrong between Seb and me. I might be a part of this Family, but I'm fully aware of where these boys' loyalties lie. And it's not with me.

'Call me,' Theo mouths to me before we break eye contact.

I nod, silently promising him that I've got Seb's back before we disappear around the corner.

"I'm glad to see you got my car back in one piece," he mutters as we approach his Aston.

"Of course."

"I can't believe she crashed," he says with a slight laugh, which is totally at odds with the wrecked look on his face. But as much as I want to focus on our current drama, I let him lose himself in Theo's for a bit. "You think she did it on purpose just to get a rise out of him?" he asks.

"I wouldn't put it past her," I confess, knowing just how feisty Emmie can be when she wants to be.

Something tells me she'd quite happily do something that dramatic just to push his buttons.

Seb falls silent, his fingers holding the wheel with what looks like a painful grip.

Reaching out, I run my fingertips over the scabs on his knuckles.

"I should have cleaned these up last night."

"It's fine. Wasn't the first time, and I'm sure it won't be the last."

"That's not the point."

He shrugs. "My knuckles are the least of our worries right now, Hellion."

I blow out a heavy sigh as I rest my hand on his thigh. I really want to tell him that everything is going to be okay, that he's not about to lose yet another member of his immediate family. But I think we both know that I'd be clutching at straws.

He's said before that he's feared this day for years. His mom's been on the brink of this for almost as long as he can remember.

She just seemed so good on Sunday. Not that I really have anything to compare her to. Okay, so she didn't exactly scream healthy, but she looked way better than the image Seb had painted of her. I was expecting her to be a complete mess, but instead, I got a woman who quite clearly loved having her family around her but was more than a little bit broken. And after the loss she's suffered over the years, I'm not sure anyone can really blame her.

I'm not sure how you deal with losing both your husband and your daughter.

I glance up at Seb, my heart swelling in my chest as I think about just how much he means to me.

Even after only these few short weeks, I can't imagine a life without him, let alone after years of marriage and four kids. How do you even begin to deal with that kind of loss?

"You okay?" he asks, feeling my stare.

"I'm here, you know. Whatever happens."

Dropping his hand to mine, he twists our fingers together and lifts my knuckles to his lips.

"I know," he whispers, his voice cracking with emotion.

We're silent once again, and only minutes later, we pull up at a different hospital to the one we've all spent time in recently.

"Sophia called an ambulance. This is where they brought her," he says when I meet him at the hood of the car, answering my unspoken question. "We'll move her if..." he trails off, but I don't need the words to know what he means.

"I'm sure they'll do a great job here."

After navigating our way to the ICU, we're finally

buzzed in and find both Sophia and Zoe in the family room.

Both of them jump the second we walk in, their faces pale, their eyes dark and pained.

"Any news?" Seb asks as we take seats with them.

"No. But they're not sounding very hopeful. I found her just in time, but even still, I'm not sure her body is strong enough to fight it."

"Then maybe they shouldn't even be trying," Seb says sadly, earning himself stunned looks from both his sisters. "What?" he asks, sounding shocked that they're surprised. "She's been trying to achieve this for years. We might as well let her go peacefully."

"She hasn't wanted to die, Seb," Zoe argues.

"Hasn't she? So just existing in a blur of darkness and drugs is better?"

Zoe's lips part to argue, but unsurprisingly, she doesn't really have a response.

"She's been so positive this week," Sophia says after a few minutes. "She even came to the park with us the other day. I really thought she might have been turning a corner."

"How many times do we have to go through this same cycle?" Seb barks, standing from his chair in a rush. "I'm fucking sick of this bullshit. You talk like she was going to get better. She never had any real intentions of kicking this. She was an addict, Soph. This was always going to kill her."

"*Is*, Seb. She's still here, still fighting."

"What's the point?" he snaps. "She hasn't been a

mother to any of us in years. What's the point in any of it?"

He blows out of the room in a rush, leaving the three of us with our chins dropped.

"He'll be okay," Sophia assures me. "He just needs a breather."

My need to follow him, to support him, burns through me.

I take a step forward to do so, but Zoe's hand lands on my forearm.

"Soph's right. Just give him a minute."

Trusting that they know him better than I do, I drop my ass back into the seat and rest my head against the wall.

That minute turns into ten as I sit on the edge of the chair in my need to flee the tension in the small room, but the second I decide to make a run for it and hunt him down, the door opens, and a doctor with a serious expression on his face steps inside.

My heart plummets, because just from the look on his face, I know exactly what he's about to say.

And not five seconds later, I discover I'm right.

Helen's not going to survive this.

She's hooked up to machines that are breathing for her right now, but there's no point in continuing trying to bring her back from this. Just like Sophia said, her body is too weak after all the years of abuse.

Sophia and Zoe's quiet sobs fill the room as the doctor backs out once more, telling them they're welcome to go and see her and sit with her for as long as they need.

"I need to find him," I say, cutting through their sobs.

I'm up and out of the room before they can say a word.

I have no clue where he's going to be. I've never stepped foot inside this hospital before, so I just start walking.

Pulling my cell from my pocket, I open the app he installed for me a few weeks ago and wait for it to load as I take the elevator to the ground floor.

Something tells me he's escaped the building, so I follow my gut while I wait.

I step out into the late morning fall sun and pull my hoodie around myself tighter as the cool air makes me shiver. Thankfully, the app finally loads and I find his cell in a green area beside the building.

Walking in that direction, I keep going until I close in on his dot.

I find a cute little charity garden that's been donated by the family of a child who lost their life a few years ago and pocket my cell, knowing that he'll be somewhere close.

I walk through some immaculately pruned bushes and find a dark figure on the farthest bench.

My heart aches for him as he sits there, looking totally defeated with his head in his hands.

CHAPTER THIRTEEN

Sebastian

I know the second she walks up because the emptiness that had consumed me since I stormed away from that family room lessens.

But I don't move or look up to confirm what I already know.

It's like my entire body has given up.

All my fight, my anger... everything has drained out of me, leaving me nothing but a shell of the person I usually am.

How is any of this fair?

How?

We've already lost so much. How can all this shit happen to just one family?

Sophia and Zoe don't deserve any of it.

Me, on the other hand... after all the shit I've done, I more than deserve the pain.

Stella lowers herself to the bench beside me and wraps her arms around my waist.

"Hey," she whispers, pressing her lips to my shoulder.

Blowing out a slow breath, I sit up a little and glance over at her.

"Shit," I gasp, taking in the expression on her face. "Did—"

"I-I... the doctor said—"

"Fuck. Fuck," I bark, my palm colliding with the seat of the wooden bench, anything to cause some physical pain to make the one inside my chest that bit easier to bear.

I push to stand in my need to flee once more, but Stella's hand wraps around my arm and she holds me with everything she's got to stop me moving.

"Baby, I need—"

"No," she snaps, slamming her palm down on my chest and forcing me to sit back.

"What are you—"

Shock cuts my words off as she climbs onto my lap, straddling me, and takes my face in her hands.

"Don't run from me, Seb. I'm right here. Whatever you need." She leans forward, pressing her brow against mine. "I'm right here," she repeats.

Wrapping my arms around her, I pull her into my body, holding her tight as I release a shaky breath.

She presses a kiss to my neck, her warmth and support spreading through me.

We stay silent as the seconds and minutes tick by, and she makes no move to try to get out of my tight embrace. She just does exactly as she said she would. She's here. And she's not letting go.

"We should probably go back up," I say eventually.

In all honesty, it's the last thing I want to do. I'd much prefer to just walk away from this hospital and forget any of this happened.

But I can't.

I can't do that to my sisters. They've been there, stood by my side, for my entire life. It's time I returned that favour and was there for them.

"Are you sure?"

Attempting to swallow down the giant lump that's clogging my throat at the thought of what's to come, I nod and release my vice-like grip around Stella's body.

Taking my hand in hers, she silently leads me back toward the building.

Long before I'm ready, we're coming to a stop beside a door where we've been told both my sisters are with Mum.

"It's immediate family only," the nurse who showed up down here says softly when we come to a stop.

My eyes lock on Stella's, panic bubbling up inside me.

"S-she's my fiancée. It's—"

"Seb, it's okay. Your sisters are in there, and I'll be right out here. I won't move from the window."

Her eyes beg me not to make a big deal out of this.

Deep down, I know she's right. She's met Mum

once—she doesn't feel that it's her place to be involved in this. But fuck, I want her there.

"I'll call Theo. I'll be right out here waiting."

"Fuck, I—" Lifting my free hand, I drag my hair back from my brow until it hurts.

I hate this. I hate feeling so fucking vulnerable. But... I fucking need her.

'It's okay,' she mouths, giving my hand a tug and dragging me into her body.

"I'm right here," she whispers, her lips brushing mine.

"I fucking love you, Hellion," I tell her firmly before slamming my lips down on hers in a kiss that's totally inappropriate for the situation, but fuck if I care.

The nurse coughs and Stella pushes me back, forcing us to break apart.

"I love you too. You can do this."

I nod once and turn my back on her. Hardest fucking thing ever.

As I push through the door, my heart feels like it's about to shatter into a million pieces, and looking at my sisters' tear-stained faces really doesn't fucking help.

Glancing over my shoulder, I find Stella standing exactly where she was, although now blurred through the frosted glass of the window.

"Seb," Sophia cries, rushing toward me and throwing her arms around my shoulders. "I'm so sorry."

"Not your fault, Soph," I say, my voice void of any kind of emotion.

Zoe's arms wrap around both of us and we stand

there for the longest time with the machines beeping behind us.

A knock at the door finally breaks us apart, and a doctor and two nurses slip inside the room.

"Okay?" the doctor asks softly and Sophia nods, the three of us taking a seat beside Mum's bed.

Unable to watch, I hang my head between my shoulders while the doctor and nurses do their thing, and after only a few minutes the beeping and whooshing of machines stops.

Both Sophia and Zoe's hands tremble in mine, but I fight everything I don't want to be feeling.

The image of Demi laid out on the road when I found her fills my mind, and my eyes burn.

"Look after Demi, Mum," I whisper, ripping my hands from my sisters'. "I'm sorry, I... I can't do this." I rush from the room, my sisters calling my name behind me, but I don't stop.

"Seb, what—" I glance over my shoulder at Stella, and she immediately swallows her words.

Knowing that she's not going to stop me, she nods.

'I love you,' she mouths before releasing me from her stare and letting me go.

It fucking pains me to do it, but I just... I can't be around anyone right now.

"ARGH," I scream, slamming my palms down on the wheel of my car over and over as the tears that were burning my eyes finally slip free.

CHAPTER FOURTEEN

Stella

Sophia and Zoe give me a lift back to Theo's once they're done at the hospital.

Both of them look totally exhausted.

I get it. My energy is almost non-existent and I haven't been through what they have today. My heart is breaking for all of them, but it's nothing compared to how they must be feeling.

"He'll be okay," Sophia says, glancing at me in the rearview mirror, her eyes red and puffy from crying.

"I know," I agree, forcing the words past the lump in my throat. And I do know he will.

The look he gave me as he left the hospital was different from when I found him out in that garden. He silently told me that he wasn't running from me. Just from the situation.

I have every confidence he's going to come back to me—assuming I don't get too impatient and go and find him again first.

"I'll let you know when he does."

"Thank you," she breathes.

With a sad smile at both of them, I climb out of the car and make my way to the door, giving them both a wave as they head off.

With a heavy sigh, I climb up the stairs and round the corner into the living room. As expected, multiple sets of concerned eyes fall on me.

I'd called Theo just like I promised I would, and he immediately told me he'd get straight to the hospital.

I'd put him off. He wasn't happy about it, but what could he have really done? I was proved right when Seb took off not long later.

"Oh my God," I breathe, finding a pair of eyes I wasn't expecting. "Toby."

He stands slowly from the couch when I move toward him and opens his arms for me.

"I didn't know you were out," I breathe, stepping into his body and loosely hugging him.

"Surprise," he says, although it lacks any kind of excitement.

"It's so good to see you. I'm sorry I haven't visited for—"

"Stop, Stella. I know. Things have been—"

"Dramatic."

"Yeah," he sighs with a pained laugh.

"Shouldn't you be at home in bed or something?"

"Yes, he should," Nico snaps.

"Give it a rest, Grampa," Toby jokes, lowering himself onto the couch and dragging me with him.

"Have you heard from him?" Theo asks, and I shake my head.

"Jesus. This is such a fucking mess."'

Silence ripples around the room, each of Seb's brothers cut up about his loss.

They might have their differences but at times like this, it's clear just how strong their bond really is.

"We all know where he is, right?" I ask, assuming they've all jumped to the same conclusion as me.

"Yeah," Theo agrees, scrubbing his hand down his face.

"Then we should go. All of us," Alex announces. "Grab some vodka and go drown with him."

"All for one and one for all," Nico adds.

Theo holds my eyes, silently asking me what I think.

I appreciate the gesture, but we all already know the answer.

We're a team, a unit, and if one falls, we're all there to pick them back up.

"Stella, you're with me," Theo says.

"Oh, you're gonna let me ride in the Ferrari?" I ask, teasing.

His eyes narrow in warning. "Do not touch anything. I'd hate to have to kill you too."

"Ha, funny. I spoke to Emmie less than an hour ago. I know she's in one piece."

A disgruntled kind of groan erupts from his throat and everyone laughs.

"I'm still pissed off I missed it," Nico mutters.

"Shouldn't have spent so much time washing your tiny cock, man," Alex jokes.

As wrong as it is to laugh at a time like this when Seb is drowning, it feels good.

I just hope we can all provide him with a similar kind of relief.

"Fuck you, bro. Everyone in this room knows it's bigger than yours."

"Jesus. Can we put the dick measuring to one side, maybe?" Theo asks, reaching up into the cupboard and pulling out a couple bottles of vodka. "Bro, you got weed?" Theo asks Alex, who taps his pants pocket. "Let's go then. Come on, Princess."

I follow the guys out of the apartment with Toby right in front of me.

"Are you sure you're well enough for this?"

"I'm fine, honestly," he says, looking over at me.

"Sure you are."

"I'm not made of glass, Sis," he says, throwing his arm over my shoulder once we're at the bottom of the stairs.

"How's your mom?" I ask.

"You mean our mum?" he asks with a smirk.

"Y-yeah."

"She's doing good. She's excited to meet you."

"You talked about me?" I ask, surprised. I know he was keeping things back because he thought her room was bugged.

"We went for a slow walk in the garden. Your dad and Aunt Penny are sorting something out."

Nerves and excitement collide at his words and my stomach turns over.

"You okay?" he asks, his large hand landing on my shoulder.

"Y-yeah. I'm just..."

"Scared?" I wince at the word, but when I look up into his eyes, I don't find any mocking, only concern and understanding.

I nod, unable to do anything else.

"She's going to love you. Now I know, I see a lot of her in you."

"Yeah?" I ask with a smile.

I've lived my entire life thinking that I'd never get to meet my mother. But she's been here all along and that despite not knowing her, that we're alike in any way fills me with a kind of comfort I've never experienced before.

"We going or having a fucking reunion?" Theo barks from the driver's side of his black Ferrari.

"Keep your hair on, Cirillo," I snap back. "See you in a bit," I say to Toby.

"He's going to get through this. Seb's stronger than he looks."

"I know. We won't let him do anything else."

Toby gives me a soft smile before stepping aside so I can drop into Theo's fancy pants car.

He remains silent as he watches the others climb into Nico's car that's parked outside the garage before the beast beneath me rumbles to life and sends a shot of adrenaline through me.

"What will it take for you to let me drive this one day?"

He glances over at me, his dumbfounded expression giving me my answer.

"I'd need to kill you first. Good to know."

"No offence, Princess, but no pussy is even close to being good enough to let a girl behind the wheel of this car."

I scoff. "Sexist pig."

"What? I wouldn't let a guy sit here either."

"So you wouldn't let Seb take me out in it?"

"Hell no. You've got him wrapped around your little finger so tight it's not even funny. He'd let you suck him dry, blow his few remaining brain cells, and then hand the keys over willingly, like he did his balls."

"And to think I was worried you didn't like me," I mutter, folding my arms over my chest.

Theo chuckles.

"I'm sorry about last night. I—"

"I'm sorry, what was that?"

"I-I... I said I was sorry."

"Shit, I should have recorded that."

He blows out a frustrated breath, pushing his hair back from his brow, and takes a moment to gather his words.

"I do like you, Stella. And, despite what I said last night, I trust you not to hurt Seb. I know how you feel about him. I always have. I just... You shouldn't have seen me like that."

"I can handle this life, Theo. I can handle the dark and the ugly as well as you can."

"I don't doubt that, Princess. You just shouldn't have to. All of us... the things we do... I wouldn't wish it on anyone."

"I guess it's a good thing I don't have a choice about being here, then. You said it last night. I'm one of you. *Terrifying*, I think you said. I'll take whatever you throw at me."

He shakes his head as if he can't quite believe the words I'm saying. But I mean every single one.

"Have you said those little words to Emmie yet?"

"What little— No," he snaps when he realizes what I mean. "I have no reason to."

"You're a fucking idiot," I laugh.

"W-what?"

"You heard. But you're wrong about her. She's not a threat to us. To you."

Theo's teeth grind, his grip on the wheel tightening.

"What? What don't I know?"

He sighs, clearly not wanting to tell me what he's thinking when it comes to my friend.

"Theo," I growl.

"I don't know anything, okay?" he spits. "I just... The Italians said that one of us was behind last night's ambush. But it wasn't just us there, and I don't remember the Reapers looking all that shocked by the whole thing."

"You think they were involved too?"

"I don't know. The Italians wouldn't change their story no matter what Daemon and I did. I just can't help feeling like we're missing something."

I sit back and consider his words. I want to agree, but then I didn't see much of the fallout of last night—I was too busy being hoisted through a window.

But I can understand where he's coming from.

Where were the Reapers when we caught the Italians? Surely they've had guys injured as we have? Surely they'd have wanted their pound of flesh for that?

"Yeah, makes sense."

"I shouldn't be telling you this."

"Why? Because I'm going to run to Emmie and squeal? Do you really think that little of me?"

"I haven't told my brothers this, Princess. I haven't even told my dad yet. I just... fuck." His curled fist slams down on the wheel, his jaw popping in frustration.

Reality suddenly dawns on me.

"You haven't told them because you're protecting her."

He glances over, but despite the fact that he doesn't utter a word, I hear his response loud and clear.

"Even if the Reapers were—are— involved in all this shit, then—" I swallow my unease at the thought of them behind all the attacks on me. "Then there's no reason to believe she'd know about it."

"I know." He pauses. "We're missing something. Something fucking important. And fuck... I just can't get it."

"We will," I assure him. "We'll win. We're better than them."

"We could have all died last night, Princess."

"But we didn't. Now, put all that bullshit aside. We've got something more pressing to deal with."

He nods as he pulls into the parking lot behind the graveyard.

We pull up next to the others, and as a group, we head through the darkness toward the headstones where I'm confident he'll be sitting.

The second we're close enough to see him, Seb looks up.

Pain is etched into every inch of his face, but the second he realizes it's us, it starts to ebb away.

"We brought presents," Theo announces, holding up the two bottles in his hands.

Dropping down beside him where he sits with his back against Demi's headstone, I rest my head on his shoulder and twist my fingers with his.

"I'm sorry," he whispers.

"Nothing to apologize for, Seb. We've got your back."

"Were Sophia and Zoe okay?"

"Yeah. They're going to call you tomorrow."

More footsteps fall around us as the others join us.

"Toby?" Seb says in surprise when he carefully lowers himself down beside Theo. "Should you be in—"

"Stella's already grilled me," he says, rolling his eyes. "I'm good. Sorry to hear about your mum, man."

"Thanks."

Seb takes the bottle of vodka that Theo passes over and twists the top off, lifting the neck to his lips and taking a generous swig before passing it over for me to share.

"So you thought you'd bring the welcome home party to the cemetery, huh?" he asks Toby.

"Wherever you need us, bro. You know that."

"Fuck," Seb breathes, his head falling back against the stone.

Lifting his hand to my lips, I press a kiss to his busted knuckles.

"Whatever you need," I whisper as Alex and Theo start bickering about something.

"Thank you," he breathes, dipping down to capture my lips.

"Fucking hell," Nico mutters. "I didn't agree to watch them go at it again."

I chuckle against Seb's lips and don't stop him when he lifts me from my place on the ground and drops me onto his lap.

"He loves it really," Seb mutters against my neck, making me shiver.

"Behave," I chastise, swatting him in the chest and swiping the bottle from where he left it on the ground.

It's November in England, and the freezing cold air whips around us as we all sit there shooting the shit and distracting Seb from his reality, but I hardly notice it while I'm wrapped in his arms.

Before I know it, Toby is fighting to stay awake and it's late into the night.

"Someone needs to get him to a bed," I say, pointing at him.

Everyone looks at each other. They're all stoned and wasted, aside from Toby, who's still on painkillers, and me, because someone needed to be fucking sensible.

"Ubers?"

"I'm not leaving my car here," Theo slurs.

"Then you either need to let Toby or Stella drive it," Alex happily announces.

Theo's eyes hold mine.

"Fuck off," he barks. "You fucking played me."

Holding my hands up in defense, I plead my case. "I didn't force you to get off your head. That was entirely your choice."

"I'm helping my brother."

I glance at Seb who's completely fucking stoned and staring at our joined hands.

"And he appreciates it. Now make a decision, because Toby needs rest."

Theo looks utterly torn as we climb to our feet.

"What's worse, handing her over to a careful driver or abandoning her in a deserted parking lot all night surrounded by ghouls and ghosts?"

"I will gut you like a fish if you hurt her." His warning might be similar to the one last night, but there's no weight behind this one. And it's not just because he's wasted.

"Don't worry, boss. I won't be testing your knife skills anytime soon."

"And if he pukes in it, you're sorting the valet."

"Fine," I agree excitedly, bouncing on my toes as I hold my hand out for the keys.

He's anything but enthusiastic as he hands them over.

I squeal in excitement, happily taking them from him.

"I'll take good care of her. Promise," I shout before unlocking her and dropping into the driver's seat. "Just get him home and in bed." I nod in Toby's direction as Seb stumbles around the hood of the Ferrari, ready to get inside.

"I can't believe you managed this," Seb slurs from the passenger seat.

"Stick with me, babe. You ready for some fun?"

"Hell yes."

I start the car and press the gas, letting the vibration of the powerful engine flow through me.

I glance over at Theo. His face is pale as he stares back at me.

Lifting my hand, I flip him off, laughing like a lunatic as I gun it out of the parking lot.

Beside me, Seb howls with laughter, the sound of it soothing my soul as I make my way through the quiet streets of London.

"You know he's expecting you to go straight home, right?" Seb slurs.

"Yep. And he's going to be disappointed."

CHAPTER FIFTEEN

Sebastian

My heart races as Stella flies through the city, taking yet another corner at breakneck speed.

"Oh my God," I laugh as my body leans into Theo's insanely comfortable seats. "I can't believe he let you do this."

My head spins from the vodka. Mix that with Alex's weed and I've almost been able to forget why we all hung out in the graveyard tonight. Almost.

"Why? He'd do anything for you. And he knows I'm about to give you the ride of your life."

Desire shoots straight to my dick at her words. The image of fucking her over the hood of this sexy-arse car vividly plays out in my mind. "Is that right?"

"Turn both our cells off," she demands, digging hers

out of her pocket and passing it over after stopping at a red light.

"Wh—oh." A knowing smirk pulls at my lips. "He is literally going to kill you."

She shoots me a look before the lights change and she floors the accelerator, throwing us both back in our seats.

"This thing is a fucking beast," she squeals excitedly.

"Yesss!" I cry, throwing my arms up. "Take this right."

Stella follows my directions out of the city without questioning me, and a little over thirty minutes later, she's pulling into the car park I had in mind.

It's deserted, exactly as I hoped. I point to a space that allows us to look out over the city beyond and she pulls the car to a stop, killing the engine and plummeting us into silence.

The lights before us illuminate the dark night sky as we both just take a breath.

Dragging my eyes from the view, I focus on my girl instead.

My heart aches just looking at her.

We grow up listening to stories about love and finding the one. Never in a million fucking years did I think it would feel like this.

That it would complete me and fucking terrify me all at the same time.

Everything about her just brings me to my fucking knees.

She should be pissed at me for walking away from

the hospital like I did earlier, but no... instead, she brought my boys to me when I needed them all the most.

And fuck did I need it.

"It's beautiful out here," she whispers, cutting through the silence.

"Yeah," I breathe, keeping my eyes locked on her profile.

Her hair is piled on top of her head. She probably thinks it looks a mess, but it's far from that. Her face is almost clear of makeup, and she's wearing a hoodie and leggings.

She's fucking breathtaking.

Realising that I'm not looking at the city stretched out before us, she turns her head toward me and my breath catches when our eyes connect.

Concern fills hers as her brow wrinkles.

There are a million things I should probably say to her, thank her for, but the words get stuck behind the giant lump in my throat, and the only way I can think about conveying everything I need her to know is with actions.

Reaching out, I wrap my hand around the back of her neck and pull her toward me.

Our lips collide over the centre console and I immediately plunge my tongue into her mouth.

"Seb," she breathes into our kiss, telling me that she hears everything.

I kiss her slowly, licking into her mouth, exploring like it's our first time, pouring every single thing I feel for her into it.

She matches my movements, keeping up with our silent conversation.

The second her teeth nip my bottom lip, though, everything changes, the deep, passionate, emotion-filled kiss turning dirty and full of desperation in a split second.

Dropping my hand from her neck, I undo her belt and wrap my hands around her waist, lifting her over the centre console and placing her—somewhat awkwardly—on my lap.

"Seb," she moans into our kiss. "We can't," she argues weakly.

"Stop thinking, Stella. I need your wild, rebellious side who just stole Theo's car."

"He'll kill us."

"He's already going to. Might as well really make it worth it."

Twisting my fingers in her hair, I drag her head to the side and lick up the column of her neck, loving the feeling of her shuddering against me.

"You wanna come, Hellion?"

"You know I do," she groans, her hips rolling as she tries to find some friction.

"You're a dirty little whore, Princess."

"You love it," she mutters against my neck as my hands slip under her hoodie and cup her breasts.

"Too fucking right I do."

Unsnapping her bra, I pull it away from her body as much as I can and pinch both her nipples.

"Seb," she whimpers.

"Lift up," I tell her, wrapping my fingers around the

159

waistband of her leggings and dragging them over her arse and down her thighs just enough to give me the access I need. "Fuck, baby," I growl when I dip my fingers between her folds and find her dripping wet for me.

"Yes," she squeals when I push two fingers inside her heat.

Her back arches and her head falls back as she rides my fingers. It's one of the hottest things I've ever seen.

"Hoodie off, Hellion. I want your tits."

Without missing a beat, she folds her arms in front of her and peels it up her body, throwing the fabric to the driver's seat before I rip her bra down her arms and throw it... somewhere.

Bending my fingers in a way that I already know will make her scream, I place my hand in the centre of her back and force her closer, wrapping my lips around her nipple.

Her fingers curl around my shoulders as her release begins to crest.

"Come for me, Hellion," I growl against the side of her breast. "Show me how good it feels with my fingers deep in your cunt."

"SEB," she screams. I pull back just in time to watch her drown in pleasure. Her face goes lax, her full, swollen lips parting, but her eyes don't close—they lock on mine, allowing me to see it all.

"Fuck, I need inside you now,' I say in a rush as we both fumble to push my sweats down enough to release my aching cock.

The second we manage it, Stella shifts herself until she's hovering right over me.

"Baby?" I growl, my patience evaporated. "Oh fuck," I cry, when she drops herself down on me, allowing me to fill her in one move. "Ride me, baby."

Needing more skin, she drags my hoodie up my body and discards it.

Her fingertips brush over my healing scar in a move that's entirely too tender for what I need right now.

"Fuck me, Hellion. Use me."

My deep, raspy voice seems to snap her out of her daydream, and her eyes flare with desire when they meet mine.

Her nails dig into my shoulders as she uses them for leverage to drag herself up my shaft.

"Fuck, your pussy is like heaven," I groan. "Shit," I bark the second she drops herself back down on me.

Gripping her hips, I help her move as she grinds down on me before she starts fucking me exactly as I crave.

"Jesus, Hellion." I have no idea how she manages it in such a confined space, but she fucks me like the perfect fucking whore she is.

By the time we both race toward our climaxes our bodies are glistening in sweat and our chests are heaving.

"Come for me, Princess. I need to feel you milking my cock."

I pinch her clit, and her walls immediately clamp down on my length as her release slams into her.

Her screams of pleasure as she pulsates around my cock, dragging my orgasm out of me, echo around the small space.

"Fuck, yeah," I grunt, my cock jerking as I fill her up.

Grabbing her hair, I drag her down, swallowing her lingering whimpers of pleasure as I soften inside her.

"I needed that," she says with a laugh.

"Yeah? Well, lucky for you, I'm not finished yet."

She pulls back and quirks a brow at me.

I roll my hips, showing her that I'm gonna be ready to go again any minute.

Desire fills her eyes but she bites down on her bottom lip, looking up at me through her lashes like she wants to say something about our next round.

"I can't feel my legs," she finally confesses.

"You don't need them."

Pushing the door open, I twist us both around until my feet hit the ground, and with one hand around her, I manage to stand without dropping her or even leaving her body.

"Seb, no. Your shoulder—" I cut her argument off with my lips, shifting her weight and grabbing her bare arse as I round the car and lay her out on the bonnet.

Reluctantly, I pull out of her. But fuck, the second I take a step back after dragging her leggings and panties down, I discover it was totally fucking worth it.

"You look like sin, baby," I groan, taking in her bare, curvy body on Theo's sexy car. "Fuck," I mutter, rubbing my hand over my rough jaw as I try to commit the image to my memory.

Placing her bare feet on the bonnet, she spreads her thighs.

"What the fuck did I do to deserve you?" I mutter, taking in every inch of her as my fingers wrap around my shaft.

"We've already been over this. Fucking nothing. But here I am anyway."

Shaking my head at her, I step up to her and grab the backs of her thighs, pushing her a little higher up the car.

"What are you—oh. Oh fuck," she screams into the night when I drop to my knees before her and suck on her clit. "Seb, shit," she cries when I don't let up, lapping at her as I push two fingers inside her.

"Tell me this is a first for you?"

"Head on a Ferrari? Y-yeah," she stutters when I rub her clit. "It's a first."

"Thank fuck for that," I mutter before dipping down once more. I've had nowhere near enough of her yet.

I don't move until I've given her two more orgasms and my cock is physically painful in its need to be inside her.

I stand up, wiping my mouth with the back of my hand, clearing away the evidence of her arousal and our previous releases.

Moving her once again, I wrap her legs around my waist and line myself up with her entrance.

Her body is limp from her releases, her chest heaving, her nipples hard and begging for attention as the cool night air whips around us, but she never complains. She just takes everything I give her, allows me to lose myself in her instead of focusing on my—our—reality.

By the time we're both racing to the end once more, Stella's sweat-slick body is allowing her to slide on the bonnet of Theo's Ferrari.

The angle, the movement, the fact that we're out in the open and that literally anyone could be watching us right now is fucking mind-blowing.

And when my restraint finally snaps only a second after Stella shatters, my release slams into me like a fucking truck.

I fall over her panting body, a weak heap of tingling nerve endings.

"Fuck, baby. That was—"

"Incredible," she finishes for me. "We're gonna have to buy this car off Theo," she suggests, making me laugh.

"Well, I'm pretty sure he's gonna want to burn it when he finds out what we've done to it. Owning it seems like a much better suggestion."

She shivers beneath me and it's the reality check I need—although I don't want—that it's the middle of winter.

"Shit, baby. You're freezing."

"I'm fine. Could do this all night."

"Whore," I breathe softly in her ear as I scoop her up and wrap her in my arms.

I hate to suggest going home, but I know it needs to happen.

We work in silence as I help get Stella dressed, her limbs like spaghetti after the orgasms I dragged out of her.

"Are you going to be okay to drive?" I ask when she has to hold onto the side of the car once more to steady herself.

"I'm not letting you, if that's what you're getting at. You're wasted and stoned."

"Doesn't stop me performing," I quip. "Arms," I demand, holding out her hoodie for her.

"Where's my bra?"

"You don't need it. Easier access for me when we get home."

Shaking her head at me, she allows me to walk her around to the driver's side. I kiss her like she's the air I need to breathe before I allow her to drop down.

"Get your drunk ass in before you pass out."

"I'm totally in control, Hellion. It'll take more than a shared bottle of vodka to knock me out."

"Sure thing. Get in before I leave you in my dust."

"You wouldn't."

"You wanna try me, Sebastian?"

She starts the engine and pushes her foot on the accelerator, making the beast purr.

"No, not really," I admit, aware that she bloody well would leave me standing right here.

I know better than to challenge my Hellion to anything.

Rushing around the car, I just reach for the handle when the locks click.

"Stella," I warn as she grins at me from the inside.

The engine rumbles again and the car pulls forward just slightly.

"Hellion."

She can't hold her laughter and throws her head back in amusement as she does it again.

After a couple of minutes, she relents and releases the locks.

"You're not coming again tonight," I grumble as I fall into the seat.

"And you are?" she shoots back.

"Too fucking right."

With her laughter still filling the car, she peels out of the parking lot, relying on me directing her back into the city.

We stop at a red light. The roads are pretty quiet seeing as it's the middle of the night, but a bike pulls up beside us.

I glance up just in time to see him look in at Stella.

He shakes his head as if he's pushing aside the idea of a drag race through the city due to the fact that the driver is female.

"He's underestimating you, baby."

"Yeah," she says, sitting up a little straighter. "I got that."

"You're not gonna let him get away with it, are you?"

"Do you know me at all, Sebastian?" Like always, shivers race down my spine at the sound of my name on her lips.

She glances over and holds the driver's eyes for a beat—not that she can see them through his dark visor.

Before I've even realised the lights are about to change, Stella floors the accelerator and we fly forward right as the amber glows.

We leave the bike in our dust and I holler in excitement, my cock hardening as I'm once again reminded of what a bad-arse my girl is.

"Fuck, yeah, Hellion. That was insane."

"He doesn't agree," she mutters, looking in the mirror.

I glance over to see him quickly catching up.

"Pretty sure that Ducati rides like the fucking wind, baby," I say, squinting and trying to make out exactly what he's riding. But I'm not exactly sober, as she pointed out not so long ago.

"I've got this."

This time when the lights change, the biker is on to her and they take off at the same time, fast enough that the next few sets of lights are still on green.

"Fuck me, where did you learn to drive like this?" I ask as she navigates the sleepy London streets like a fucking race car driver.

"Calvin and I used to race," she confesses, changing the gear so fast I almost miss it.

The bike keeps up with us.

"What the fuck, asshole?" Stella screams at him, scaring the ever-loving shit out of me.

Glancing over, I find him right at the side of the car.

"Move over, you fucking cunt," she barks.

"Do not scratch this car."

She shoots me a 'shut the fuck up' look before taking a sharp left that almost has me crushed up against the door with the fucking speed.

"We're going to spend the night in a cell, aren't we?" Although I'm pretty sure no cops could even catch us right now if they tried.

"I need to get rid of this cunt before he kills us."

I look over at him; he seems far less in control than my girl as he weaves about on the road.

"There's no one behind us. Slam the brakes on and take a left."

"You're not fucking serious?"

"What, scared of losing?" I deadpan.

"Fuck you. We all know who won this shit."

"Exactly, now end it before we all die."

"Fine."

Her foot slams on the brake as she pulls the handbrake doing a seriously impressive wheelspin, leaving the bike to continue flying down the main road as we start weaving through the backstreets that eventually lead us, unharmed, back to Theo's.

"Holy shit, that was epic," Stella says once we've come to a stop. Her chest is heaving and her eyes are sparkling with excitement.

"I'm so fucking hard for you right now," I confess. "You are literally the most incredible person I've ever met."

"You think Theo's parents can see us?"

"Nah, the house is dark. Why?" She moves faster than I thought possible and has my cock out of my sweats and in her mouth before I've had a chance to blink.

"Fuck, I love you."

CHAPTER SIXTEEN

Stella

I knock quietly on the door. Part of me is secretly hoping he's already asleep, but I know I'm only lying to myself.

I saw him standing like a creep in the window after Seb came down my throat in the car.

"Yeah," he calls, and my stupid body sends nerves shooting through my veins.

Shaking my head at myself, I push the handle down and slip into the room.

Theo's sitting in his bed, shirtless, with his laptop resting on his thighs.

"Come to explain?" he says coolly as he spins the screen toward me, showing me exactly what's put that scowl on his face.

It didn't occur to me when I told Seb to turn his cell

off that the idiot back here who probably spent the last few hours worried about his beloved car was following us on the car's app.

"Whoops," I say, completely insincerely as I stare at the speed tracking he's showing me.

"Whoops?" he asks, mocking me.

"Whatever," I wave him off, walking farther into the room and dropping down on the edge of the bed.

It's been a long day, and I'm fucking exhausted.

"How is he?"

"Passed out," I say, thinking about how I left Seb snoring on his back. I only went for two minutes to pee, but it was all he needed. "He's going to be okay."

"I know," Theo says confidently. "We won't let him be anything else. Plus, you seem to have inventive ways to get him out of his head."

I raise a brow at him.

"I should tell him you were watching."

"You really think he'd care?" He quirks a brow.

"Ugh, whatever. We had an issue on the way home," I confess.

Theo's laptop gets thrown to the end of the bed and he's out and standing at the window faster than I think I've ever seen anyone move.

"I didn't crash your car, Cirillo," I snap. "Glad to know you're that confident in my skills." I roll my eyes.

"You hit one hundred in the fucking city, Stella."

I shrug, dismissing his comment.

"I wouldn't have if some douche on a bike hadn't taunted me into it."

He turns away from the window, his eyes locking

on me.

"Go on," he demands, slipping back into bed.

Guilt washes through me that I never said anything to Seb at the time, although to be fair, there wasn't really time for a fucking conversation.

"It was dark, I couldn't see much, but he was wearing a cut."

"Shit," he hisses, scrubbing his hand over his face.

"It could be a coincidence and was just a chancer up for a late-night drag race."

"You really believe that?"

My lips part to tell him that I do. But there was something about my reaction to whoever the guy was when our eyes locked that stops me.

"No," I mutter. "It felt like he was waiting for us. That he knew it was me. Not sure he was expecting me to cream his ass, mind you."

Theo groans. "Stop, please."

"Your girl's seen all kinds of excitement tonight," I smirk. "More than you're giving her, anyway."

He stares at me, clearly unimpressed, but he can hardly moan. Seb lost his mom today, his only parent. I think that trumps wanting to keep your car safe.

"You really think he was a Reaper?"

"As I said, it was too dark to see. I got the license plate though."

"Great, what is it?"

I rattle off the numbers and letters I've memorized and he writes them in his cell.

"I'll run it and see what comes back."

"You can do that?"

Again, he just stares at me, silently telling me to stop underestimating him.

"Okay, so you'll let me know what the results are."

"Of course. Go and get some sleep. You look wiped."

"Yeah," I say, pushing a few loose strands of hair from my face. "It's been a long day."

"Go," he says, reaching for his laptop again. "Look after him," he whispers when I get to the door.

"Always."

Silently, I slip back into our bedroom, finding Seb still snoring, although as I crawl back into bed he immediately tucks me into his body and holds me as if he'd drown without me.

Lacing my fingers with his, I make him a silent promise to be there through whatever hits us next.

———

S eb's still asleep when I come to the next morning. His arm is still wrapped around my waist possessively, but I manage to slip out without waking him, and when I emerge from the bathroom a while later after freshening up, he's still out cold.

"Morning," I say, finding Theo on his favourite seat with his laptop once again.

"Those plates were fake," he says in way of a greeting.

"Of course they were," I mutter, going straight for the coffee machine.

"Would you remember the bike if you saw it?"

I think back to the night before and shake my head. "Seb said it was a Ducati, but I don't know bikes. It was a fast black one."

"And here I was thinking you were a petrol head."

"Just cars."

"Speaking of, I found this." Lifting his hand, he swings my black bra from his finger. "Do I want to know how it ended up under the seat?"

"Probably not. Thank you," I hiss, swiping it from his finger.

"She smelled like sex."

"She had the time of her life."

"We rocked her fucking world," a very rough and sleepy voice says from behind me. "Stop smelling my girl's underwear, Cirillo," Seb grunts, pulling me into his body and cupping my face with his hands.

Theo huffs in frustration. "At what point did I say that I—"

"Morning, baby," Seb's lips brush against mine and all of Theo's words just melt away.

"How are you feeling?" I ask when he releases me.

"Better than I should, I'm sure. You making coffee?" he asks with a wink.

"Sure, go sit down."

"Yep, I need to tell my boy all about my hot-as-sin car racing girl."

"He already knows," Theo mutters. "I was tracking her fucking speed."

"You're telling us you'd have turned down that little drag race?"

Theo's eyes find mine and Seb looks between the two of us curiously.

"W-what? What did I miss?"

My lips part to explain, but Theo beats me to it.

"Stella thinks it was a Reaper."

"R-right. And that's a problem why?"

Seb and Theo are still discussing theories when the doorbell rings a while later.

"I'll get it," I say, rolling my eyes when neither of them makes a move to get up.

I press my finger to the button beside the screen that shows me who it is. "It's my dad," I tell the guys before letting him in.

"Stella," he says, his brows pinching in concern when he sees the healing cuts on my bare legs.

"I'm fine, Dad. Just a few scratches."

His brow lifts at my attempt to smother just how serious Friday night could have ended up being.

We've spoken on the phone since that night, but he couldn't exactly come rushing to my aid seeing as he was sent to the other end of the country soon after.

Seems to be a theme these days.

"When did you get back?" I ask, opening the door wider and allowing him inside.

"Late last night."

As I follow him up the stairs, I can't help but feel the huge cavern between us that never used to be there. All my life, I've been his little girl, but since being here, everything has changed.

I don't feel that I've changed, but maybe he would suggest differently.

In only a few short weeks really, I've fallen headfirst into a relationship with Seb and moved in with him.

It probably wouldn't have all happened so fast if my life wasn't constantly on the line. Maybe the two of us would have had a slightly more normal and slower-paced start to things.

I can't even imagine what that would be like now—going out on dates, to the movies, getting to know each other and then sneaking him into my bedroom like other teenagers.

I'm laughing to myself as we emerge into the living area where I left the guys.

"Galen," Seb greets casually while Theo just nods, grabs his stuff, and makes a quick exit to give us some privacy.

"You two don't look ready," Dad says, looking between the two of us.

"Ready for... Oh shit," I gasp, Toby's words coming back to me. "Today?"

"Yeah, if that's okay with you," Dad says hesitantly, studying me closely.

My stomach explodes with nerves, but I keep my expression neutral, not wanting to show anyone, even my own father, just how scared I am about meeting a woman I've believed was dead my entire life.

"Yes. I just really need to shower first." I look down at myself. I had a wash yesterday morning but I'm still gross from the fire and then the events of last night.

Screw the Band-Aids littering my body, I *need* a shower.

"Can you give me thirty minutes?" I ask Dad before

looking at Seb.

"Yes. Jonas is away all day. Penny is waiting for me to tell her we're on our way."

I clench my fists to stop them from visibly trembling.

"Okay, great. Are you two..."

"We'll be fine," Dad assures me, holding Seb's stare. "Give me a shout when you're done."

I nod and take a step away from them. My need to demand that Seb comes with me is almost too much to bear, but I think after everything that's happened over the past few weeks, that just might push my dad over the edge.

It's almost an hour later by the time I'm ready and walking down the short hallway toward the kitchen where I assume my dad's waiting.

"Stella, you look beautiful," he breathes, taking me in.

I had no idea what the hell to wear to this. I'm so out of my comfort zone it's not even funny. Give me a gun and tell me to shoot someone and I wouldn't bat an eyelid. But meet the woman who gave birth to me? Yeah, I'm a fucking mess.

I glance down at my simple black prom dress and run my hands over the fabric.

I've teamed it with a leather jacket and a pair of biker boots that Emmie would be proud of. My silver hair is hanging straight around my shoulders like a curtain, although I refuse to use it to hide behind, and my makeup is dark. I feel good. Like myself. Like the badass mafia princess that I am, I guess.

Seb's pacing the living room on his cell when I enter, but it only takes him another few seconds to notice me, and when he does, his words falter and the look he gives me is pure sex.

"I... I'm... uh... gonna call you back, Soph, Hang on." He jabs his finger into the screen despite the fact that Sophia is still talking on the other end. "You look insane," he says, walking up to me and making me spin for him, Dad watching us with a frown.

When I turn to face him once more, his eyes are dark, and the fire within them makes desire burn in my belly.

"I hate to do this, but Soph and Zoe need me. Are you okay to go with your dad?"

"Of course, but if you need me then—"

"No," he says firmly but quietly so Dad isn't forced to overhear. "You need to go and meet your mum."

Guilt floods me. While I'm here possibly— hopefully—starting a relationship with my mother, he's just said goodbye to his. We haven't even had a chance to talk about what happened yesterday.

"Are you sure? I can—"

"I'm just meeting Soph and Zoe at the house to go through some things. You should do this with your dad and Toby."

"But—"

"No." He cuts me off, brushing his thumb over my cheek. "You need to do this." He can clearly sense that I need more, because he quickly adds, "We'll talk later, promise."

"Okay," I breathe, not entirely happy about letting

him go but knowing he's right. He needs to deal with his own family stuff just like I do.

"I love you, Hellion."

"I love you too."

Seb grabs his wallet and keys from the side and disappears before I get a chance to change my mind and call him back.

"Ready?" Dad asks, pushing from the stool he was resting on.

"Uh..."

"I know this is weird. And I know it's all my fault. We just felt that..." He lets out a heavy sigh. "Once we knew them coming to be with us was out of the question, we just thought it would be easier for you to deal with. We—"

"Dad," I cut him off, "it's all in the past. I might not like it, or agree with it. But it's done. You both made your decisions, and there's nothing we can do about it now."

He stares at me and shakes his head. "You're so like her," he says, a sad smile playing on his lips.

"Do I look like her?"

He nods.

"How have you looked at me every day if—"

"Because you're the little bit of her that I got to take with me. A part of us. The best part."

A lump clogs my throat at his words.

"O-okay. Let's do this. I need to meet the woman who clearly owns your heart even after all these years."

CHAPTER SEVENTEEN

Stella

My heart is slamming against my rib cage by the time Dad pulls up on a quiet street. We drove farther than I was expecting.

With how close all the others live, I assumed Toby's house would be around the corner.

I was wrong.

It seems that Jonas wanted to keep his family away from prying eyes by moving them to the other side of the Cirillo territory.

What I'm also not expecting is to stop by none of the houses.

"Dad, what's going on?" I ask, looking around, seeing nothing but the trees lining the street and giving the huge houses some extra privacy.

"We can't just walk through the front door."

"Jesus," I mutter, running my fingers through my smooth hair.

"I know. Come on. They're waiting."

We climb from the car and Dad leads me toward an alley at the end of the street.

A lush green park spreads out before us. There are kids playing and dogs running around, but as we get closer, Dad turns to the side and we keep walking until he comes to a stop beside some thick bushes.

"What are—" Realization hits. "Fuck off. We're breaking in, aren't we?"

Dad winces.

"This is fucked up, Dad."

"I know," he sighs, sounding and looking utterly exhausted. "Maria's got a few more weeks of treatment and then we'll be able to come up with a plan. But until she's finished, I'm not rocking the boat."

"No more than breaking onto their land and spending time with someone else's wife?" I ask, raising a brow.

He glares at me, clearly unimpressed with my attempt at humor. It was lame, I know, but I don't know how else to deal with the nerves that are beginning to make my entire body tremble.

"Come on," he says, reaching for my hand and tugging me through what I now see is a gap in the plants.

In seconds we're engulfed by the trees and bushes, the park no longer visible as Dad treks through the undergrowth like he's done it a million times—which, of course, he probably has.

"Oh wow," I breathe when we finally start to emerge to find that we're beside a small lake. But the pretty scenery only captures my attention for a few seconds, because movement on the other side of the water catches my eye.

I find Toby first as he stands from the bench he was sitting on, but my gaze doesn't linger on him. They drop to the woman beside him.

The second our eyes connect, all the air rushes from my lungs.

Mom.

Even from this distance, I can see the similarities between us.

My heart aches as I take a step closer, and with the help of the bench arm, she pushes to stand, Toby quickly rushing to her side to steady her.

I don't even realize that my legs have carried me closer until I'm standing right before her.

Silence ripples around us as we just stare at each other—until a broken sob erupts from her throat and tears spill from her eyes.

I move on instinct, wrapping my arms around her slim body and holding her to me.

I'm not a hugger; I never have been. But the second she returns my embrace, I realize that I never want to let go.

"Oh my God," I whimper, barely holding myself together as she trembles.

I have no idea how much time passes as we stand

there, but when she pulls back and takes my tear-soaked cheeks in her hands, I know it wasn't long enough at all.

"My baby," she whispers, her voice full of awe as if she can't believe I'm actually standing here before her. "You're so b-beautiful. I've seen photographs but..." She shakes her head. "I'm so sorry."

She crumbles before me and I pull her into my arms once more as I sense both Dad and Toby take a step closer to us.

I look up at my brother over her shoulder and hold his concerned stare. His eyes are full of unshed tears, which doesn't do anything for my unsteady emotions.

'It's okay,' I mouth to him. 'I've got her.'

He gives me a lopsided smile as I gently lower our mom to the bench.

"I can't believe you're actually here," she says, taking my hand in her cool one and holding it tight.

"Tell me about it," I mutter, but there's no malice in it.

"I'm sor—" she tries again, but I cut her off.

"I don't need your apologies. We don't need to rehash the past," I say, similar to what I said to my dad not so long ago. "It's too painful, for everyone."

She nods, her bottom lip trembling.

I look over her features. Her skin is pale, her eyes are dark, showing her exhaustion from her treatment, and she's wearing a hat with a huge pink fluffy bobble on the top which makes me smile, and a thick winter coat. But despite all the treatment she's been through, she still looks gorgeous. I can totally see why my dad fell head over heels for her all those years ago.

"We're going to get through all of this," I promise her.

"She's right," Dad confirms, coming to stand behind us and placing his hands on both of our shoulders.

Maria lifts her free hand and holds his. The look that passes between the two of them is pure, unfiltered love. It gives me the final push I need to ensure that we all come out of this and that they get the time together that they deserve.

Lifting my arm, I gesture for Toby to come and join us.

Maria and I have time to properly get to know each other—I hope—but right now, we just need to be together.

Toby takes my hand and squishes in beside me.

Maria sobs as she looks between the two of us.

"I've made so many mistakes in my life," she tells us. "But I've never regretted having either of you. I just wish I could have been the mum you both deserved."

"Mum, no," Toby says, his voice cracking with emotion. "None of this is on you. It's *him*," he spits. "And he's going to get what's coming to him."

Maria nods. "It's time. Nothing he has over us is more important than this." She squeezes my hand. "I want my family. My babies." She looks up at my dad once more. "You," she whispers.

We spend almost an hour sitting by that lake, talking about nothing of any significance. We avoid all the heavy subjects of our reality as Maria and I get to know each other a little.

It's utterly surreal.

And when a woman—Penny, I assume—appears through the trees to see how her sister is holding up and I get a look at Maria, I know our time is coming to an end. She's still in the middle of treatment and recovering from surgery.

"I'm not ready," she tells us all, holding my hand tighter.

"You need to rest," I tell her softly. "But this isn't the end. It's only the beginning. We need you strong, yeah? Because we're going to win."

Tears drop once more as she sighs, "Oh, Galen. You raised me the most perfect daughter."

My heart shatters once more as she pulls me into her arms.

"I can't wait to get to know you better," she whispers in my ear. "I've spent all these years imagining all the things we could do together."

"I want that."

She holds me for a few more seconds before releasing me.

Taking my face in her hands once more, she wipes my tears away with her thumbs.

"I can see why the boys are so taken with you, sweetheart."

"Mum," Toby warns.

She rolls her eyes at him. "You really should have seen the resemblance, Tobias," she jokes.

His grip on my hand tightens, and I can't help but smile.

"Should I be keeping an eye out for any others or..."

"You're safe," Maria confirms. "From my side... at least."

She noticeably cuts herself off from saying any more. But none of us needs to hear the words.

"Jesus Christ. I'll order some DNA tests then, shall I? Just in case."

"Just keep it in your pants, son," Dad suggests helpfully.

Maria and Penny snort a laugh.

"Not sure you can be giving out that kind of advice, Dad," I deadpan. "And anyway, I'm clearly going to have to vet any girl Toby considers worthy now, and nothing will get through me."

"Because you have such good taste," he mutters with a laugh.

"Hush now."

"Yeah," Penny mutters. "You two are definitely siblings."

Toby and I stand as our parents embrace, allowing them to have a whispered conversation between them.

"How's Seb doing?" Toby asks, dragging my attention away from watching my dad with a woman for the first time ever. The way he holds her. Damn. He's so utterly smitten with her. It would be adorable if the situation weren't quite so dire.

"He's okay. He's gone to meet his sisters to get everything sorted."

"He doesn't deserve any of this shit," he admits, rubbing the back of his neck.

"I think we of all people know just how unfair life can be," I say, shooting a look over my shoulder at our parents once more.

"Yeah. It's fucking shit."

"We're gonna fix it. Your dad's going to get what's coming to him, and we'll start over. All of us."

"Sounds good, Sis," he says with a wink, pulling me in for a hug.

"Go get your—our—mom inside where it's warm. You should be resting too, remember." I pin him with a warning look.

"Sure thing, kid."

"Eleven months, Tobias. Don't fucking start with *that* shit."

He laughs as Maria calls for him.

After dropping a quick kiss to my cheek, he steps around me but pauses when I press my hand against his stomach.

"I know it's weird after... But I just want you to know that... I'm glad it's you."

A smile twitches at his lips. "You were always going to be Seb's, Stella. I'm glad too. Looking forward to making up for lost time."

"You got it," I promise him.

Dad steps up behind me as I watch Toby wrap his arm around Maria and help her back toward the house. We can just see the roof in the distance.

"You're going to get her back, Dad. We're gonna make it happen."

"I know," he says confidently. "Toby and I are working on it."

"You are?" I ask, ripping my eyes from the three of them and back toward him.

"Yeah. I've been planning that man's death in my head for most of my adult life, sweetheart. It can't come soon enough."

"You're gonna give Toby the final shot though, right?" I ask as if we're talking about something as simple as the weather.

"You really are my daughter, aren't you?" he mutters lightly, not turning away from Maria until she's out of sight.

"You trained me. Which I really should thank you for. You should have seen the guys' faces when my marksmanship wiped the floor with them."

"They took you out to the range?"

"Yeah," I say with a smile as I remember that afternoon. "Taught Seb a lesson too. The bullet was less than an inch from his head," I confess as I remember just how right he was to be a little concerned that day.

"Glad to hear it. He needs it."

"He's a good guy really, Dad."

Dad laughs as we make our way back through the trees.

"I know, sweetheart. You think I'd trust any of them with you if I didn't know the kind of boys they are?" I don't get a chance to reply because he follows up with another question. "You hungry?"

"What kind of question is that?" I mutter. Dad

knows as well as anyone that I can pretty much always eat.

"I found this place that you're going to love. Spend the afternoon with me?"

He turns back to me, his brow creased as if he's scared I'll say no.

"Sure. But I hope you're armed. There's someone out there trying to kill me."

"Really, Stella?"

"Joke. It was a joke."

"You're a pain in my arse, kid." He waits for me to catch up with him and wraps his arm around my shoulder, dropping a kiss to the top of my head.

"Love you too, Dad."

———

Seb was still out when Dad dropped me off after our lunch date. He took me to the most insane restaurant that only served desserts. It was heaven. Although, I must admit I felt pretty sick by the time we left.

I grabbed my laptop and made myself comfy on the opposite couch to Theo, and we just sat there together and worked.

It was... nice.

I kept an eye out for Seb's call, and it was long dark outside by the time he messaged to let me know he was on his way home.

"I'm going to go out, give you two some time," Theo says when I tell him.

"You don't have to do that. This is your home."

"S'all good. I could do with blowing off some steam anyway."

I quirk a brow.

"Don't even start," he warns.

"Did I say anything?"

"No, but I can read that filthy mind of yours, Princess."

"Hmm. Any news on the Reaper thing?"

"No. I've got a meeting with Dad tomorrow. I'm gonna see what he thinks."

"You have to book a meeting with your own father?" I balk.

"He was out of town with yours. They're up to something."

"Are they ever not?"

"Good point."

"Dad said he's working with Toby to fix the Jonas situation. Was it something to do with that?"

Theo shrugs. "Contrary to popular belief, I don't get told all the Family secrets. Everything is on a need to know basis. I have no clue what's going on with Jonas other than they need Maria's treatment finished first. I think all bets are off after that."

"Fair enough." I look back down at the assignment I was working on as Theo tidies up the kitchen.

"It's coming to an end," he says, almost as if he's talking to himself instead of me. "I can feel it. Something big is going to happen, and we're going to catch that motherfucker."

"Should I be worried?"

"Nah. It'll take more than a deranged psycho to put you down, Princess."

"Glad you agree."

"Just be ready," he tells me before disappearing to his room.

Seb and I spend the night as something resembling a normal couple. We order takeout and sit and watch some shoot 'em up movie on Netflix while we catch each other up on our days.

I still feel guilty about the fact that I met my mom for the first time while he was planning his own's funeral. But he was insistent that he wanted to hear all about it, and as I've discovered, I'm not very good at saying no to him.

Theo went out dressed in his killer black suit not long after Seb got in, and he hasn't reappeared yet. When he said he wanted to blow off some steam, I assumed he was going out with Alex and Nico to get wasted and laid. But seeing him dressed for work made me wonder if he has something else entirely planned.

"What are you going to do about your mum's house?" I ask Seb after crawling into bed beside him and wrapping my arm around his waist.

"I have no idea. You wanna live there?" he asks, surprising me.

"Uh..." I hesitate, not wanting to say no quite as quickly as I wanted to.

He chuckles. "It's okay, Hellion. It's the last place I want to live as well."

"What will happen to it?"

"They generally go down the family. So, Sophia is technically next in line for it, if she and Jason want it."

"Do you think they will?"

"Maybe. It's bigger than their place. They're more than welcome to it."

"What about you?"

"What about me, Princess?" he asks, tugging me closer and dragging my leg over his hip.

"Where are you going to live?"

"You mean we, right? Where are *we* going to live?"

"Uh..." I hesitate. I haven't really thought much beyond right now and being here with the guys while whoever is trying to kill me plays his twisted games. I guess I just assumed that I'd go back to Dad's at some point, although the thought of it makes my chest ache.

"You're not going back to your dad's, Hellion. Well, not unless I'm with you. And something..." He rolls his hips, grinding his hard length against my core, making me gasp. "Tells me that your dad wouldn't want that."

"S-so," I stutter, trying to keep my head focused and not just push the serious shit aside in favor of riding his talented dick. "W-where will we live? Here? Don't you think we've already cramped Theo's style enough?"

"He loves it," Seb growls as he drags me closer, ramping up the pleasure as he teases me.

"I'm not so sure about that," I admit. I actually feel pretty sorry for him having to put up with us.

"What if I were to say that I had something up my sleeve," Seb confesses quietly.

"I'd say, go on."

"But," he starts, rolling me onto my back, "it might be a secret."

"We don't have those, remember?" I groan as he slips his hands under his shirt that I'm wearing.

"Okay, so it's more of a surprise then," he confesses, dipping his head to my neck.

"I don't like s-surprises," I gasp as he bites me.

"Tough. Now, enough talking. I just want to hear you screaming."

"If you insist," I moan as his lips tease me, allowing my legs to fall open in invitation.

"Whore."

"Yours."

"Hell yeah, Princess. All fucking mine."

CHAPTER EIGHTEEN

Sebastian

S tella wasn't happy about it when I announced the next morning that I was going back to school and that life was going to continue as usual.

We'd lost Mum, and yeah, it hurt like a fucking bitch, but life couldn't stop because of it, and I certainly wasn't going to let Stella go to school without me.

The wounds from the weekend are still both physically and mentally too raw. It's bad enough that I've had to let her go to class without me.

Thankfully, though, she agreed with me, and she hasn't gone back to gymnastics and cheer yet. She might think she's fine, but she seems to be forgetting that she got fucking stabbed only a few weeks ago.

I know that everything is healing well, I can see that

with my own eyes, but still. Given half the chance I know she'd push herself to the limit and probably end up hurting herself in the process.

That did mean that I had to follow my own rules, and she banned me from football training, too—something I'm pretty sure Coach was going to enforce on me anyway seeing as I have a bullet hole in my shoulder, but still, I was willing to give it a shot.

The past week has been weirdly normal. No one's tried to kill any of us, we've been to school, Theo and the guys have worked. The boss has put me on full-time babysitting duties which, of course, I'm taking very seriously. Although we have spent more time out of the house than I'd like in the hope of tripping this motherfucker up, but he seems to have gone to ground again.

I'm not stupid enough to think that he's given up. I think it's obvious to all of us at this point that he's just waiting to make a move.

Theo's told all of us more than once that he senses something, and as irritating as it is listening to him, he's usually right.

Stella stirs beside me and I tighten my grip on her, needing her to keep me grounded. She mumbles something in her sleep and curls into my body, wiggling her arse back against my morning wood.

Lifting my head from the pillow, I press a light kiss to her bare shoulder to see if she's awake. She shows no signs of life, other than her arse shifting again.

"You're a tease, Hellion," I whisper, lifting my hand from her belly to pinch her nipple.

I have no idea what time it is, but I'm confident it's still early enough that we've got time for a little fun. Anything to take my mind off what today holds.

A whimper of pleasure passes her lips, making my cock ache for her.

Memories of watching her get herself off in her sleep in her bedroom all those weeks ago come back to me.

After everything that's happened, that feels like a lifetime ago. Back when I was trying to convince myself that I hated her. That every single part of my shit life was her fault. Little did I know, all I needed was her to make everything that much more bearable.

I shake my head at myself. Fuck. I was a cunt to her back then.

I'll never understand why she ever decided to give me a chance. I didn't—I don't— deserve it. Yet here we are, all these weeks later, and she's right beside me, in my bed, my home for all intents and purposes, naked and driving me as fucking crazy as ever.

I pepper kisses across her shoulder as I skim my hand down her belly.

Her breathing is still even, and I can only assume that she's asleep. Either that or she's playing me, letting me take whatever I want. I'm happy either way, because I know that she wants it too.

Pushing my leg between hers, I open her up for me and continue lower.

She moans, urging me on.

"Fuck, baby," I breathe when I dip my fingers into her pussy. She's fucking drenched.

I push two fingers inside her, getting her ready before I shift behind her and line up with her entrance.

I swallow a moan as I sink inside her burning heat.

So. Fucking. Good.

"Seb," she moans as I push deeper, my grip on her hip tightening as her body sucks me deeper.

"Need you, baby," I whisper.

"I'm right here. Anything you need, Seb. I'm right here," she repeats sleepily.

"Fuck, you're perfect."

I rock into her slowly, taking my time, memorising every feeling of her pressed against me, wrapped around me.

No more words are said between us. They're not needed. As she twists her fingers with mine where I hold her hip, I feel everything she's trying to tell me, the strength she's giving me for what's to come.

When I sense she's getting close, I free my hand and find her clit, slowly rubbing her until she shatters beneath me.

A low moan rumbles deep in her throat as she rides out her release and her body trembles against mine.

"Seb?" she whispers once it's subsided.

"Yeah, Hellion."

"Fuck me. Take everything you need from me."

"Jesus, Princess."

"I know you need it. Don't even try telling me that you don't."

"I don't deserve you."

I almost cry out when she rolls away from me and I slip from her hot, tight body. But the second she gets onto her hands and knees, I breathe a sigh of relief and get with the program. Climbing to my knees behind her, I grab her hips and put her exactly where I need her before lining myself up and slamming balls deep inside her.

"Yes," I groan when I bottom out. Digging my fingers into her hips, I pull out and do it again, over and over until the bed is banging against the wall and she cries out with every powerful thrust of my hips.

Everything in my head falls away like it's nothing. The only thing I'm able to focus on is her. After all, she's really the only thing that matters.

"Fuck. Stella. Princess. Fuck. Baby," I chant as my balls draw up and her pussy clamps down on me.

Threading my fingers into her hair, I drag her up onto her knees so her back is to my front.

Banding one arm around her chest, I slide the other from her hip, dipping it between her legs and finding her clit.

"Need you to come for me, Princess," I growl in her ear.

She turns to me, her lips capturing mine in a wet and dirty kiss as my tongue licks into her mouth, mimicking what my cock is doing lower down her body.

"Come for me," I demand again into our kiss, my fingers pinching her clit.

"Seb, shit. Seb," she screams as she crashes. Her head falls back on my shoulder as she rides wave after wave of pleasure.

Two more sharp thrusts into her slick pussy and my release slams into me.

I sink my teeth into her shoulder as my cock jerks, filling her up.

The second I'm done, I fall forward, taking her with me and crushing her into the bed.

"Morning, Sebastian," Stella purrs beneath me, her voice rough from crying my name and her lingering sleep.

"Mmm," I mumble, kissing the burning skin on her neck. "Fucking love waking up with you, Princess."

"You just like easy access."

"Always." She chuckles. "You were awake, weren't you?"

"Yeah."

"Why didn't you say anything?"

"I was enjoying myself. And I wanted to know what you'd do to me when you thought I wasn't aware."

"You're a filthy little whore, Princess. I fucking love it."

"Seb," she moans when I roll my hips, showing her that I'm ready to go again. "Already?"

"With you, Hellion, always."

She wiggles and I reluctantly pull myself from her body to let her roll from beneath me.

She turns on her side and I do the same so I can look at her.

Reaching out, she cups my jaw and stares into my eyes. I hate the sadness, the sympathy oozing from them, but I also know she's only trying to help.

"We really should get ready," she says quietly.

I nod once. "I know."

Today's the day that I've known has been coming for years. I thought I'd accepted that it was going to happen sooner rather than later. But now it's here, I don't feel at all prepared for it.

Obviously, I have no memory of when we said goodbye to my father. But I remember every second of Demi's funeral, and knowing that we're going to be heading to the same church for the service this morning fills me with dread.

"It's going to be okay. Whatever you need, I'll be right there by your side, Seb."

I swallow, trying to force down the giant lump that's crawled up my throat.

"Come on," I say, pushing everything aside and rolling from the bed. "I want to dirty you up some more in the shower before we get clean."

"Sounds like a plan," she says, hopping from the bed and running toward the bathroom before I have a chance to grab her.

"Hellion," I warn, marching after her, taking in every inch of her bare skin.

My movements are almost robotic as I pull my suit from the wardrobe and dress.

I keep my mind focused on Stella and this morning. It's easier than thinking about what the rest of the day holds.

"I'm going to find Theo," I tell Stella. My voice is

cold and empty as I meet her eyes in the bathroom mirror before pressing my lips to her shoulder.

Placing her makeup brush down, she reaches back and takes my hand in a tight grip.

"I'll be five minutes."

"No rush," I breathe, although we both know it's a lie. We spent way too long in the shower together, and any extra time we might have had seemed to vanish.

With another kiss to her shoulder, I force myself to walk away from her.

"Hey," Alex says when he's the first one to see me coming.

The guys, including Daemon and Calli, are sitting around on the sofas, waiting for us. Their support means everything, and I hope they know that because I sure as shit don't have the capacity to tell them right now.

"Stella will just be a few minutes."

"Here." Theo passes me a hip flask when I pass him.

I give it a shake, and the second I discover it's full, I twist the top and knock back a shot.

It burns as it hits my throat, and the temptation to keep going is almost too strong to deny.

"Maybe save the rest for later, yeah?" Alex says, clearly sensing my need to down the lot and make this whole fucking day blur in front of me. "You can have it with this later," he says, passing me a rolled joint. "It's the good shit."

"Thanks, man."

I fall down on the end of the couch and silence fills

the room. Tipping my head back, I stare up at the ceiling as we wait for Stella.

"Boss has security locked up tight for today," Daemon finally says, breaking the unbearable silence.

His words make me jolt forward.

"He thinks something is going to go down today?"

Daemon gives me a one-shoulder shrug.

"Can't be too careful."

"Fuuuck," I groan, dragging my hand down my face.

Surely that crazy motherfucker wouldn't be deranged enough to try something with almost the entire Family there.

Would he?"

"Maybe it would be better if he did something," Alex says, shocking the shit out of me. "What?" he says when I give him a death glare. "We'd be more likely to catch him."

"I guess," I mutter, although that doesn't make me feel any better about this whole thing. "You sure you want to be a part of this, Baby C?" I ask Calli, who's sitting ramrod straight on the very end of the sofa, looking kinda hot in her fitted black dress and her new dark hair.

She twists her hands nervously in her lap.

She's been kinda absent recently. Ever since the shit that went down at Halloween. I know she's been checking in with Stella, but she hasn't hung out here as much as she was before. I get it. She's probably scared this place is going to go up in smoke any second.

"Of course." She throws her shoulders back. "Family. Right?"

I nod at her in appreciation.

I know we've pretty much forced her to remain in the shadows all this time, but I'm under no illusion that suddenly coming out and being a part of all of this—especially under the current circumstances—must be pretty terrifying.

A door opening down the hall drags my eyes away from Nico's little sister, and I watch as my girl walks down the hall toward her.

Someone—Alex, I think—wolf whistles when he sees her.

"Looking hot, Princess," Nico announces happily. "Ow," he complains when someone hits him.

"That's my fucking sister," Toby barks.

"Didn't seem to stop you checking out mine when she walked in."

"Shut the fuck up."

Ignoring their bickering, I focus on my girl as she steps up to my side.

Standing, I wrap my hand around the back of her neck and press my brow to hers, needing her strength.

"You've been drinking," she says, but there's no accusation there.

"Theo gave it to me," I say, incriminating him.

"Hey," he complains. "It should be Alex you're moaning at. That shit he gave you will make you lose your mind later."

"Can't fucking wait. High sex is the best."

Stella rolls her eyes at me before looking over at everyone else.

She smiles at Toby and then focuses on Calli.

"You look beautiful, Cal."

"T-thanks."

"Right. Shall we go and get this fucking over with?" I say, already antsy as fuck to just put this day behind me.

"Whatever you want," Theo says.

"What I want is to get wasted and forget it's even happening, but I'm not sure I'll get away with that."

Everyone stares back at me.

"You've only gotta say the word, man. We've got your back. No matter what."

My breath catches at the sincerity in everyone's eyes, but I swallow down my fear and stand tall.

"As much as I appreciate that, I need to do this."

"Then let's do this," Theo announces.

Calli stands and rushes over to Stella's side.

"Is Emmie coming?" she asks quietly.

"She said she was."

Looking up at Theo, I find him distracted by Daemon.

"Is that a good idea?" I ask.

Stella shrugs. "Probably not, but she insisted. I think she secretly likes you and just wants to be there for you."

"As sweet as that might be, I'd rather not be the one responsible for Theo killing her. You know he's still suspicious of—" Stella cuts me a look that stops my words, and I glance at Calli, who's staring at me with her brows pinched tight.

"Suspicious of what?" she asks.

"N-nothing," I say, looking between her and Stella, begging my girl for an out of this conversation.

Calli's lips purse in anger as she realises that we're still keeping her in the dark.

"I'll fill you in in the car, but you can't say anything," Stella concedes.

"I'm a fucking Cirillo, Stel. Family above all else, remember?"

"I know that," Stella assures her before flicking her eyes to the guys. "They don't. You still need to prove yourself."

"Ugh, whatever. Fucking wankers," she mutters, heading for the front door, making Stella snigger.

"I trust you, Princess," I tell her, lifting her knuckles to my lips.

"Good. You should. Now let's get this done so we can share that joint." She winks before leading me out to the cars.

We climb into her Porsche after Calli crawls into the back and the others spread out in the other cars. With Theo's Maserati still in the garage, he's had to cope with not being the go-to taxi driver.

The second we're out of the driveway, Stella reaches over for my hand, and she doesn't let go for the rest of the day.

I couldn't fucking love her more.

CHAPTER NINETEEN

Stella

The funeral was... heartbreaking.

The whole time we were in that church, Seb held himself with such solid composure that even I was impressed. I've seen him wear a mask before, put on a front. But never anything like that.

I might have been shocked by it, but mostly I was terrified because I knew that when he broke, it was going to be fucking brutal.

No one else might have seen it, but deep down, he was shattering into a million pieces.

Being back in that church, I knew he wasn't just saying goodbye to his mom, but he was reliving every single moment of being forced to say goodbye to Demi too.

He kept his eyes on one single spot the entire time

we were inside that building. And no matter what happened, who was speaking or what was being said, his point of focus never changed.

Neither did the trembling of his hand in mine.

I held tight. As tight as I fucking could. But I knew it was never going to be anywhere near enough, and it fucking killed me.

Sophia, Zoe and Jason stood in the row with us with the guys all directly behind.

I didn't need to look back to know their attention was on Seb. They sensed his impending crash just like I did.

One look over my shoulder at Theo and I knew just how concerned he was.

He'd even managed to ignore Emmie's presence, along with the Reapers she arrived with.

I don't know why I expected this to be a Cirillo Family only thing, but I was proved wrong quite quickly when I saw the size of the crowd that was here before us.

It seemed that losing a member of the Family meant that everyone—friends and enemies alike—all turn out to pay their respects.

Emmie stood between two tattooed bikers. I could only assume that the oldest one was her grandfather and the other her uncle.

My eyes caught hers through the crowd, and my brows pinched in concern.

Apparently, her dad is still unaware that she's been spending time with the club. This seems a little too public for my liking.

I smiled at her despite my concern, silently thanking her for coming.

As far as I knew, the Reapers had no idea we were looking into their possible involvement with my stalker. I just hope for Emmie's sake—for all our sakes—that we're wrong. That the things we've noticed really are just coincidences.

"Can we go home now, please?" Seb whispers in my ear later that afternoon while we're sitting at the venue for the wake, watching everyone around us.

Seb has had an endless stream of people to deal with as they've given him their condolences, and I've been forced to watch as he's fallen deeper into his despair with every word spoken.

He didn't want to come here. I told him that he didn't have to if he really didn't want to, but his pride stopped him from ducking out early.

I got it. Everyone was here, and certain things were expected of him.

I glance around the room, my eyes landing on Damien Cirillo where he's talking to the man I correctly guessed as Emmie's grandfather earlier, along with another man, who is quite clearly Italian, over by the bar.

"They seem very civil," I say, ignoring Seb's question in favor of my curiosity.

I've had a million questions on the tip of my tongue all day, but we've barely had a second to be able to talk.

"It's all an act. A ruse to keep the truth under the radar. We might know things, others might suspect things, but until a full-out war is announced, this is how it always is.

"On the surface, we work together, we follow the rules that have been set out over the years—"

"But in the background, you're all killing each other?" I finish for him.

He laughs, but it's empty, hollow. "Yeah, something like that."

"So trust no one then?"

"Same as every other day of our lives, baby."

I blow out a long breath. "And people think it's glamorous?" I think of some of the people at school, Teagan and her bitches, who clearly just want to be a part of the action, to claim the status. They have no clue what it's really like, and they never will because they couldn't cope with the reality. I'm not sure many people could.

"People are idiots."

"Amen," I joke. Leaning over, I brush my lips over his cheek before pausing at his ear. "Let me go to the bathroom and then you can take me home." His hand lands on mine that's resting on his thigh, and he drags it higher until I'm cupping his already hard dick. "Seb," I growl.

"You mention home and that's what happens, baby."

"You're insatiable."

"You're complaining?"

"Hell no. Give me five."

I drop a kiss on his lips and give his cock a teasing squeeze before taking off across the room.

Calli and Emmie's eyes follow me, and I know that I'm about to have company.

"How's he doing?" Calli asks the second we step through into the bathroom and find that—by some miracle—we're alone.

"Yeah, you know."

Calli shakes her head. "I can't even imagine what it must be like for him. Losing one parent is bad, but two? So fucking cruel."

Emmie remains quiet beside us.

"What about you?" I ask, turning to her. "Your dad know you're here with the big bad bikers?"

She snorts a laugh. "Oh yeah, I totally fessed up." She rolls her eyes. "He'd kill me for hanging out with them, let alone this." She gestures to what's happening out in the main bar.

"So why are you? Don't you trust him that you should stay away?"

"Yeah, of course. My dad's smart. Crazy fucking smart but—"

"You can't help rebelling despite knowing it's the wrong thing to do?" Calli finishes for her.

"Something like that. I'm not saying I want a part of all that. I just..." She lets out a long sigh. "It's a part of my family, my history. Just like you two, I want to know about it, understand it."

"You want to make your own decisions about it?" I guess. It's exactly how I feel about the Family.

"Yeah. My pops and uncle, they've done some bad shit."

I scoff a laugh. "Has anyone out there not?"

"True. I just... I dunno, I'm just curious, I guess."

Calli's eyes hold mine for a beat. I told her the basics on the way to the church earlier about us looking into the Reapers, so she's aware that Theo at least is suspicious as fuck about Emmie and her current involvement with her family's club, but I don't need to ask her how she feels about it. I can sense her loyalty to Emmie from here.

I feel the same. I don't think she'd cross us like that. But I can't ignore the facts, either.

All of it is giving me a fucking headache.

"Fair enough," I say. "You have every right to be able to form your own opinions. Just... please, be careful."

"I am. It's my dad I need to worry about, not those scary-ass motherfuckers. Cruz has made it very clear to all of them as to what would happen should anyone hurt a hair on my head."

"Well, that's something at least," I mutter, heading for one of the empty stalls.

The girls change the subject to something a little safer to be discussing in public. Even if we are surrounded by all these power-hungry and dangerous men, it seems sensible not to be openly talking about them and our connections.

Calli is happily relaying to Emmie how Teagan fell flat on her face from halfway up the pyramid at their last cheer practice as we make our way back to the bar.

Someone walking toward us, his wide, leather-covered frame taking up damn near the whole fucking hallway, makes us move to the side.

I look at him and recognition hits me. His face is looking a little healthier than the last time I saw him, but I know it's him. I recognise the eyes.

He nods at me, clearly knowing exactly who I am as well.

"Joker," I say in greeting, needing him to know that I'm more than aware of who he is.

"Princess," he snarls, making my brows draw together in confusion. No one calls me that aside from my boys. But when I focus once more, I find him looking over my shoulder at Emmie—who just growls in frustration.

"Fuck off, Joker, before I fucking castrate you."

"You weren't saying that the other night." He winks as he leers at her. The look makes my skin crawl. He's not much older than us, and without all the blood covering his face, he's not bad to look at, but something about him just gives me a major case of the creeps.

He disappears down the hall toward the bathroom before I get a chance to respond.

Spinning on my toes, I place my hands on my hips and pin Emmie with a look. "The other night?" I ask with my brow quirked. "Something you need to tell us, *Princess?*"

She flips me off, her lips curled in disgust at the nickname.

"He just took me for a ride. His bike is fast as fuck. It was amazing."

"Adrenaline junkie," I mutter, laughing.

"Oh, like you're one to talk. What did I hear about a midnight drag race?"

"How'd you know about that?" I ask, my voice a little harsher than I was intending.

Emmie frowns at me in confusion. "Uh... Calli told me."

Calli nods in agreement.

"I need a fucking drink," I mutter, turning away from them, more than ready to find Seb and get the hell out of here.

I agreed to drive so we could flee if he needed it, but I'm starting to regret it because some alcohol would really fucking help right now.

"I was about to come and find you," Seb says from behind me a second before looping his arms around my waist and resting his chin on my shoulder.

"Sorry, we got to talking." I nod to Calli and Emmie.

"You two be good. No fucking the bad boys in the backroom," Seb warns both of them. Emmie rolls her eyes, her usual resting bitch face firmly in place, while Calli's eyes widen in shock.

"Keep your knickers on, Baby C. It was a joke. Jesus." Calli's tiny fists curl and her lips purse. "Someone really needs to get laid," Seb whispers in my ear.

"Sebastian," I warn, reaching behind me and slapping wherever I can reach.

"What? I meant me. I need to get laid."

"Jesus. We'll see you tomorrow, yeah?" I say to the girls, holding Emmie's eyes a little longer to get the confirmation I need from her about something we've been planning.

"Sure thing. She's going to need to be able to walk tomorrow," Emmie warns Seb, who just scoffs in my ear.

"I can carry her anywhere she needs to go."

"All right, caveman. Let's go. Have you said goodbye to your sisters?"

"We're good to go. Come on."

"**D**o something crazy with me," Seb slurs from the other end of the couch.

We're both laid out with our legs tangled, him in just a pair of sweats and me in just his hoodie.

My entire body feels like it's sinking into the soft cushions beneath me, thanks to the mind-blowing orgasms Seb forced on me like a man possessed from the second we stepped through the front door, along with the vodka and Alex's weed.

I feel fucking fantastic. And it's even better seeing Seb with a lazy smile playing on his lips and a little of his usual wicked sparkle back in his eyes.

"Anything," I say honestly.

"Come on then. Grab some shoes," he says, pocketing his cell and grabbing what's left of the bottle we've been passing back and forth.

"Uh... okay," I say, pushing aside any hesitation, because even half-cut, I know he wouldn't do anything to put me in danger. "Do I need more clothes?"

"Baby," he growls, closing the space between us

until my breasts brush against his bare chest, "you never need more clothes, only less."

He dips down, capturing my lips in an all-consuming kiss before pulling away all too soon, taking my hand and leading me from the apartment.

Wearing only his hoodie and a pair of Ugg boots, we emerge into the bitterly cold night. I have no idea where the others are; I can only assume the wake has finished by now. I guess they've planned something to give us some time alone.

We walk around the Cirillo house. There are some lights on, showing that someone is home, but Seb doesn't make a move to head inside so I just trail behind him. The cold air breezes under his hoodie, making my skin prickle and a shiver race down my spine.

Seb leads me toward the building at the bottom of the garden where I already know a state-of-the-art gym sits.

"You'd better not be expecting me to work out," I tell him as he pushes the door open and allows me to step into the warmth of the building first.

I've had nowhere near as much vodka or weed as him, wanting to keep my head somewhat in case something crazy happened, but I've still had too much to start fucking running.

"Nah, baby. I've got something much more fun in mind."

"Okay, I'm all in then."

A wicked smile curls at his lips and my heart rate picks up at the sight.

"Right answer, Hellion." He kicks the door closed

behind us but doesn't turn the lights on, leaving us with only the glow of some security lights.

He steps up to me, forcing me to take one back and making me bump up against the wall.

His dark and dangerous eyes bore into mine, and it sends a shot of arousal through me despite the fact that my muscles still ache from our sexcapades when we got back earlier.

"What are you planning, Sebastian?" I damn near purr his full name, knowing that it'll drive him crazy.

His fingers brush my thighs as he wraps his hands around the bottom of his hoodie.

In a heartbeat, he's dragged the fabric from my body, leaving me in nothing but my boots.

"Fuck, you're perfect," he growls, grabbing my breasts roughly, making a moan rip from my throat.

He makes the most of my parted lips and plunges his tongue into my mouth, finding my own.

Lifting one of my legs, he hooks it around his waist and grinds into me.

It drives me fucking crazy, and in only seconds I'm trying to climb him like a tree in my need to get more.

My hands go to his waistband so I can free his cock, but just before I grab the fabric, my feet leave the ground and I'm thrown over his shoulder.

"Seb, what the fuck?" I squeal, grabbing handfuls of his firm ass and squeezing until I'm sure it must hurt. "Ow," I scream when he retaliates by slapping mine. It burns like a motherfucker, but his hot palm soon comes back to soothe it.

"How wet are you, baby?"

"Fuck you," I hiss.

He chuckles, and the sound of his joy after the day we've had makes my heart flutter.

I've done that. I've helped drag him from the pits of hell he was drowning in earlier.

"That is most definitely the plan, Hellion."

He continues walking, but with the building in darkness, I don't get to see much. Although the smell that hits my nose when he opens another door and steps through sure gives me a solid clue about what his plans are.

I'm still hanging hopelessly over his shoulder as he tugs my boots off and lets them hit the floor with a thud.

My wanton moan rips through the silence of the room when he runs his palms up the backs of my legs and squeezes my ass hard.

"Seb," I groan when he slides a finger between my cheeks until he finds my aching core.

He pushes one digit inside, dipping it into my wetness and curling it in a way that makes my eyes roll back.

"Such a dirty whore, Princess. Do you know what I think you need?"

"No," I moan as he pushes a second finger in, despite the fact that I know exactly what's coming.

"You need a good clean," he says through his laughter before I find myself flying through the air.

"Gonna kill you," I scream just before the warm pool water swallows me whole and my surroundings vanish.

CHAPTER TWENTY

Sebastian

I toe my trainers off and place my cell on the lounger beside me but keep my eyes on Stella as she flails around in the pool.

I drop my joggers just in time for her head to pop back up.

She wipes the water from her eyes, but her gaze doesn't move from my dick, fully hard and desperate for her.

"That wasn't nice," she hisses.

I take a step forward, my toes curling around the edge of the pool.

"I'm sure I can come up with a few ways to make it up to you."

She bites down on her bottom lip as she watches me, waiting for me to do something.

"Want some company?"

"I guess that depends on whether you're going to give me what I need or not," she sasses, moving backward toward the shallows, slowly exposing more of her naked body to me.

"Don't I always give you what you need?" I growl, watching her with hungry eyes as her arse hits the edge.

"Well, you're pretty wasted," she says with a smirk, taunting me. "I might have to question your skills."

"Is that right?" I ask, amused as hell that she has the audacity to even question my ability while under the influence. She should know by now that I always do my job. Always.

She tilts her head to the side and studies me as she hops her arse up on the side, letting me see her body.

My cock jerks with my need to push inside her tight cunt. But I stay still, willing to play her game, for a bit at least.

"Yeah," she says, finally answering my question as she leans back on her elbows, places her feet on the tiles and spreads her legs.

It might be dark in here, but that doesn't mean I can't see every-fucking-thing.

"I think that maybe…" She gasps as she cups her breast, pinching her hard nipple between her fingers. "I should…" Her hand descends down her stomach and mine mimics, my fingers wrapping around my cock as I watch her. "Do it myself."

"And you think you can come as hard as I make you come?" I growl.

Her sharp gasp fills the silent room as she pushes two fingers into her pussy.

Fuck my life.

I stroke my cock, but it's not enough. It never fucking is anymore. Anything less than her is never fucking good enough.

"Yes," she cries, her back arching, putting on one fucking incredible show for me. I don't even care that she's faking it.

I dive off the edge, and a split second later, my body cuts through the water until I come up right in front of her.

"Want a close-up?" she asks, her breaths coming out in short, sharp gasps.

Okay, so maybe she wasn't faking it.

"I want more than that, Hellion."

Wrapping my hand around her wrist, I drag her fingers away from her cunt.

"Mine," I growl, pushing the two digits she was fucking herself with past my lips.

I suck them, lapping at her juices, letting her taste coat my tongue.

Her eyes darken as she watches.

Dragging her fingers from my mouth, I let her arm drop to the side.

"Now, tell me, Princess. Who does this cunt belong to?" I ask, stepping closer and running one finger lightly down the length of her.

"You," she breathes, her eyes holding mine. "I'm yours, Sebastian. All. Fucking. Yours."

Pressing my hands against her knees, I push her legs wider and drop my lips to the faded brand on her thigh.

I lick around my initials, wishing that I'd thought to bring my knife down here with me so I could rebrand her.

The knowledge that she walks around every fucking day with my name on her skin does some weird fucking shit to me that I'm sure a well-trained psychologist would have a field day with.

But fuck it, we're both as twisted as each other.

The only therapy I need is this. Her.

She's my fucking saviour.

My fucking everything.

"Seb, please," she moans when I take my time kissing up the soft skin of her inner thigh instead of diving for what we both want.

"Horny, baby?"

"You fucking know it," she barks, threading her fingers into my wet hair and dragging me closer to her pussy. "Now lick me. Suck me. Fucking anything. Just make me come. Please."

"Only because you asked me so nicely."

Pushing her legs even wider, I completely expose her to me and lick up the length of her cunt while she writhes on the tiles.

"Yes," she screams when I suck on her clit and slide two fingers deep inside her.

Her grip on my hair becomes painful, but I don't let up—not until she's riding my face as she cries out my name, her juices flooding down my hand.

221

"Fuck yeah," she groans her chest heaving as she lies back on the tiles, trying to catch her breath.

"Good?"

"It was okay," she says with a laugh, pushing to sit up once more.

"Switch," she demands.

I quirk a brow at her.

"What? You think you're the only one who can make demands? Get your ass on the side, Sebastian, and let me suck your cock."

She hops down into the water, her body sliding down mine.

I grasp her chin.

"You really have a way with words, Princess."

"Funny, because I thought you might prefer I use my mouth for something else, Sebastian."

"I fucking love your mouth no matter how you use it." To prove it, I slam my lips down on hers, pushing my tongue into her mouth and letting her taste herself on me.

Spinning us around, I bump against the pool wall and wrap my fingers around the edge, ripping my lips from hers when I jump up.

"All yours, baby," I say, shooting a look down at my painfully hard cock.

Her gaze follows mine and she licks her lips.

"Make it good," I tease.

She scoffs. "When don't I?"

Sliding her hands up my thighs, she leans forward and licks up the length of me.

"Always fucking mind-blowing," I confess as she takes me in her mouth.

Despite already coming more times than I can count today, it takes an embarrassingly few minutes before I'm balancing right on the edge again.

She fucking knows it too, because she keeps pulling back right at that moment before I come down her throat.

"You're killing me, Hellion."

She chuckles around me, making the delicious torture even worse.

She takes me deep, and I've got my cock buried in her throat when the sound of a door opening and voices in the distance sound out.

Her eyes shoot up to me, widening in shock.

"Don't fucking stop," I tell her, tightening my grip on her hair.

She's got her back to the door, so whoever's about to join us won't see anything of her, and that's all I really have the capacity to give a shit about right now.

"Fuck, Hellion," I groan, so fucking close to exploding.

The voices get closer, the footsteps louder, and then the lights around us come on, giving everyone a really good fucking view of what's happening.

"Oh fuck—"

My eyes lock with Theo's as he, Alex, Nico, Toby, Calli and Emmie all stand in the doorway with wide, although not entirely shocked, eyes. Knowing that they're watching is the final push I needed, and my release slams into me.

"FUUUUCK," I roar, my cock jerking violently as I fill Stella's throat. "Fuck, Princess. I love you. I fucking love you so much," I tell her, reaching down and cupping her jaw as I stare deep into her eyes.

"Fuck. Did he just—" A horrified female voice fills the space around us.

"You really need to lose that V card, Baby C," Alex tells her, amusement laced through his voice.

"What the fuck would you know about my V card, Alexander?" she growls back.

"Jesus, can we please stop talking about my little sister's virginity?" Nico snaps, marching farther into the room.

Pushing from the edge of the pool, I let the water swallow me up and wrap my arms around Stella.

"What the fuck are you guys doing?" I ask when they make their way over to the loungers and start getting comfortable.

Theo pulls his phone out and syncs it with the speakers, filling the whole room with music a few seconds later.

"Pool party, bro," Alex says, as if it's fucking obvious.

I run my eyes over all of them now that I'm not in my post-orgasm blissed-out state and notice they're all in shorts and t-shirts.

"Fucking hell," I mutter.

"Come join us," Theo says, his eyes flashing with amusement.

"Tell me they're not actually fucking serious," Stella mutters.

"Sorry, baby."

"I'm not walking out there naked."

"Too fucking right you're not."

"You guys are mean," Calli snaps, walking over to both of us and holding something out for Stella. "It's all I had. It might be a little small," she admits with a cringe.

"Thank you," Stella says, accepting the scraps of fabric Calli passes over.

"The guys have yours. Good luck getting them to bring it over, though."

"Fucking cunts," I mutter under my breath, releasing Stella so she can dress and march toward the shallow end, not giving two single fucks about everyone getting an eyeful. The guys have seen me naked more times than I'm sure they're willing to admit.

"What the fuck is wrong with you?" Emmie barks, clapping her hand over her eyes. "I'm not fucking high enough for this shit." Her other hand reaches out in Alex's direction, demanding the joint he's got to his lips. Unlike the others, she's the only one still wearing the same outfit she was earlier.

"No one invited you, biker bitch," he scoffs, although he does hand the blunt to her.

"Calli invited me, bellend. She wanted some kind of relief from all the macho alpha bullshit."

"She doesn't need to be here either," Nico adds as I snatch up the pair of shorts Theo was hiding behind his lounger.

"Just tell me you brought more alcohol," I demand.

"Of course, bro. What kind of pool party would this be without it?"

I drop down on a free lounger and gesture for Emmie to share, taking a pull on the joint as Stella emerges from the pool.

"Holy fucking shit," I gasp, quickly proceeding to choke on the hit I just took.

"You're a lucky motherfucker, man," Alex announces, clearly eye-fucking my girl.

"Yeah, I know." I scoot back on the lounger and pat the space between my thighs. Stella holds my eye as she walks over, her hips swaying, almost all her curves exposed and making my cock stir to life again.

Calli was right—the bikini is a bit small but in all the right fucking ways.

She takes a seat between my legs and rests back against me, tilting her face up to drop a kiss beneath my jaw.

"Love you," she breathes.

I hold her tighter, dropping my nose to her wet hair. I breathe her in.

"Can't believe these cunts gatecrashed."

"Oh, I totally can. They knew exactly what they were doing, too."

"Arseholes."

"Nah, Seb. They're just the best fucking friends you could ask for."

I look over at all of them, laughing, joking and passing around another joint and cans of beer and bottles of vodka.

"Yeah, they're all right, I guess."

"Fuck you, man," Nico barks, having clearly overheard. "We're the best and you damn well know it."

"What did you guys do with Daemon? Was he not up for a pool party?" Stella says, her body shaking slightly with a laugh.

"Daemon wearing anything other than his suit? You'd be lucky," Alex barks. "He's probably gone home to worship the devil or some shit. How the fuck we share the same DNA I'll never know."

The conversation moves on, the drink flowing along with the weed, and I keep my hold on Stella as I lose myself in my friends.

The events of the day might be up there with some of the worst of my life, but things are going to be okay.

I've got my boys, and most importantly, my girl, by my side. What more could I need?

CHAPTER TWENTY-ONE

Stella

"Oh my God," I groan quietly as I come to.

My mouth is like the bottom of a freaking bird's cage, my stomach is rolling, my head is spinning, and my body is covered in a sticky sheen of sweat.

Gross.

Rolling onto my back, I pray my stomach will hold and still for a few seconds as I wait for the result.

Seb snores loudly beside me, and when I glance over, I'm relieved to see that he actually looks relaxed.

Yesterday was all kinds of painful, saying goodbye to his mom and then having to endure everyone who wanted to offer their condolences.

Understandably, it was the last place he wanted to

be, and I feared I was going to lose him for longer than I did.

Thankfully, some—or a lot—of weed, a handful of orgasms, and good company seemed to help banish some of the shadows from his eyes.

I'm not naïve enough to think that's all it's going to take. But it was a good start.

My need for the bathroom eventually gets the better of me, and I silently sit up, swinging my legs from the bed and padding across the room.

Seb doesn't even stir. I come to a stop in the doorway and just watch him for a beat.

He's on his back, naked, the sheets draped low on his waist, so low they barely cover anything. And despite the soreness I feel between my legs from helping him forget last night, heat blooms at the sight of him.

Damn him. He's just too pretty.

I laugh quietly at myself. He'd hate me for calling him that.

My big bad mafia soldier tries to be all hot and scary, but right now, that whole persona is gone. He's just my broken boy with a pretty face and a sinful body.

My heart races as I watch him.

How is it possible that my feelings toward him flipped as fast as they did?

I hated him. I hated him so fucking much.

I smile as I recall some of our worst times.

But now...

Now he's my everything, and I can't imagine my life without him in it.

"I can feel you staring." His deep, raspy voice startles me. "Either come make use of this body or continue with what you were doing."

I chuckle at him. He doesn't even open his eyes as he shifts slightly, getting more comfortable.

The covers fall lower, and I'm gifted with the sight of all of him.

Hot damn.

I bite down on my bottom lip as I continue staring.

But my pressing need for the toilet forces me to move. That and my need for some painkillers.

I pee, turn the shower on and brush my teeth while I wait for it to warm up. I throw myself under the torrent of water in the hope that it'll help wake me up a little before finding one of Seb's shirts from the bedroom floor and dragging it over my body.

I add a pair of panties, brush out my wet hair, and call it a day.

I have no idea who's still here, but let's be honest, they've all seen me in a worse state before.

I pull the door open and quietly make my way down the hall.

Loud snores come from Alex's room, and I reach in and pull the door closed as I pass. But when I get to the living room and find three passed-out bodies, I discover it wasn't actually Alex, because he's on one of the couches with Nico and Calli on the other two.

I try to keep any noise to a minimum, but my need

for coffee means that only a second later the starting of the machine makes all three of them stir.

"Fuck off," a deep male voice rumbles. "Make it stop."

I can't help but laugh when Nico drags a pillow over his head to muffle the noise.

"I'm dying," Calli adds.

"Welcome to the world of hangovers and regrets, Callista," Alex sings.

"Oh God, what did I do?"

I can't help but laugh at the panic in her voice.

"You expect me to remember?" I ask with a laugh.

"You're good, Baby C," Alex mumbles. "You didn't fuck anyone in the pool, or give anyone a blowy in the steam room."

His words might reassure her somewhat, but when his eyes find mine, I realize that he's only recalling some of my actions from the previous night.

"You're gonna need to work harder to embarrass me, Deimos. We both know it's nothing you haven't seen before."

"We should have invited our own pussy," Nico grunts. "Partying with my little sister is a buzzkill."

"You could have left," Calli snaps.

"Guys, it's too early for this shit," Alex grumbles. "Coffee," he groans. "I need coffee. Princess?" He bats his eyelashes at me and I roll my eyes so hard it hurts.

"Fine. But you're ordering food."

"Deal," he says, pushing to sit up a little and reaching for his cell on the coffee table.

I grab a box of painkillers and swallow two before

throwing the box at a needy-looking Alex while the mouthwatering scent of coffee fills the air around us.

Calli stumbles her way down toward the bathroom, and I can't help but laugh as she bounces off the walls as she goes. Like me, she's dressed in one of the guys' shirts from last night, although I don't remember whose. They weren't wearing them long before they all dived into the pool.

Calli and Emmie refused for a while, preferring to watch them act like children from the loungers, but as they should have predicted, it didn't last long before Alex and Theo wrestled them away and unceremoniously threw them both into the pool, clothes and all.

Calli had a swimsuit on under her dress, but Emmie had apparently point-black refused to wear the pink bikini Calli had offered her and ended up just in her black underwear, much to Theo's faux horror and barely-concealed delight.

That sly fuck is so gone for her it isn't even funny.

He spent most of the night watching her every move, and I'm pretty sure it would have been the case whether she was walking around in her tiny thong and bra or fully dressed. All we need to do now is convince him to admit it to his pig-headed self and make a move.

The sound of someone moving around down the hall catches my attention as I deliver the first coffee to Calli—much to Alex's disgust.

"Ladies first," she sasses as she drops back down to the couch, clearly having come back to life a little after her trip to the bathroom.

"You're no lady, Baby C." He winks at her like he knows something I don't.

"You weren't thinking that last night while you were staring at her tits in that itty-bitty swimsuit." Alex cuts me a scathing glare while Nico groans, letting us know that he's not passed out under his cushion.

"My head hurts too much to listen to a conversation about my baby sister's tits. Ow," he complains when Alex throws another cushion at him.

It's not until I'm placing two more mugs on the coffee table that a door down the hall opens and a sleepy Toby emerges.

"Mornin'," he grunts, lifting his hand to run his fingers through his messy hair.

He's shirtless, just wearing a pair of sweats, but as impressive as his body is—just like all of them, assholes —it's the fresh scar on his chest that catches my attention.

Pain slices through my own as I remember what he went through recently, and all because of me. Me and my fucking deranged stalker. My stomach twists, much like it did when I first woke up, and I prepare to have to run to the bathroom.

Thankfully, it subsides with a couple of deep breaths.

"Hey," Toby says, clearly sensing where my head's at.

He walks over and grips the back of my head, pulling me into his body and pressing a kiss to the top of my head.

"I'm okay. And it's not your fault."

"But—"

"No, Stella. Just... no."

I nod in his hold and take a couple of seconds just to soak up his strength.

Seb isn't the only one who became a vital part of my existence almost overnight, because Toby did too. And long before I discovered how we were connected. I had no idea at the time, obviously, but I felt something... something stronger with Toby from that first day he dropped into my car and offered to sit with me while I waited for recovery. If only I knew how deep that connection ran, I might not have spent the entire night checking him out and trying to use him to drive Seb crazy.

"That's better," he says, noticing the smile on my face as I remember those early days. "Wanna share what's making you smile?" he whispers so the others can't hear us.

Taking a step back from him, I shake my head. "Just remembering how completely inappropriately I looked at you those first few weeks."

He barks out a laugh, but I don't miss the cringe that accompanies it.

"Yeah, well. You weren't the only one," he says. "I'm just glad your dad stopped us when he did."

"Jesus," I say, scrubbing my hand over my face. "I can't even—"

"Stop discussing your almost incest and get the poor guy a coffee," Alex shouts with a laugh.

"What the fuck did your last slave die of?"

"You'd probably rather not know, Princess."

I narrow my eyes at him. "Did you order food yet?"

"Yes," he drawls as if I'm boring him.

"Good, now shift your ass and let Toby sit down."

He salutes me with a wink and moves over a little.

"Where's Emmie?" Toby asks, looking around as if she's about to pop up from behind the couch.

"No idea," I say.

"I don't even remember getting back here, let alone how anyone else did," Calli confesses. "What the hell was in that weed?"

"Uh... weed?" Alex suggests, laughing when she flips him off. "I like you more now Stella has corrupted you, Baby C."

"Fuck you."

"I mean, Nico would probably kill me, but sure, I'm up for it if you are."

"You're a pig," Calli scoffs.

"Did she go home?" I ask, ignoring their bickering.

"Maybe she called an Uber to get away from Theo's desperate stares," Toby offers up.

"You noticed that too, huh?" I mutter, starting the coffee machine again.

"He just needs to fuck her."

"Who needs to fuck whom?" a familiar deep voice asks, sending a shiver down my spine.

Seb appears around the corner of the kitchen and my mouth waters when I find him also only in a pair of grey sweats.

Undiluted lust shoots straight through my veins at the sight.

"Hey," I purr, turning to him and running my hands over his bare chest, linking them behind his shoulders.

"Hey, Princess."

I brush my lips over his with the intention of keeping it chaste, but he has other ideas and crushes my body against his, sliding his hand under the shirt I'm wearing and gripping my ass roughly.

"Put her down, Neanderthal," Calli mutters.

"She loves it," Seb answers, although he does do as she said.

"Too fucking right, I do."

"So who needs to fuck?"

"Theo and Emmie."

"Oh, well, yeah. That's not fucking news. Go sit down, baby." Seb places his hands on my shoulders and pushes me toward the couches to take over playing barista.

I watch as he moves around the kitchen, making the final coffees before dropping down beside me and dragging me into his side.

"So, what did we miss?" he asks the others.

"Uh... other than not knowing where Emmie went, not a lot."

I think back over the events from the night before and try to remember how it all ended, but much like Calli, I don't really remember getting back here. I do have flashbacks of Seb and I in bed, though, and against the wall and...

"She came back here with us," Seb confirms, clearly having a better memory than the rest of us.

"Okay, so where is she now?"

"I'll call her," Calli says, reaching for her purse.

But she doesn't get a chance to make the call, because a door opens and heavy footsteps follow it.

All of us look up as Theo emerges.

I have to smother my laugh at the state of him. He's usually so put together that it almost hurts to look at him, but right now, he's hanging out of his ass.

His hair is sticking up in all directions, he's got more scruff than I think I've ever seen on his face, and he's got a...

"Dude, have you got a black eye?" Alex barks.

"Just..." Theo holds his hand up in the hope of stopping them. I can't help but laugh because... does he not know his friends at all? "Don't. Okay? Don't. I need coffee. Strong fucking coffee."

He just takes a step toward the kitchen when I hear something else. I'm not the only one either, because every head turns toward Theo's bedroom as someone else steps out.

"Oh my fucking God," Alex damn near squeals. "Hell yes, bro."

Emmie legit looks like she's been dragged through a hedge backward. Her hair is a matted mess on her head, she's got last night's dark makeup everywhere, and she's wearing Theo's shirt. But the most startling thing is what looks like dried blood down the side of her face.

"Em, what happened?" I ask, clearly the only one to see the real damage and not just get carried away about the two of them emerging from the same bedroom.

"I don't know," she hisses, "and that prick won't tell me."

I turn my angry stare back on Theo, but he's too focused on the coffee machine to appreciate the pure death in my glare.

"Someone order her a fucking Uber," he snaps. "I'm going back to bed."

The second he's got his coffee made, he disappears back down the hall and slams his door so hard the entire building vibrates.

"Well, I'll make my own then," Emmie shouts after him, flipping him off.

"I'll do it," Seb offers, making my heart sing.

"Thanks. Can I?" she asks, pointing at the box of painkillers on the coffee table.

"Help yourself," I say, and she does. Throwing two small pills into her mouth, she swallows them down dry, making my eyes widen in surprise.

"So?" I ask when she falls down beside me.

"So nothing. I'm having coffee then leaving." Her head falls back against the cushion and her eyes close.

"What happened to your head?" I ask, my eyes zeroed in on the blood.

She shrugs. "Ask that arsehole."

"Did you two—"

"No," she snaps, sitting up so fast it must make her head spin, because she squeezes her eyes tight and takes a deep breath. "No, we didn't. I don't even know how I ended up in there."

"Are you sure?" Alex asks, looking way too amused by all of us. "If you can't remember what happened, then how do you know you didn't..."

"Because I know," she snaps. "Either that or his cock is so small it didn't touch the sides."

Alex laughs as Nico sprays coffee everywhere.

"I've seen it. That's entirely possible," Alex happily supplies.

"Whatever," Emmie scoffs, turning back to me. "We didn't. You know?"

I nod, knowing what she means. Reaching for her hand, I squeeze gently. "I believe you," I whisper.

Seb passes her a mug and settles back on my other side.

Silence fills the room for a few minutes, the guys all lost in their cells until Alex feels the need to read out some lame-ass joke that he finds hilarious.

"You wanna come and use our bathroom to freshen up?" I ask Emmie. "We can take you home to change before..." I trail off, wanting to remind her that we've got plans but not wanting anyone else to know.

We had originally planned to get up and go to school today. Seb was insistent that life continue as normal despite everything, but I think we all unanimously agreed to forget about it somewhere between the vodka and the weed last night.

The clock is already showing that it's past lunch, so I think we all thoroughly fucked the idea of attending any class today, but thankfully, we've still got plenty of time for the surprise I've planned for Seb.

"Before what?" Seb asks, not missing a thing.

"You'll see." I drop a kiss on his cheek. "Come on, Em. Let's go fix you up."

CHAPTER TWENTY-TWO

Sebastian

I'm still feeling a little delicate when Stella, Emmie, Toby and I climb into my car a few hours later, although I'm confident that I'm okay to drive. The same can't be said for Nico and Alex, who were once again asleep on the sofas when we walked out—although not before I found a permanent marker and Stella and Emmie went to town drawing cocks on their faces.

The journey across town, first to drop Toby off, and then to Emmie's is pretty quiet, everyone still suffering from the night before, but I'm more than happy while I've got Stella's hand locked in mine.

Every time I look at her, my chest aches as I think about her strength and support yesterday.

I couldn't have done it if she weren't beside me. There's no question in my mind about that.

I wouldn't have been able to stand there while my sisters fell apart, while people who didn't have a clue about our real lives stood up and talked about Mum like she was someone who actually cared more about her kids, her life, than she did the poison she filled her body with. But worst of all, the memories. Stella helped keep them at bay.

She glances over at me as I pull the car to a stop outside of Emmie's house.

'I love you,' she mouths before pushing the door open and climbing out.

I follow because I'm powerless to do anything else.

"Are you going to tell me what you're up to yet?" I ask, trailing the two of them into the house.

It's empty, Emmie's dad is at work and Miss Hill is at school, although probably not for much longer seeing as the day is almost over.

"Nope."

"I won't be long," Emmie says, quickly disappearing upstairs and leaving us in the middle of the hallway.

The house is nice, although pretty modest compared to the homes I'm used to, living the life I do. But it's homely, comfortable, and as I look over the array of photographs that line almost all the surfaces, I quickly realise that it's full of love.

"Hey, look," I say, staring at one picture. "It's Miss Hill as a kid."

Stella comes to stand beside me and looks at the image of the two smiling teenagers before us.

"Emmie's dad was hot back then," she announces, the twinkle in her eye telling me that she's just trying to get a reaction.

"Just back then? I thought you were pining after him now," I say, playing along.

"Oh yeah. He's got that bad boy biker thing down to a T."

"Bad boy biker grandad," I mutter.

Stella throws her head back and laughs. "He's not that old. He had Emmie at like, eighteen."

"Still too old for you to be lusting after, Hellion."

She shrugs as if it's not a big deal before walking over to some more photographs.

"We should send this one to Theo," she laughs, giving me little choice but to walk over and see what she's found.

"What is it with parents taking photos of their kids naked in the bath?" I mutter, knowing that Mum has the exact same images in an album in the house somewhere.

"No idea. But look how cute she is."

"Sure cuter than she is now."

Stella looks over at me, her eyes narrowed. "She's not involved in any of this."

She's so confident in her friend, and I want to agree with her, but these kinds of coincidences don't usually exist, and I can't get Theo's theories out of my head. He's convinced that she's somehow involved. Even if she's not aware that she is.

"Only time will tell, baby."

Her lips purse in frustration, but she doesn't get a

242

chance to argue with me because feet pounding down the stairs stop her from saying anything.

"Ugh, really?" Emmie complains when she spots what's holding our attention. "You couldn't have just gone and helped yourself to something in the kitchen?"

"Aw, you've got a cute butt, Em."

An angry growl rips up her throat and she quickly swallows her frustrations and tosses her hair over her shoulder.

"Are we ready to go?"

"Yep," Stella agrees happily.

"Go where?" I ask, looking between the two of them. It's more than obvious they've been conspiring about something, and curiosity is killing me.

"Surprise," Stella says, turning to me with a wide, mischievous grin.

She slips her hand into mine and pulls me out of the house behind Emmie, but she doesn't release me so I can walk around to the driver's side of the car. Instead, she drags me into her body and backs me up against it.

"Hey." She smiles up at me through her lashes.

"H-hey. What's going on, Hellion?"

She reaches up and cups my jaw, and I'm powerless but to lean into her touch.

"Do you trust me?" she asks, making my brows pinch.

My fingers curl around her waist. I tug her closer, using her body to pin me against the passenger door.

"You know I do," I breathe, dipping to capture her mouth but quickly finding that she's got other plans.

Right before my lips connect with hers, her hand dives into my pocket and her fingers wrap around the key before she pulls it out with a triumphant smile.

"You know I'd have given you that if you'd just asked."

She shrugs. "Where's the fun in that?"

I shake my head at her, unable to wipe the smile off her face.

"Are we going or what?" Emmie sasses from behind Stella.

"Yeah, we're going," Stella agrees, dropping a quick kiss to my lips. "Remember you said you trusted me," she warns before skipping around to the driver's side and dropping behind the wheel.

"I'm going to regret this, aren't I?" I ask Emmie, who doesn't look half as excited as Stella.

She shrugs. "Get in the back, Seb," she demands, pushing me out of the way and pulling the door open.

"Oh sure, yeah," I mutter, rolling my eyes at her as I move.

"You look cute in the back, Sebby."

"Sebby?" I ask, the roughness of my voice relaying just how much I hate that nickname.

Demi used to use it to annoy me as I got older.

My fists curl and my jaw tics as I think about her.

As if she knows, Stella's eyes catch mine in the rearview mirror and she blows me a kiss.

"Come on then, I want to see what you're up to," I demand, forcing the memories aside.

As Stella pulls out onto the street, Emmie takes over

the music and some hard rock booms through the speakers.

"Really?" I mutter.

"Quit bitching," she scoffs. "We're in charge right now."

"Ain't that the fucking truth," I mutter, making Stella laugh.

Slouching back in the seat, I focus on watching her drive across the city to save me from diving headfirst into memories from yesterday and the constant ache in my chest.

Her hand grips the wheel tightly. Unlike everyone else, letting her drive my car doesn't really bother me—not that I'm going to tell her that. I'm pretty sure it's got something to do with just how hot she looks while she's driving.

She's got her hair up in a messy bun, allowing me to see down her slim neck before her skin gets covered by her leather jacket.

"I can feel you staring," she says, shooting me a quick look over her shoulder.

I shrug, totally unfazed at being caught.

"You're mine," I state like it's the answer to everything.

Sitting back, I rip my eyes from my girl, watching the shops and houses pass outside, trying to work out what they've got planned. But as we navigate the streets with Emmie directing, I'm no closer to guessing where the hell we're going.

"Just pull up over here," Emmie eventually says,

pointing to a space on the side of the road a little farther down.

Stella parks with ease, kills the engine, and then turns to look at me with a wide smile playing on her face.

The little bit of unease I was feeling about what we're doing immediately disappears. I wasn't lying when I assured her that I trusted her. I do implicitly.

"We don't have time for this," Emmie mutters, pushing the door open and climbing out.

"What's her problem?" I ask with a laugh, although I think we all know full well what her issue is. It comes in the form of my best friend.

Stella shakes her head at me and climbs from the car.

It's not until I'm on the pavement beside them and looking down at the businesses that line the street that I start to get a clue as to what we're about to do.

"Hellion," I growl as she grabs my hand and starts moving forward.

"What's wrong? Not scared, are you?"

"Scared? No, baby. Just intrigued."

"Good. Although something tells me you're going to love it." With that said, she drags me through the front door to a tattoo studio called Rebel Ink.

A pink-haired woman sitting behind a desk welcomes us, but the second she smiles at Emmie and addresses her by name, I realise that there's much more to this than I first thought.

"This is Stella and Seb," Emmie says, introducing us.

"Hey, I'm Biff. It's so good to finally meet you. Emmie's always talking about you, little chatterbox she is," Biff teases while Emmie's lips purse in frustration.

"She's lying. She didn't think I had real-life friends until you just walked in."

"She's right," Biff agrees with a laugh. "Her daddy is always telling us about her imaginary friends. He—"

"Right, are we about done here?" Emmie snaps, her face beginning to turn a little red as to why we're in this specific studio hits me.

"Yeah, he's all ready for you and already settled your bill. Have fun, kids." She winks.

My teeth grind at her calling us kids. I haven't been a fucking kid for years. Sometimes I wonder if I ever actually had the chance to be a real one.

I think back to those photographs of Emmie as a baby. Yes, there are a few in Mum's house of me. But mostly, all those kinds of photographs are of my sisters. Back when they had two excited parents watching them grow and learn. By the time I got there... I push those depressing thoughts from my mind as Stella drags me in the direction Emmie disappears in.

"We're here," she announces, throwing a door open dramatically and marching inside. "Dad, this is Stella and Seb. Your victims for the afternoon."

"Fantastic. I love young meat. As long as it's not yours," the inked-up biker says, ruffling Emmie's hair and instantly pissing her off.

I squeeze Stella's hand as she laughs.

"One day soon, old man." She winks at him before

falling down onto a sofa in the corner of the room as if she lives here.

"Right, well. I'm D, that brat's long-suffering father. Apparently, I get to cause you both some pain today." He rubs his hands together, excitement twinkling in his eyes.

"It's nice to finally meet you properly," Stella purrs, her voice dripping in lust.

I know she's baiting me by flirting with him. But fuck. It works.

Wrapping my hand around her waist, I drag her back into my body and growl quietly in her ear.

Sadly, Emmie's father doesn't miss the move, and his eyes flash with something.

"So, Sebastian Papatonis," he mutters walking back to his little wheelie stool.

"Yeah, what of it?"

He chuckles as he continues getting his kit ready.

"Nothing. Nothing at all. I trust Emmie's judgment."

"Oh yeah, of course you do," Emmie scoffs.

"Ignore her. If you're friends, then I'm sure you're well aware of what she's like." He sticks his tongue out at his daughter and she flips him off.

Their relationship makes my heart ache and forces me to wonder how my life would have been if things turned out differently.

"Okay, so who's first?" he asks, dragging me from my morose thoughts.

Stella looks over at me, a wicked smile playing on her lips.

"I'm first," she damn near purrs.

"Fucking hell," I mutter, scrubbing my hand over my face.

"Take a seat, Seb. You get to watch." Motherfucker winks at me. He knows too damn well how torturous this is going to be. I don't even know where or what he's tattooing yet and I'm already a mess.

All the things Stella's ever said about Emmie's hot dad flicker through my mind as I fight to keep my jealousy at bay.

I know it's irrational. I'm sure he's completely professional. Hell, his fucking daughter is sitting beside me. But still. She's mine.

M. I. N. E.

She holds my eyes as she undoes the button on her skirt and lets it drop to her feet, leaving her in just a pair of black boy shorts.

My arse barely hits the leather of the sofa before I'm up once more.

"What the fuck?" I bark, much to Stella's amusement.

"Chill out, caveman," Emmie mutters. "My dad's hardly gonna feel her up with us watching."

"I can make you sit out in the waiting room if you'd prefer," D offers, a knowing smirk on his lips.

"No," I state, sitting back down and folding my arms over my chest.

Stella's eyes hold mine. I have no idea how she doesn't just give in to her amusement. It's written all over her face.

"Some fucking surprise," I mutter, resting my

elbows on my knees as I prepare to watch some other guy with his hands on my girl.

"It'll be worth it. Promise." She blows me another kiss, and dammit, it helps.

"Chill the fuck out, man," Emmie hisses. "You're starting to lose your bad boy image."

"Oh yeah?" I ask, glaring at her. "Luckily for me, I don't really give a fuck what you think."

D clears his throat.

"So how's Miss Hill?" I ask, looking back over at him. "You had her in that chair yet?"

His eyes darken enough that I don't really need an answer.

"Oh my God, Dad," Emmie huffs.

"What? You've seen her ink."

"Yeah, it's amazing but... ugh. Can we just get on with this? I can't stand the tension vibrating from this dick." She shoots me a look.

"Do you need to be here?" I ask her, my brows raised.

"And miss my dad causing you some pain?"

D's low chuckle of amusement fills the room as he wheels himself into place and tells Stella to move her leg.

"Fuck my life," I whisper to myself as I realise where this is happening.

D sucks in a breath when he sees the scar I left behind on her inner thigh.

His hard eyes hold mine before they move to his daughter. "Any guy carves you up like this, Em, I'll fucking kill him. Okay?"

"Yeah, whatever, Dad," she mutters, not even lifting her eyes from the screen.

He gives me another warning stare that I meet, my gaze never faltering.

He might be an ex-Reaper, but he hasn't been active for years despite his family connections. Safe to say, I'm far from scared of him.

I shrug, finally resting back on the couch as a familiar buzzing fills the room and he sets to work on my girl.

At least he's fully aware of who she belongs to now.

CHAPTER TWENTY-THREE

Stella

I knew this was going to be fun, but man, I didn't know Seb's reaction was going to be this good.

"Is he still growling at me?" D whispers, and I have no choice but to throw my head back and laugh as he lifts his machine, giving me a little reprieve from the pain on my thigh.

"Oh yeah," I say after a few seconds. "I'm not expecting that to stop anytime soon."

"I'm not sure whether I should be warning you off him or telling you you're brave for being anywhere near him."

"Maybe he's the brave one."

"From what I've heard, you might be right. What do you think?" he asks, shooting a glance down at my very sore-looking thigh.

"It looks amazing, thank you so much," I say sincerely.

When Emmie first spoke to him about doing this, he was super reluctant. Both of us are old enough, but knowing that we were Emmie's friends made it a little weird for him. Especially as he's adamant that Emmie is not getting any ink anytime soon—well, not from him at least—so I think it made him feel like a bit of a hypocrite. But the second Emmie showed me some of his work, there was no way he wasn't doing this.

I knew what I—what we—wanted. I'd already put a design together. Emmie had taken it off my hands and added to it in her own way, and then it finally went to D, who just made it sing.

I'm obsessed with it. And I can't wait to look at it every day for the rest of my life.

Seb though can't see fuck all right now, and it's killing him.

"Seb?" I ask, my voice all innocent.

"Yes," he growls, his eyes that have been drilling into me the whole time we've been here narrowing in curiosity.

"Theo's name is spelled T-h-e-o-d-o-r-e, right?"

His lips purse as the meaning behind my words hits him. I also don't miss Emmie's head fly up from her cell in curiosity. She's seen the design, but still, hearing Theo's name causes a reaction.

Damn, to have been a fly on the wall between them last night.

"You'll need a reminder, because if you have any of

their fucking names on your skin they'll no longer be breathing to see it."

D chuckles, and after stretching out his back a little, the buzz returns and he gets back to work.

"We'll see. He's all talk," I tell D.

"Fucking am I?" Seb scoffs.

D shakes his head at our bickering. I can only assume that he's fully aware of just how dangerous Seb and the rest of the Cirillo Family are, but he never says anything—aside from Seb's name when we arrived—to confirm or deny that.

I thought the time was going to drag as I laid here torturing Seb. But all too soon, D sits up and announces he's done, a triumphant smile on his face.

"Can I see?" Seb asks, sitting forward.

"Nope," I say happily. "Wrap me up, D. Then I want to see what a wuss my man is." I wink, not even trying to hide my teasing.

"Wuss. You know I've already had both sleeves done, right?"

"Inner thigh is no joke," D adds, happily joining in.

"Whatever. Get your arse out of the chair, baby."

Without waiting for instructions, he drops his pants, making Emmie and D's eyes widen in amusement before hopping up in the spot I waddle away from, the wrapping over my thigh and a wide smile on my face.

"You good?" Emmie asks as I drop onto the couch beside her. She passes me over a can of soda, and I don't waste a second in taking it from her.

"So good."

"That didn't hurt?" she asks, glancing down at my sore thigh.

"It was worth it."

She shakes her head at me. "You're a lost cause, you know that right?"

I look over at Seb getting comfortable on the chair and his eyes find mine.

"Yeah. I don't even care."

"I seriously hope you're not about to ink some cute pink fucking teddy or something into my thigh," Seb grunts as the buzzing restarts.

"I'm brave, Seb. But I'm not that brave," I joke. "Trust me, yeah?"

He nods at me and then to D to get started.

"I'm hungry," Emmie whines a few hours later.

"Go get us all food then," D tells her, pulling his wallet from his pocket and throwing it down on the couch.

"Sure. You coming?" she asks me.

"Yeah, I'm starving."

I put my skirt back on a while ago but quickly shove my feet into my boots and head over to where Seb's laid out with his eyes closed on the chair.

To start with I wondered—sickly hoped— it was just hurting him so much that he couldn't focus on anything else, but it soon became apparent that he was actually asleep. Fucking weirdo.

He's clearly not totally out of it though, because the

second I press my hand to his chest, his eyes flicker open and he stares up at me with a softness in his expression that melts my heart.

"We're going for food. Any requests?"

"Yeah, take someone else with you."

"Seb, we'll be fine." I tap my purse, silently telling him that I'm more than equipped.

His eyes narrow, but he doesn't argue.

As it happens, the second we get to the reception area, Biff is pulling her coat on, ready to go out.

"How's it going?" she asks when she spots us.

"It's good." I pull the hem of my skirt up, showing her my new ink. "We're going for food."

"I'm getting coffees for the guys. Let's go."

She might be a few years older than us, but as we walk down the street, I fall into easy conversation with Biff about her job and life in general. It's quite refreshing, talking to someone who doesn't have the faintest idea about the drama surrounding my life right now. It makes me realize just how oppressing it is, looking over my shoulder every second and waiting for that sick fuck to make his next play.

Thankfully, the trip that results in burgers, fries and a huge trayful of coffee is uneventful, and when Emmie and I manage to get back into D's room, he's just putting the finishing touches on Seb.

"That looks insane," I tell him, although Seb doesn't look down. He hasn't since D started. His restraint is impressing me, because there's no way I'd have been able to wait, especially if I had no clue what was happening to my own skin.

"Let me wrap your boy and we can eat," D says, his deep voice rumbling around the room.

How he's sat in that position inking us all afternoon and evening I have no idea. His back must be aching like a bitch.

Emmie and I unwrap our burgers, eating in silence as D asks Seb if he wants to see.

"Nope, just wrap me up."

"You don't want to see?" I ask around my mouthful of food.

"Of course. But I'll look later. With you."

My heart flutters at his words.

"You know, you two are almost cute," D admits as he finishes up.

"Cute?" Seb scoffs. "There's nothing fucking cute about either of us. My girl's a bigger bad-arse than you. I fucking guarantee it."

"Oh yeah?" D asks, sounding all kinds of amused.

Dragging his eyes from D's, Seb looks at one of the many, many sketches covering the walls.

"Amazing resemblance of Miss Hill, D," Seb mutters. "Real bad boy biker of you."

"Fuck you, squirt." Seb just chuckles, knowing that he's touched a nerve. "I walked away from that life a long time ago. Best decision I've ever made. Emmie comes above everything."

I glance over at my friend just in time to see her swallow nervously. It only confirms what I already knew. D has no idea that Emmie has been hanging out with the exact people he's tried to keep her away from.

Rather her than me when he discovers that.

I raise a brow at her and she just waves me off, clearly not wanting to visit that little issue right now.

But she's not stupid. She knows it's coming.

D runs through the after-care instructions for our new ink before he grabs himself some food and Seb comes to sit beside me on the couch.

He drops a kiss to my bare shoulder before wrapping his arm around my waist and proceeding to eat his burger one-handed.

"I can't believe you didn't look," I whisper as D and Emmie lose themselves in an argument about when she can get her first ink.

"I will. When we're alone."

I shake my head at him. "You're crazy."

"Crazy for you."

I can't help it, I swoon so fucking hard. "That was cheesy."

He shrugs, biting into his burger.

Feeling eyes burning into the side of my face, I look up to see D staring at us.

"You two remind me of Piper and me when we were younger," he muses.

Emmie might not have given me any real details, but she did say that they knew each other as kids and that club bullshit ripped them apart.

"Want some advice?" he asks, deadly serious.

"Daaad," Emmie whines as if he's the most embarrassing person to ever walk the planet.

"Sure," I say, intrigued.

He holds my eyes for a beat before looking at Seb.

His lips part but no words come out for a second,

although when he does finally speak, it hits exactly where I think he was intending.

"This," he says, pointing between the two of us, "is a once-in-a-lifetime kind of thing. Fuck what anyone outside the two of you says or tries to do. Hold on tight and never fucking let go. Ever."

Seb's hand tightens around my waist as silence falls around us.

"I'm sorry you and Miss Hill lost so much time," I say softly.

"Yeah. I got her instead," he says lightly, nodding his head to Emmie.

"What he means is that he got wasted and fucked my mum without wrapping it."

"Yeah, did you need more advice?"

"No, no," I say with a laugh before he dives deeper into that conversation. "Got it covered, thanks."

"Good to hear it." Putting that to bed, he turns back to Emmie. "Speaking of the witch, you heard from your mother?"

Emmie shakes her head. "Still nothing."

I narrow my eyes at her. I knew something was going on with her, but I assumed it was the shit with Theo and the secrets she's keeping from her dad. I had no idea it was anything to do with her mom. She's barely ever mentioned her.

"I'll put some more calls out. She can't have just vanished off the face of the Earth."

"It's fine, Dad. If she wanted to be here, she would be."

He parts his lips to argue but quickly cuts himself

off when it becomes clear that Emmie really doesn't want to talk about it.

"Do you want us to take you home?" I ask Emmie once we've finished eating and D is cleaning up after us.

"I can take her. You're on the other side of town, right?" he asks without looking up at us.

"Uh, yeah. But it's okay," Seb says.

"S'all good. You two head off. You can spend the night comparing your ink."

"Okay," I say, jumping up. I'm more than ready for Seb to get his first look. "We'll see you at school tomorrow?" I ask Emmie.

"Hopefully you'll all be more successful at getting there tomorrow," D says, still with his back to all of us.

Emmie stills, realizing that she's been caught.

"It's my fault," Seb confesses. "We got a little carried away last night. You know, after my mum's funeral."

"It's okay, Seb. I get it. I'm not completely old and uncool."

Seb nods at D and moves toward the door.

"Thank you so much for this," I say.

"You're welcome. Try to stay out of trouble, yeah?"

Seb laughs. "Yeah, we'll see. Come on, Hellion. We've got things we need to do."

Heat rushes between my legs at his suggestive tone.

"Bye," I shout as Seb all but drags me from the room and down the hallway.

The reception desk is empty as we pass, but there

are voices coming from somewhere suggesting that Biff isn't too far away.

Seb doesn't stop until we're at his car.

With one quick flick of his arm, he has me pinned between the car and his body.

His eyes hold mine for a beat, and I prepare myself for what he might have to say about all that, but I soon discover that he has no words, because instead of telling me what he thinks, he shows me.

His lips crash down on mine in a brutal, bruising and claiming kiss.

My arms rest over his shoulders, my fingers in his hair as my lips part, deepening our connection and allowing his tongue to sweep into my mouth.

"Fucking love you, Hellion," he growls into our kiss.

"I love you too. Take me home. Please," I beg, my hands running down his body and slipping under his shirt. I can't help but smile against his lips when his muscles bunch at my touch. "I want you naked."

"Mmm..." he mumbles, still kissing me. "Not as much as I want you naked, I'm sure."

"Seb, please," I whimper when he starts kissing down my neck.

"Fuck, baby. Do you have any idea what you do to me?" he asks, although I get a good idea when he rolls his hips against me, allowing me to feel just how hard he is against my stomach.

"I'll demand you fuck me right here if you don't move."

"And you know I would, too."

Heat rushes through me, making my knees weak.

He fucking would as well.

Thankfully, he thinks better of it, and instead of just laying me out on the hood, he lifts me to the side, opens the door and places me in the passenger seat.

The drive home is almost as thrilling as what I know is coming once we get there.

Seb's grip on the wheel never loosens as he takes every corner too fast and jumps every light he can get away with.

By the time we pull into the Cirillos' huge driveway, my heart is racing and I've got a better understanding of just how he felt watching me race that bike the other night.

"Let's go," he barks, not wasting a second.

Clearly not quick enough, he rips my door open and drags me out, throwing me over his shoulder and racing up the stairs with me.

"Oh hey, where have you—"

"Go out," Seb barks, cutting off Theo's question.

"You know, I'm getting fucking sick of being kicked out of my own home."

"Then don't go. But don't say I didn't warn you," Seb mutters, sliding his hand up the back of my non-inked leg until he dips his fingers under my panties and finds my aching cunt.

"Oh fuck," I moan loudly when he pushes his finger deep inside me after discovering I'm more than just a little wet for him.

"Fuck it. I'm out. I can't do this again," his angry

voice booms through the apartment. I wince, feeling bad.

Once all this shit is over, we really need to sort out where the hell we're living, because Theo deserves his space, his peace, back.

As it is, Seb kicks the door closed behind us and throws me down on the bed. The look in his eyes when I find them makes everything else in my head vanish.

"Have I told you how fucking perfect you are recently?" he asks, dragging his hoodie over his head and discarding it on the floor beside him as he toes off his shoes and drops his pants.

The dark ink on his thigh catches my attention as he steps toward me and presses his knee into the mattress. But still, he doesn't look down at himself.

"What are you waiting for?" I whisper.

"Arms up," he says, wrapping his fingers around my tank and dragging it from my body. His hand wraps around the back of my neck as he claims my lips once more before he begins a teasing trail of hot kisses and painful nips, working his way down to my waistband.

He pops the button and pulls my skirt down my legs, quickly followed by my panties so that I'm naked before him.

"Seb," I whimper.

"Now," he drawls. "Now I'm going to look."

His eyes rip from mine and he trails them down my body until they lock on the ink on my thigh.

"Fuck," he breathes, lifting one hand to push his hair back as he stares down at D's handiwork.

In the center of the images are his initials, right on top of where he carved them, and surrounding those two letters is the most stunning sketch of things that remind me of us.

"You designed this?" he asks, hovering his fingertip slightly above the wrapping as he takes it all in.

"Yeah. I mean, I had a little help, but the ideas were all mine."

"Baby, it's—"

"Look at yours."

Standing from the bed, he pushes his boxers down his legs and kicks them from his feet.

His tattoo is almost identical to mine. The only differences are that he's obviously got my initials and his is entirely black, whereas I've got flashes of color to make mine a little more feminine.

"D is fucking talented," he breathes, alternating between looking at both of our thighs.

"Uh-huh," I agree. "So you like it then?" I ask. Even after seeing his reaction, I'm a little nervous that I got this inked on his skin without checking it with him. Although, he didn't have to just agree like he did.

"Like it? I fucking love it." His lips find mine and he kisses me until I'm breathless and grinding up against him, desperate for more of him.

CHAPTER TWENTY-FOUR

Stella

As promised, we all went back to school the next day and tried to return to normal. Or as normal as our lives ever have been.

Emmie still refused to talk about what happened with Theo the night of Helen's funeral, and Theo has been just as tight-lipped about it. I'm curious as fuck, but I won't push them about it. If they want to talk—hell, if they even remember—then they will when they're ready.

"We should probably go out," Alex says from the other couch on Friday night as he lights a joint.

"He's right. This fucking psycho has turned us into boring motherfuckers," Nico adds.

"You're more than welcome if you wanna go out and get your dicks wet," Seb says, his fingers squeezing my thigh where his hand has been resting as we've hung out as a group.

"Do you have to be so fucking smug?" Theo mutters, tipping his beer back.

"You're telling me you'd be different if you had what I have?"

"Seb," I warn. We both agreed that we'd tone it down a little for Theo's sake. We might be no closer to making a decision about what we're going to do, but we do need to stop banishing him from his own home.

"What, baby? It's true."

"We haven't had a guys' night in ages," Nico complains.

"Don't let me stop you if you all want to go and get wasted in a strip club." Nico and Alex's eyes light up at my suggestion.

"That wasn't what he meant," Theo points out.

"No, and I'd rather watch you strip any day," Seb whispers in my ear.

"Well, go out and do whatever it is you used to do before I gatecrashed your party."

They all look at me like I've grown an extra head.

"What? I'm not some bunny boiler who doesn't want Seb to have a life, to have fun without me. I can call the girls over to have a slumber party," I say, knowing exactly where their dirty minds are going to go.

"Maybe we should stay in," Alex says. "Get our pyjamas out and have a pillow fight."

"With Seb's girl and my sister? Sounds like a wild night," Nico deadpans.

I sip my drink while they all debate whether they want to actually go and do anything or not until Theo's phone pings on the coffee table, making Toby pause mid-sentence and all of them still.

"Well, I guess we just got our answer, boys," Theo announces, although he sounds anything but happy about it. He reads whatever is on his phone before muttering, "Suit up, we're needed."

"You're fucking kidding me," Seb complains.

"Do I look like I'm kidding? Boss wants us in."

"All of us?" Toby asks.

"Yep. His office, forty-five minutes."

"Fucking hell. Let's move."

Before I even have a chance to ask anything, they all scatter.

"I'll call the girls then, shall I?" I shout after them all.

Knowing I'm not going to get a response until someone reappears, I pull my cell from my hoodie pocket and find my group chat with Calli and Emmie.

It only takes three minutes to discover that Calli has plans with her mom but that Emmie is bored out of her head at home and more than happy to come over, as long as the boys aren't here.

I assure her they're about to leave and climb from the couch.

"Hey, Emmie's going to come over," I say, resting back against our closed bedroom door as Seb dresses in his suit and then runs some wax through his hair.

"Good, I'm glad we're not leaving you alone."

"Any idea why you've been called in?" I ask, walking up to him and helping straighten his tie.

He doesn't need me to help, he's more than capable, but he humors me nonetheless.

"You know as much as me, baby."

"Do you think it's got anything to do with me?"

"I'm fucking hoping the boss has got some stupid fuck strung up by the balls for ever hurting you."

"Aw, you say the sweetest things," I say, running my hands up his chest and resting them over his shoulders.

"I'll be back as soon as I can."

"It's okay. We'll just hang here, watch a film or something."

"If you order in, you know to—"

"Only order from Cirillo restaurants. I know. I've got this, Seb."

"No crazy trips to the Avenue?" he asks, quirking a brow.

"Nope. We're having a night in. Promise."

It's the first time all five of them have been called away together in weeks. The thought makes my stomach knot, because it's obviously something serious.

"Okay." He drops a kiss on my lips and takes my hand, leading me down the hallway to meet Theo, who's already waiting.

"Anything?" he asks Theo, who shakes his head.

"Nothing, but I fucking hope it's a lead."

"Same," Seb agrees. "Keep your phone close and don't—"

"I'll be right here when you get back."

He nods, although I can see his concern shining bright in his eyes.

"I'm safe here. I'll lock up once you go and after Emmie gets here."

"Come on," Theo says, clapping Seb on the shoulder.

"I love you," Seb says, looking at me over his shoulder as Theo directs him toward the door.

"I love you too. Stay safe."

"Always." He blows me a kiss before disappearing.

"You're so fucking whipped, it's pathetic," Theo mutters as they descend the stairs, making me laugh.

"Just you wait," Seb says. "It'll happen to you one day and I'll remind you of all this."

"What the fuck ever," Theo scoffs before the door slams closed, leaving me alone for the first time in... a long fucking time.

Knowing that Emmie won't be long, I quickly tidy up and throw the dirty dishes sitting on the counter into the dishwasher before making us both a drink and putting some music on.

The bell rings only a few minutes after I sit down on the couch.

Just like I promised Seb, I'm sensible and check the camera before opening the door. It's completely unnecessary, because it's just my girl standing on the other side.

Theo's wrong about her involvement in this. I know he is. He's just clutching at straws, trying to find a reason to dislike her so he can convince himself to push her away.

269

I see you, Theo Cirillo.

"Hey," I say with a wide smile, moving aside to let her in.

"I can't believe they left you alone," she says, looking around the living area as if one of them is about to pop out and shout boo.

"I know, right. It feels... weird."

Emmie kicks off her boots and falls down on the couch like she owns the place.

"So what's the plan then?" she asks, accepting the weak cocktail I made her seeing as she's probably going to want to ride home later.

Shrugging, I drop onto the opposite couch. "I don't have one. Thought we could just hang."

Her brows rise in shock. "And here I was thinking I was being tricked into some crazy plan that would drive Seb insane."

"I don't have the energy," I admit, slouching back.

"Who are you and what have you done with Stella?" she asks, mocking me.

"I know, I know. The last few weeks have been fucking mental. I just want to chill the fuck out. Watch some shit on the TV and... I dunno," I confess. "Breathe a little."

"I get that." She lifts her glass and takes a drink. "Have you eaten?"

I shake my head. "No. You?"

"Chinese? I could murder some chilli shredded chicken."

"Sounds good to me."

I pull up the menu on my cell and select what I

want before throwing it at Emmie so she can add whatever else she's craving.

After I hit order, I fall back on the couch and stare at whatever is playing on the TV. Silence surrounds us, but it's completely comfortable.

I glance over at Emmie, desperate to question her on Theo, amongst other things. She wants to talk; I can see it in the slight frown on her brow and the darkness in her eyes.

"Emmie, are you—"

"I'm fine," she snaps, predicting what I was about to ask, inadvertently giving me the truth.

"Em," I breathe, twisting to give her my full attention. "What's going on? You can tell me anything, I promise it won't go any further."

She laughs, but there's no humor in it. Only pain.

"I trust you, Stella. I do. I just..." She shakes her head. "I don't want to talk about it."

"Okay," I say, but I refuse to change the subject completely. "Your dad have any idea that you're hanging out with Cruz yet?"

She visibly pales at my question.

"He's going to literally kill you, you know that right?" I thought it before, but after spending all that time with him the other night as he inked us, I'm now more confident than ever that he'll blow his fucking lid when he finds out.

"I know. I just—"

"Want to know the truth about who you are. I get it, I really do, Em. But is it worth it?"

She lets out a heavy sigh.

"When I'm there, no one treats me like a kid," she confesses. "My name alone makes most of the guys treat me with a level of respect I don't get anywhere else. It's... refreshing. It makes me feel like I'm part of something. Like I belong somewhere."

"You do belong somewhere. You belong here."

Her brow lifts. "Do I? Theo hates me. He hates me being here. The others just put up with me because they're scared of you. And don't even try to tell me that I belong at school."

I can't help but laugh at the way her face twists at that point.

"No, Em. I think I can safely say that neither of us belongs there. But we're in that together."

"I didn't want any of this. I just wanted to..." I don't say anything in the hope that she'll continue. "Disappear," she finally says after long, silent seconds.

"What's going on with your mom, Em?"

Her eyes drop from mine in favor of the coffee table, but not before I spot the tears that well in her eyes.

"It's nothing I didn't expect," she mutters quietly. "She was never going to win mother of the year or anything, but for her just to fuck off and not look back..." She sighs. "It hurts more than it should."

I smile sadly at her.

"I—" I cut myself off from my knee-jerk reaction of telling her I'm sorry. I hate that fucking saying when something's gone wrong, or someone's died. It wasn't my fault, so why am I accepting blame? "Wanna get wasted?" I ask.

"And still be here when the guys get back? No thanks."

I want to argue with her, but I bite the words back when I see the fierce determination on her face. There's no way I'm going to be convincing her to do anything she doesn't want to do tonight.

"I'll just drown myself in Chinese and sugar instead."

"Sounds like a plan. Any preference?" I say, pointing the remote toward the TV.

"Something where someone gets shot."

"Done," I say, flicking through until I find some action movie I've never seen before and hit play.

"What are the guys doing tonight?" Emmie asks a little later, while the hero of the movie meets the woman who will obviously become his love interest.

"No clue. It was all cloak and daggers."

"Must be important if they all left you."

I shrug. "Boss is probably fed up with them babysitting me."

"I dunno, I reckon he probably wants you safe just as much as they do."

"Why? He doesn't even know me." I've spoken two words to the man, and that was only because he attended Helen's funeral. If it weren't for that, I have every confidence that I wouldn't have seen him in person.

"He knows you well enough to protect you and your dad when all that shit went down. He protected you when you first came back, even if it was to put those arseholes on your case."

"I guess."

"It's family, Stella. It's how it's meant to be... apparently," she adds quietly.

"Your dad is amazing, Em," I tell her. "Most kids would kill for a dad as cool as him."

"Jesus, Stel. Promise me you'll never tell him he's cool."

I can't help but laugh at her. "Of course not. He is, though. You've got to admit that."

"He is. I deserve it after the shit show I got for a mother."

"You've got Miss Hill now."

Emmie smiles softly. "I'm glad they've found each other again. I've never seen my dad smile like he does now that she's back in his life."

"See, happily ever afters and miracles do happen."

Emmie's blank expression tells me that she isn't entirely on the same page as me.

"So you mean that I might wake up in the morning and miraculously have my A-levels and some kick-arse place at uni somewhere very far away from Theo Cirillo?"

The fact that she even puts his name into that little dream tells me he's way more in her head than she'd ever admit.

"We can all hope, right?" I say but quickly panic. "Not about you leaving, though. I'd miss you."

"Aw, don't go all soft on me," she mocks. "You really think a uni would ever accept me? I'm a complete fuck-up, Stel. The fact that Knight's Ridge let me in was possibly my miracle—that I didn't want, I might add."

"It'll all work out how it's meant to," I tell her.

"You really believe that?"

My cell pings with a message and I reach for it in a rush, hoping that it's Seb, but I still smile when I see Harley's name on the screen.

It's Friday night. Game night.

Despite being happy here, a wave of homesickness washes through me. It's almost Thanksgiving. This time of year was always my favorite. The football games, the cheering, the pumpkins, bonfires, parties, turkey. Everything.

But it's different here. Halloween was... well, the less said about that the better, but the guys did try to ensure it was something special. I'm guessing Thanksgiving will pass them all by.

I open the message before I get too hung up on everything I've left behind, and a smile plays on my lips as I find a selfie of Harley, Ruby, Kyle and Ash all smiling and kitted out ready for the big game.

Stella: GO BEARS! Good luck tonight. I miss you guys x

I hit send and wait to see if it's going to be read. It never is, and the thought of them getting ready for their night makes my heart ache.

"You okay?"

"Yeah. It was just Harley. It's game night."

"You miss it all, huh?"

"Yeah, but when I was there, I missed here. Trust

me when I tell you that I understand not belonging. That's pretty much been my life."

"You want to be here though, right? With Seb?"

"Yes, of course. If you handed me a plane ticket and the keys to my old life in America, I wouldn't go. A few weeks ago maybe. But not now."

She nods, seemingly happy with my response. "Good. And you're wrong. You do belong. This is where you were always meant to be."

"Maybe," I breathe, thinking of how happy Dad is here compared to when we were on the other side of the pond. I think of Toby, Maria, Seb. I might miss my family from Rosewood, but they're always going to be there. But here, I've got a real family. I've got parents. Okay, so it might be completely unconventional and an utter disaster right now. But they're here, and if the doctors are right, Maria—Mom—still has time, and I might actually get to know her, to have the kind of mother/daughter relationship I've always dreamed of.

The sound of the doorbell cuts off any more conversation about my life, and I hop up to go and grab the food.

Just like before, I check the screen before opening the door to a delivery guy I'm starting to become familiar with.

The guys have a handful of favorite Cirillo-owned restaurants that they order from—too often—and most days one of their delivery drivers is here at least once.

We really should make more effort to cook, but with everything going on, standing in the kitchen cooking for whoever might or might not turn up doesn't sound like a lot of fun.

Despite never really having to cook for myself, I can. Angie taught me from an early age.

I pause as I think of her.

"Shit," I hiss as I step back into the living room.

"What's wrong?" Emmie asks, pushing from the couch.

"Oh, uh... nothing. I haven't visited Angie."

"Who's Angie?" she asks, trailing me, or more the food, toward the kitchen for plates.

"Our housekeeper, but pretty much the woman who brought me up."

"I'm sure she knows you've been busy."

"I know," I agree, but it doesn't lessen the guilt that washes around in my belly.

The last time I saw Calvin, I was pissed at him and pretty much stormed out of the house.

Both of them deserve more from me than that after all the years they've supported me. None of this has been their fault. If Calvin knew someone had been in the house, he'd have put a stop to it, I know that without a doubt.

"Hey," Emmie says, resting her hand over mine, the shock of her move makes me look up at her. "Just go and see her tomorrow. No one can blame you for anything over the past few weeks. It's been fucking stressful."

"I know. Thank you."

"Gotta be useful for something, right?" she asks, loading her plate full of food.

"More than just getting Theo's cock hard, you mean?"

The look she shoots me is pure death, and all I can do is laugh.

"Sorry, I'm sorry," I say as I try to catch my breath.

"No you're not," she sulks, dropping onto the couch with her plate.

"Meh, maybe not. You should just take him for a test drive, shatter some tension. It might fix everything."

"Or make everything fucking worse?" she mutters, shoving a forkful of food into her mouth.

"You don't know until you try."

She doesn't need to give me a verbal answer. I get everything I need from her eyes.

"I was just making conversation," I mutter lightly before spearing a piece of pork with my fork.

She shakes her head at me as she continues eating.

"Have you got any ice cream here?" Emmie asks a couple of hours later.

It's almost midnight. I was hoping that the guys would have been back by now, or at least heard something, but my cell is sitting silently on the couch.

"Are you serious?" I ask, eyeing her suspiciously. "You just ate your weight in Chinese. How can you want ice cream?"

She shrugs. "I just need something sweet. And ice cream isn't really food so..."

Knowing exactly what she means despite the amount of takeout we both consumed, I push from the couch and head toward the kitchen to search the freezer.

Something tells me it'll be empty. I can't imagine the guys sitting around with tubs of Ben and Jerry's and face packs on.

I burst out laughing at the visual that pops into my head.

"What?" she asks, looking at me from the couch, her brows pinched in confusion.

"N-nothing," I stutter, still chuckling to myself. "Nothing. I think those cocktails were a little strong."

"So…" she asks, her eyes flicking to the freezer door that my fingers are still wrapped around.

"No. No ice cream."

"Dammit," she pouts before taking off across the living room.

"What are you doing?" I ask when she shoves her feet into her boots.

"Going to the shop."

"You need ice cream that bad?" She raises a brow at me in response. "Okay, fine. I'll come with you."

"No, you stay here. You're not allowed to step out of the house," she jokes. "You might set off an alarm or something."

"Jesus, I'm not a dog, Em."

She shrugs.

"It's just the shop down the street. We'll be back in less than ten minutes."

"Okay, fine," she concedes.

"Oh shit," I shriek when I lift my first foot to put it into my Ugg boot and instead wobble and collide with the dresser.

"What the hell was in that cocktail?" Emmie asks, catching me before I hit the floor.

"Er... vodka and... whatever the bottle was at the back of the cupboard."

"Jesus. Seb is going to kill me."

"I can handle Sebastian." I shake my head. Even I can hear how slurred my voice is. "The fresh air will clear my head," I tell myself out loud.

"Come on then." Emmie threads her arm through mine as if she thinks I need support down the stairs.

I'm tipsy, not freaking wasted.

"Oh shit, wait," I say once we step out the front door.

I was half expecting to find Carl and Cass on watch duty, but clearly, the guys believed that I would stay put tonight, or just didn't trust that they could stop me if I went against the rules again.

Guilt hits me as I pause, trying to remember why I stopped in the first place.

"I forgot my cell. Wait there."

"Do you really need it?"

"One minute," I shout, bolting for the stairs.

"I'll be by the gate."

CHAPTER TWENTY-FIVE

Sebastian

Theo catches my attention from across the room and nods.

My lip twitches at one side, confirming that everything is good but also showing him just how pissed off I am with this fucking job.

Apparently, Evan had some big bust or something going on tonight and he needed all the men. That resulted in us being called in to play security in the back rooms at the hotel.

And by back rooms, I mean the ones that the majority of our customers don't even know exist.

Alex and Nico are in their element, their eyes locked on the women spinning around the poles that are suspended from the ceiling in clothing so small I'm not entirely sure why they bothered.

I've been in here a few times over the years, so I knew what I was expecting when we walked in earlier. It's only Nico and Toby who've put shifts in back here before, seeing as they're older than us. We might be more than capable of handling the assholes who push their luck with our dancers too far, but the boss does try to keep the staff of legal age where he can.

"You've railed her, haven't you?" I ask Nico as he blatantly eye fucks the woman up on stage.

"No, actually. Fucking want to, though. You seen that arse?"

I mutter some kind of agreement because yeah, her body is pretty incredible—all the girls are, but no big surprise there seeing as they spend their nights doing that.

I'd still take the one at home waiting for me over them any day.

"So fucking whipped," Nico mutters.

"Yeah? And what of it?" I ask, taking a warning step toward him.

He holds his hands up in defence. "I was just pointing out a fact, no need to hit me for it."

"You're an arsehole," I mutter, walking away from him and doing a sweep of the room before I come to a stop at the end of the bar.

"What can I get you, sweetie?" Missy, our bartender, asks.

"Vodka. Neat."

She gives me a warning look.

We're not allowed to drink on the clock, but recently I've been finding that I've been following the rules less and less. Especially when we're put on bullshit jobs like this one and the hen do a few weeks ago.

Our skills can be put to way better use.

I'm sure whatever Evan is up to is much more exciting than this.

"Just one," I promise Missy, who thankfully complies and pours me a more than generous shot. "Thanks," I mutter, throwing it back.

I pull out my phone and check Stella's tracker. I should just trust her, I know I should, but fuck, after the last time...

I breathe a sigh of relief when it shows her phone as at home and a genuine smile plays on my lips as I think about her hanging out with Emmie. Thoughts of finding her already asleep and naked in my bed when we get back later fill my mind, and my cock swells as I imagine sliding in behind her, taking her from behind to let her know that I'm home.

The temptation to message her is strong, but I resist, knowing that I'll end up spending all night talking to her instead of working if I even start.

Pocketing my phone once more, I thank Missy and take off.

The patrons are well on their way to being utterly wasted, and as the clock ticks around, I just know we're getting closer to someone getting a little too handsy with one of the girls and forcing us to do something.

My fists curl, my knuckles crunching. Maybe throwing a couple of punches tonight is exactly what I need.

"All right?" I ask, coming to a stop beside Theo.

"You shouldn't be drinking."

"Gonna tell your daddy on me?" I quip.

"His security team have probably watched you do it. You don't need me snitching on you."

"Surely they've got better things to do than watch us." Although as I say the words, I remember the boss's warning before we walked out of his office earlier, our role for the night having been laid out quite clearly. No fucking about with the girls, no drinking, no showing him up. *I will be watching.*

"He wasn't being serious," I mutter, although I know it's a lie.

"Your funeral, man."

Silence falls between us. Theo might be okay with pushing his father at every opportunity, but that doesn't mean he thinks it's a good idea for us to do the same thing.

"Stella okay?" he asks after a few minutes of silence.

"Her phone is still showing as at home, if that's what you mean."

He snorts. "You should have tagged her. She'd happily leave that at home to give you the slip."

"I trust her."

He turns to me and quirks a brow.

"As long as Emmie is gone before we get back," he says quietly. So quietly I wonder if he wasn't meant to say it out loud at all.

"You ready to talk about that?"

"About what?" he asks, pushing from the wall he was leaning against and taking off across the room.

"I'll take that as a no then," I mutter to myself.

I'm still watching him move to where Alex is staring up at the woman on stage when someone screams and he quickly changes direction, running toward where I'd left Nico instead.

"Fuck's sake," I mutter when I join them and find Nico with some old dude in a headlock, the woman Nico was lusting after sitting on the edge of the stage with some guy's jacket around her shoulders as her body trembles.

"What happened?" Theo barks.

"This stupid fuck tried pulling her off stage and onto his lap."

"Dumb fuck," Theo scoffs as Toby finally joins us. "Take him out back and show him what happens when stupid cunts even try to touch our girls."

"You got it, boss," Alex quips, grabbing the guy's other side and helping Nico drag him out through one of the security doors at the back of the room.

Toby is already sitting next to the woman, talking to her softly, so I leave him to it. After a couple of seconds, he takes her over to the bar and Missy slides a couple of shots in her direction to steady her nerves.

"Go help if you want," Theo says to me, knowing that no one else will try shit immediately after watching someone get dragged out to have their arse handed to them.

"Nah, I'm good. They've got it covered."

"Yeah, they do. This is fucking—" His phone

blaring in his pocket stops whatever he was going to say and he pulls it out.

The second he swipes the screen his face drops, the blood draining from it in a split second.

"What's wrong?" I demand, my own heart slamming against my chest from his reaction alone.

His eyes meet mine a beat before he turns the screen around.

"Is that... Fuck. Is that the coach house?"

"You need to go. I'll sort something out and I'll be right behind you."

I hear his words, but they don't register. The only thing I can see is the bright orange flames that were engulfing our home, the place where I left my girl.

Fuck.

FUCK.

"Seb, take my car. Just fucking get back there." He shoves the keys to his Ferrari into my hand and closes my fingers around them.

"I-is she—"

"I don't know, Seb. That was from the security camera on the house. Just fucking go."

"Y-yeah. Shit. Fuck."

Theo jabs his finger into the screen of his phone and brings it to his ear a beat before I take off running.

His car is parked right out the front of the hotel, unlike Alex's, who drove us here and parked in the underground car park.

My entire body is shaking in fear. The tires of Theo's Ferrari screech as I round the final corner to get to his house.

There are already fire engines blocking the entrance, so I'm forced to slam my foot on the brakes and abandon the car in the middle of the road.

Smoke and flames billow high into the inky night sky as I race toward the devastation.

"Please, please. Fuck. Please don't have been inside," I whisper to anyone who might fucking listen as I get closer to the firefighters who are beginning to get the blaze under control.

"I'm sorry, but you can't come—"

"Get the fuck out of my way," I bark, cutting off what the firefighter was going to say.

He reaches out to try to stop me, but I dart forward too fast for him and round the high wall that surrounds the Cirillo estate.

"Holy fuck," I breathe, my eyes wide in shock when I take in the mess that used to be Theo's coach house.

One side has completely collapsed, both Stella's and my car somewhere beneath it.

My hand trembles violently as I fight to drag in the air I need. Smoke burns my lungs as I stand there, my vision blurring as I try to force myself not to believe that she could have been inside.

"No. Please. I don't fucking deserve this." A sob rips up my throat as I stare at the flames. "FUUUUCK," I scream, my fingers twisting in my hair, pulling, but I don't feel it. The only pain I feel is that of my heart shattering into a million pieces.

The sound of someone calling my name makes me stand a little straighter, but when I don't hear it again, just the sound of something collapsing in front of me, I begin to think I imagined it.

"Sebastian."

"Shit." Spinning around, I find myself face to face with Selene, Theo's mum.

"I-I can't—"

"She's inside." She cuts me off, her own cheeks wet with tears as she takes a step closer.

"W-what?" I ask, thinking that I misheard her.

"She's inside. They're both inside the house."

"Fuck." I run around her and toward the front door.

I fly through the hallway and into the living room. I have no idea if it's where they are, but it's as good a guess as any.

My fingers barely grip onto the doorframe as I spin around, my heart in my throat.

The second my eyes land on people huddled on the sofa, all the air rushes out of my lungs.

"Seb," Stella cries, pushing a child off her lap as I run to her.

We collide with an audible thud, my arms wrapping around her so tight she probably can't breathe, but I don't give a shit.

"Fuck, baby. I thought you were dead."

"I'm sorry," she sobs into my chest, her own body trembling.

Tears stream down my cheeks as I stand there just holding her. Fear like I've never experienced still rages through my body as if this is just a dream, as if she's not really here in my arms.

"Shh, it's not your fault," I tell her after she

apologises again. "Fuck. Are you really okay?" I ask, finally releasing her so that I can inspect her for injuries.

"I'm really okay. W-we weren't inside when it went up."

My eyes narrow, knowing that she'd left the house, but I can hardly be mad about it. If she hadn't then... I look over my shoulder and out the window at the burning building.

"Fuck."

Movement on the sofa catches my attention, and I find Emmie with Theo's brother and sisters huddled into her. Her eyes are wide as she stares at the two of us, clearly still in shock.

"You okay?" I ask her.

"Y-yeah. I'm good. Thank fuck I wanted ice cream, huh?"

"Emmie," a little voice chastises.

"Sorry."

Stella's body trembles again, but when I look back at her, I find a wide smile on her face. She's fucking laughing.

"Umm... did I miss something."

She shakes her head and tries to compose herself, but she quickly discovers that she can't as she barks out another laugh.

I look at Emmie, who just shrugs in confusion at her friend's state.

"Baby?" I take her upper arms in my hands and give her a little shake.

"She drank a lot," Emmie helpfully adds.

"I'm sorry. I'm sorry," Stella finally says, getting herself under control. "It's just... we were saved by fuc — freaking ice cream."

"Okay," I say, pulling her back into my body and twisting my fingers into her hair as I press her face to my chest.

It only takes thirty seconds tops for her laughter to turn into tears, and she clings onto me like she never wants to let go.

I know that fucking feeling.

"Okay, I've got drinks and cookies," Selene says, lowering a tray to the coffee table.

The kids attached to Emmie scoot forward and immediately grab a glass of milk and a homemade cookie as Selene walks over to the window and pulls the curtains closed. I shouldn't be surprised by her coolness in this situation. She's been married to Damien for years. She must be used to dealing with this kind of drama.

"Damien and Evan are on their way."

"I'm so sorry about your home," Stella says, lifting her head from my chest.

"It's okay, sweetie. I'm just glad no one was injured. It was just bricks and mortar. There are much more important things in life."

She squeezes my shoulder in support as she passes and drops onto the sofa with her younger kids, pulling them all in for a hug.

CHAPTER TWENTY-SIX

Stella

I'm still sitting on Seb's lap with his arms locked around my waist when the others come piling through the door almost an hour later.

"What the hell happened?" Theo barks, his face blank but his eyes dark with barely concealed rage.

Selene managed to get his younger siblings back to bed about thirty minutes ago after they were woken by the explosion of the coach house and then the blaring sirens of the fire trucks.

"I'm so sorry, Theo," I say, but Seb squeezes my waist in warning. He doesn't want me to take responsibility for this, but let's be honest, this wasn't a strike on Theo, or even the Family. It was on me.

I'm the one whoever they want dead.

"It's not your fault, Princess. You didn't ask for any of this," he says, pacing back and forth.

"Nor did you, and it was your home."

"It's just stuff," he says, much like his mom did not so long ago. "I'm just fucking relieved you weren't inside." He shoots a quick look in Emmie's direction. "Either of you."

Emmie's eyes widen in surprise, but she doesn't say anything.

"So what happened? Why *weren't* you inside?" he asks, lowering his ass to the other end of the couch to Emmie, his eyes locked on me.

"Emmie wanted ice cream, so we were going to the store to grab some. We got to the end of the driveway and..." I wave my hand toward the window, although the curtains are still closed so we can't see the disaster that was our home. "That happened," I finish sadly.

Theo turns to look at Emmie, his eyes narrowing.

"What?" she hisses.

"Okay, tell me exactly how it happened."

"Uh... like I just said."

"So you both left together?"

"Yeah. Well, no," I quickly add. "I went back in to grab my cell because I left it on the coffee table and..."

I trail off, holding Theo's eyes.

Fuck.

"Do you really think..." I trail off, praying that we're not thinking the same thing.

"Does he think what?" Emmie snaps.

"Nico," Theo barks. "Take Emmie home, please. And get an ETA on our fathers."

292

"What? No. I'm not leaving. No." She jumps up from the couch, looking totally affronted by even the suggestion.

"Emmie," Theo growls, turning to look at her with a dangerous expression on his face that I'm sure would make grown men piss themselves. Unfortunately for him, my friend, much like me, isn't normal, and instead of backing down she places her hands on her hips and holds his eyes.

"Make me," she hisses at him, taking a step closer.

"Nico," Theo barks, his fists curling at his sides.

"What the fuck?" Emmie squeals as Nico picks her up as if she weighs nothing more than a feather and throws her over his shoulder. "No. I'm not fucking leaving." She kicks and flails around, but I think we all know that she's not going to win.

It's not until the front door slams with their departure that anyone speaks.

"Bro, you don't really think that—"

Thundering footsteps make Alex's question end abruptly, and not ten seconds later does the living room door widen and three larger-than-life men walk inside.

Damien, Evan, and my dad come storming into the room.

"Stella," Dad breathes, his entire body relaxing when his eyes land on me.

"I'm okay," I say, stepping away from Seb for the first time since he got here so I can embrace my dad. His eyes run all over me, looking for cuts and bruises. "I'm okay. I promise."

His strong arms wrap around me and he drops his lips to the top of my head.

The same overwhelming rush of emotions I felt when Seb first burst into the room slam back into me.

I could have died tonight. Both of us could have. If Emmie didn't want ice cream, we would have been inside when the house went up.

Or would we?

Is Theo right? Is this connected to Emmie?

She'd left the apartment.

A shudder rips through me at the thought.

"My office," Damien barks, while Dad still holds me. "We're finding this motherfucker. Tonight. He's not going to get away with this."

Damien's voice is cold, deadly as he makes that statement, and Dad releases me, ready to follow the boss's orders.

"Come on, baby," Seb says, wrapping his arm around my waist and pushing me to follow everyone out of the room.

"I-I don't think he meant me," I try to argue when he turns us to follow the others.

"You're a part of this, Stella."

Damien's eyes track me as I slip into the room beside Seb, and I brace myself for him to demand I leave.

But he never does.

"Estella, come and take a seat."

He gestures to the chair that Evan lowered himself into, and his second immediately jumps to his feet, allowing me to sit.

"U-uh..." I stutter, feeling completely out of place, and still a little drunk, but Seb's hand on my lower back pushes me forward.

"Theo, pull up the security footage. There has to be something we can go on."

"Boss." He nods, walking over to another desk with multiple computer screens mounted on the wall behind it.

"Tell me everything," Damien demands, his hard, angry eyes holding mine.

Seb's hand squeezes my shoulder, letting me know that he's right behind me, and I start talking.

"It's got something to do with the Reapers, Boss. I'm telling you," Theo adds once I've finished. "There are too many coincidences where Emmie Ramsey is concerned."

Damien sits silently for a beat, his expression and body language completely unreadable.

And then he says two words that turn my blood to ice.

"You're right."

Fuck.

"Do you have the footage ready?"

"Yes, Boss."

We all shift around to see the screens as Theo hits play. There's a different angle of the coach house on each one, and my eyes flick around for the longest time, just waiting for something to happen.

We've seen the guys leave and Emmie is already inside. We've watched me invite her in, but it seems like forever before something catches Theo's eye.

"There," he says, pointing to the bottom right screen.

I squint, staring into the darkness, but after a couple of seconds, I discover that he's right.

A dark figure cuts through the night from around the back of the coach house.

"How'd he get there?" Seb muses. The wall behind the coach house is at least ten feet high, with barbed wire on the top and an alarm, I've discovered.

"No idea," Damien mutters, his eyes laser-focused on the screen.

The black-hooded figure walks around the building, but he keeps his head down the whole time.

"Motherfucker," Nico grunts, noticing just like I am that he turns his back on every camera.

"He knows our security system. How?"

"The Italians were right," Dad says quietly, making a ripple of unease flow through the air.

"What's he doing?" I ask, not really able to take in what I'm watching.

"Planting explosives," Evan answers for me.

We keep watching long after the figure vanishes, and eventually the front door opens and Emmie and I appear before I shoot back inside for my cell.

"Where did Emmie go?" Theo asks.

"She... uh... she shouted that she was going to wait by the gate," I confess quietly.

"Why?"

"To... uh..."

"Stop herself getting blown up?" Alex suggests, saying aloud exactly what everyone is thinking.

"She wouldn't have done this," I say, but my voice doesn't come out sounding as confident as I'd hoped it would.

Theo scoffs, clearly disagreeing with me.

"She wouldn't. She wouldn't hurt me, or try to, like this."

On the screen, I appear back at the front door and pull it closed behind me.

I barely make it ten steps before the building lights up behind me and I'm thrown forward, thankfully landing on the Cirillos' front lawn to save me from the damage the gravel of the driveway would have caused.

The screens before us become nothing but the glow of the flames as the coach house is engulfed.

Theo lets the recording run until the fire trucks pull up, and then he turns it off.

"She wouldn't do this," I say again in the hope that someone will believe me.

"She walked away and left you there, Stella. The evidence is pretty damning," Seb says softly.

"Well look harder. This wasn't her," I bark, my heart thundering in my chest and my hands balled into fists in an attempt to stop them trembling. "She wouldn't." My voice comes out softer this time, emotional, and I hate it.

"Do you need us for anything else?" Seb asks, wrapping his arm around my waist and pulling me from the chair.

"We'll pull the footage from the street, follow this fucker. I've got guys outside searching the wreckage. If we find anything, we'll call you."

"Thank you," Seb says on my behalf before ushering me out of the room.

"Where are we going?" I ask, my voice barely audible.

Seb doesn't respond, but when he turns me toward the stairs and encourages me to climb up, I get a good idea.

We move in silence until Seb comes to an ajar door and gently pushes me inside.

My breath catches as I step into the room, the orange glow from the huge windows capturing my attention, and without thinking, I walk toward it.

"Baby, don't," Seb breathes, but it's too late. I'm already there and staring down at the charred remains of Theo's home.

"This is all my fault."

"No, baby. It's not. The security on this place should have stopped it."

"But it didn't. And look." I wave my hand in front of the window, tears filling my eyes once more as I watch everything about our lives together burn into nothing but dust.

"I know, Princess," he says quietly, reaching out to close the curtains. "I know."

He turns me into his body. Cupping my cheeks in his hands, he brings his face down until his nose is almost brushing mine.

"I thought I'd lost you again tonight, Hellion," he says, his voice rough with the lingering fear and emotions that statement drags up.

"You didn't," I assure him, pulling our bodies tighter with my arms around his waist. "I'm right here."

He stares into my eyes for the longest time, as if he's trying to convince himself that those three words are true.

"We need to find this fuck, Princess. I can't keep doing this."

A humorless laugh falls from my lips. "Tell me about it."

Tilting my head up, I brush my lips against his. But unlike usual, he doesn't immediately dive into our kiss. His movements are unsure, hesitant.

"Seb," I breathe, lifting my hand to his cheek and brushing my thumb back and forth. "I promise you, I'm okay."

"Fuck, baby."

Finally, I crack his resolve and his lips move, his tongue diving into my mouth and twisting with mine.

Desperation, relief and fear ooze from him. I feel it in every brush of his lips and swipe of his tongue. Yet I have no idea how to make any of it any better.

Until we put an end to this—to him—the risk is always going to be there.

The fear that next time, he might just succeed in his mission.

CHAPTER TWENTY-SEVEN

Sebastian

I slide my hands around her body, ready to close even more space between us. My need to feel every inch of her against me to make myself believe what she's telling me is too much to deny.

I thought she was inside that house.

I thought...

A shudder rips through my entire body as the memory of flying through the entrance and seeing the house engulfed in flames for the first time hits me once more.

"I'm okay," she mumbles into our kiss. But as I slide my hands down her back, ready to grab her arse, she flinches.

"What's wrong?" I ask, ripping my lips from hers.

"Nothing. Seb, I just need—"

Placing my hand on her shoulders, I spin her around and lift her top.

"Motherfucker," I bark, seeing the red, angry skin all the way up her back.

"It's fine," she argues.

"It is not fine," I hiss, peeling her hoodie and tank from her body before unhooking her bra and letting it drop to the floor. "Don't move," I instruct, dropping a kiss to her shoulder and racing from the room.

I navigate through the Cirillo mansion quickly until I locate one of the many first aid boxes in the master bathroom and pull out what I need.

When I slip back into the room I've claimed as ours, I find she hasn't followed orders at all.

Although, I'm not really sure I expected anything less.

"Stella," I growl, following the slither of light coming from the adjoining bathroom.

Pushing the door open, I can't help my breath catching when I find her standing behind the glass shower screen, totally naked with water rushing over her mouthwatering curves.

She's standing with her front to me, but her face is tilted up, allowing the water to rush over her skin.

My fingers curl around the tube of cream in my hand as I push aside just how badly I need her, my anger taking over.

"What the fuck are you doing?" I bark out.

Her entire body flinches at my deep, booming voice,

quickly followed by the slam of the door as I kick it hard behind me.

"Shit," she hisses, her eyes wide in fear.

"What the fuck, Seb? You scared the shit out of me."

Taking a step forward, I suck in a deep breath through my nose.

"I told you to stay put." I narrow my eyes at her, letting her see how fucking pissed I am, but as ever, she just waves it off, a smile curling at her lips as she takes in the tube of antiseptic cream in my hand.

"It's just some friction burn, Seb. It's fine."

"You were nearly fucking blown up. Nothing about this is fine."

"I know. I know, but..."

The broken, exhausted look on her face forces all the anger and tension from my body. She sags back against the wall, gasping as the cold tiles hit her sore skin.

"Baby," I breathe, dropping the tube, kicking my shoes off and pulling my already loose tie from my neck.

Still dressed in my shirt and trousers, I step into the shower stall with her, the water immediately soaking my clothes.

"Just... just let me look after you, okay?" I whisper into the top of her head as she clings to me.

She nods, her body beginning to tremble.

She puts on a good show for everyone else, appearing like this is just another normal day. But it's not. It's anything fucking but, and she needs to stop pretending that it's okay.

"It's okay to break, baby. I'll hold you together. I fucking promise."

A sob rips from her throat as her grip on me tightens.

We stand there, just holding each other, with the water raining down on us for the longest time.

"Let me wash your hair?" I ask when she begins to shiver despite the warm water.

Nodding, she releases her hold on me and turns around.

I don't need to worry about there not being anything to use. Selene keeps every bedroom and bathroom stocked in this house as if it's a fucking hotel.

Reaching for the bottle of shampoo, I squirt a blob into my hand and begin massaging it into her hair. The scent of smoke and burning is almost instantly replaced by its floral scent, and Stella immediately leans back into my body as my fingers work.

Her moan ripples through the air as I massage her head and she reaches back for me, wrapping her hand around my hip and holding onto me as if I'm her anchor.

"Good?" I whisper loud enough for her to hear over the water.

"So good," she moans, just like she does when I'm balls deep inside her.

I rinse out the bubbles before running the conditioner through her lengths, using my fingers to untangle the knots.

"You're good at this."

"I grew up with three sisters. Couldn't help learning a few tricks."

"Well, I appreciate it."

Leaving her hair for a bit, I reach for the shower gel and squirt a generous amount on my hands before rubbing them over every inch of her body.

Her breaths come out in short, sharp pants, her nipples pebble, and her moans are downright fucking filthy as I work, but I refuse to cave to it.

I told her I would look after her, and that's what I fully fucking intend to do.

"Seb," she moans, her hand reaching behind her in search of my cock.

"Baby, I'm trying to do the right thing here."

"Fuck the right thing, Seb. Fuck me against the tiles, please."

I chuckle at her. "Nice try, Hellion."

I make quick work of rinsing the conditioner from her hair.

Reaching out, I turn the dial, cutting the water off and step out of the stall, much to her frustration.

I grab a thick white fluffy towel from the heated rail and gesture for her to step into it.

"You're getting water everywhere," she points out, nodding at the puddle that's forming around my feet.

"Go sit on the edge of the bed. I'll be right there," I promise before attempting to peel the sodden fabric from my body and dumping the lot in a pile in the shower.

With a towel around my waist, I head out to find my girl.

Thankfully, she allows me to apply the cream that I found discarded on the bathroom floor, and after pulling the sheets down, she crawls inside.

She looks exhausted with dark circles around her eyes and her bottom lip red and swollen from where she's been worrying it.

Wrapping her arms around her tucked-up legs, she watches me as I squeeze the towel around her hair to get the excess water out, then encourage her to lie down with me.

I tuck her body against mine and hold her tight.

Silence falls around us, and I focus on her soft, shallow breathing, reminding myself that she's here and okay.

"Talk to me, baby," I breathe softly, not wanting to startle her but also knowing that she's not asleep.

"W-what will happen if... if Emmie is involved in this?" she asks hesitantly.

"I guess that all depends on how involved she is," I reply honestly. "If she had a knowing part in any of this, then I'll kill her my-fucking-self."

Stella sucks in a breath, the deadly tone as I issue my threat enough for her to know that I'm serious.

"No one gets to try to hurt you and live, Hellion. It's not going to fucking happen."

She lets out a shaky breath.

She already knew what my answer was going to be, and I'm not sure hearing it from my lips makes her feel any better about what's to come.

"Try to get some sleep, baby. I think we might have a few hard days ahead of us."

I drop my lips to her head and press a kiss there, hoping like hell she can feel even just a bit of the love, the relief, I do holding her in my arms.

I don't get a wink of sleep. I'm too keyed up to even try. I end up just lying there, staring at the shadows moving around the room as the glow from the fire outside lessens and the morning winter sun takes over.

There are voices and noises from somewhere in the house all night, so I know I'm not the only one who can't rest after what happened.

I hear footsteps long before the bedroom door opens and soft light from the hallway fills the room.

"Hey," I say as Theo pokes his head around the door.

"Couldn't sleep either, huh?"

He shakes his head.

"I've got clothes and things for both of you. You need to come down to Dad's office, though."

"You found something?" I ask, sitting up in a rush before I realise my move exposes Stella, who's still fast asleep beside me.

"Yeah. Sooner rather than later," he says before ducking out of the room.

"Shit," I hiss, scrubbing my hand down my face. "Stella, baby," I whisper, wrapping my hand gently around the side of her neck and brushing my lips against hers.

"Mmm," she moans, her body leaning into mine, her leg lifting over my hip and dragging us closer.

"Baby, I need you to wake up."

"Just kiss me."

I swallow my groan. How badly do I just want to lose myself in her right now and forget everything else?

"We can't. We need—"

Her body tenses in my arms, and I know that reality has just slammed into her.

Concerned blue eyes meet mine as her eyelids fly open. "What's happened?" she asks in a rush, pushing her hair from her face and sitting up.

The sheets fall from her body, and I have to give myself a little pep talk when her nipples harden with the cool air.

"I-I don't know," I say after clearing my throat. "Theo just came in and—"

"Why the hell are we still here then?"

She's out of bed in a flash and damn near running to the bathroom.

The sight of her sore back brings everything crashing down around me, and after blowing out a breath, I flick the covers back and follow her.

Damien, Galen, and Theo are in the office when we knock and slip inside. The rest of the house is quiet, but I don't think for a second that everyone is actually sleeping.

"What have we found?" I ask, immediately taking one of the free seats in front of the screens and dragging Stella down on my lap so we can watch together.

"There's nothing from here. This motherfucker covered his tracks well," Theo hisses. A shiver of unease rushes through me.

This really was an inside job.

And only one fucking name comes to mind.

My eyes lock with Theo's. We discussed possibilities late one night when Stella was asleep after hearing the Italians' confession and I'd started to wonder if I was wrong about all of this.

"But we pulled the CCTV from his escape and we managed to find this."

Theo hits play on one of the videos.

The time shows that it's almost an hour after the blast, and the footage is of a street that I don't recognise.

"We tracked his escape," Galen says, probably seeing my confusion.

"Here," Theo says as the hooded guy ducks into a late-night café.

"Wha—"

"Wait."

My pulse races as I stare at that screen, waiting for something to happen, for someone to appear.

And when they do, despite the fact that I was expecting it, my jaw damn near hits the floor.

"Is that... shit," Stella gasps, leaning forward to study the screen. But it's not necessary; we can all see who it is clear as day.

"But what's the connection here?" I ask as the two

men turn away from the café, the one on the right giving us an almost perfect shot of his Reapers cut.

"Now," Theo says, his hands rubbing together and a twinkle of excitement in his eyes, "this is where it gets interesting."

CHAPTER TWENTY-EIGHT

Stella

"Stella!" Calli screams when Seb and I walk hand in hand to the kitchen after our need for caffeine overtook our shock. "Oh my God. I'm so glad you're okay."

She's off the stool she was perched on and collides with my body not two seconds later.

"Now that is something I can get on board with," Alex mutters suggestively, earning himself a very hard slap around the head from Nico.

"If you don't have anything constructive to say, shut the fuck up."

"Fuck off, if it was Emmie molesting Stella like that you know he'd be all over it," Alex says, tilting his head toward Theo as he stalks in behind us.

"Shut up or get out." Theo's voice is cold and so

fucking lethal that it actually sends a shiver of fear down my spine.

"What's happened?" Calli whispers in my ear after peeking at her cousin over my shoulder.

"Nothing I can tell you yet. I'm sorry," I say with a wince.

Instead of the frustration I was expecting to cover her face from being shut out, I'm pleased when she just nods in understanding.

"You got him though, right? This is all coming to an end?"

"Yeah. It's ending."

"Thank fuck for that. My nerves can't take this shit."

"Man, up, baby C. You're a fucking Cirillo," Theo snaps, storming past us and toward the array of food on the counter.

"Arsehole," she mutters after him, but he doesn't react.

"Do you all want coffees?" Selene asks, appearing from somewhere behind me.

"Yes please," Seb says politely, making me smile.

She gives her son a curious glance before moving past him toward the coffee machine. I'm sure she's more than used to Theo angry. And if not him, then his father.

Until recently, I would have told anyone who'd have listened that Theo was nothing like his father—or the image of his father that had been explained to me, seeing as I hadn't actually met the man—but after the other night in the apartment, and then this morning, I realize just how wrong I would have been.

Theo Cirillo really is his father's prodigy.

"Eat," he demands, looking over his shoulder at me before shooting a knowing look at Seb.

"Come on, Hellion. We're gonna need our strength."

His hand lands on my lower back as he pushes me forward, toward the food and away from Calli.

"Have you spoken to Emmie?" she asks behind me.

Theo doesn't look back, but I don't miss the way his entire body locks up at the sound of her name.

"Not this morning. Was she okay when you dropped her off last night?" I ask, looking at Nico.

He grunts in response. "Her usual delightful self."

The guys all share a knowing look.

Even though it's only the three of us who know the truth about last night right now, they're all aware of Theo's concerns, and recent events can only be feeding their suspicions.

"You should call her, Stel. Check in," Calli says innocently.

"Yeah, I will." I force a smile onto my face and grab the plate Seb holds out for me, filling it with pastries and fresh fruit that I already know I don't have the stomach for.

"Nico," Theo barks, "get Toby here."

"He is here. He crashed up with me," he says, narrowing his gaze at Theo.

"Then fucking get him."

"Yeah, all right. Jesus."

Nico stalks out of the room before bellowing up the stairs for Toby.

My stomach knots as I stare down at my food.

I knew this was a fucking mess. But didn't appreciate just how fucking bad it was.

Seb's warm hand lands on my thigh, dragging me from my own head. I look up at him and find myself relaxing the second I look into his eyes.

'It's going to be okay,' he mouths.

"I know." I force a smile on my face because I do believe it. I just hate the pain it's going to cause to those we care about.

We've all been through too much. We don't need more.

A door in the house somewhere slams before Evan blows through the kitchen with Charon hot on his heels.

"Calli, Stella, boys." He greets us all as he passes to join Damien and Dad.

Silence ripples around the room as we all sit there. Only Alex eats despite the fact that both Theo and Seb instructed us all to do the same.

Footsteps run down the stairs and I hold my breath as Nico, and finally, Toby, join us.

"Sorry, those painkillers knock me the fuck out," Toby says as if everything's okay. I watch as he moves across the room. "Oh sweet, your mum got the good shit." He's just stuffed the end of a croissant into his mouth when he looks up and his eyes lock with mine. "What the fuck has happened now?" he asks, correctly reading my face.

"Mum, Calli, could you give us a few minutes, please?" Theo asks, his voice not quite as cold as it was when he first walked in.

"Sure thing, sweetie. We'll go and check on the kids in the den."

Together they leave the kitchen, but not before Calli shoots me a worried look over her shoulder before Selene closes the door, giving us all some privacy.

"Guys?" Toby asks, meeting Theo and Seb's eyes before looking at Alex and Nico.

"Fuck knows, bro. I'm hoping someone's going to start talking," Nico hisses, clearly pissed that he's in the dark right now.

"Sit down and shut up and I might be able to fucking talk, dickhead," Theo mutters.

It's only as he speaks and I look over that I recognize his position at the head of the table.

Sensing my attention, he looks over at me, his brows pinching when he sees that I'm smiling at him.

'What?' he mouths.

Shaking my head, I look away and watch as Toby lowers himself to the chair beside me.

"This isn't good news, is it?" he asks, forcing a lightness into his tone that I'm sure no one in the room is feeling.

"No," Theo confirms.

"Lay it on us then, bro. Tell us how many motherfuckers we need to go kill for this," Alex says, slouching back in his chair as if we're discussing the fucking weather.

"Okay," Theo says, resting his elbows on the table

314

and looking everyone in the eyes before continuing. "You know how we've been concerned about the Reapers' involvement in all of this."

Everyone nods.

"That's because they are."

"Motherfuckers," Nico scoffs, throwing his pain au raisin down on the table. "Emmie?" he asks, shocking the shit out of me.

"We don't know how deep this runs yet. But we know who's been doing the hits, and we know who's planned it all."

"The Italians?" Alex asks, leaning forward and suddenly looking interested.

"They were right. It is an inside job."

"Who?" Nico snaps, his patience quickly running out.

Reaching out, I take Toby's hand that's resting on the table beside his place.

Suddenly, the room is so silent we'd hear a fucking pin drop. Hell, I fucking do. I hear the exact moment that realization hits with Alex, Nico, and then finally Toby.

"No," he breathes. "No." His chair goes crashing to the floor as he stands, ripping his hand from mine.

"Toby?" I whisper, twisting so that I can get to him quicker.

"He's been doing this? *He's* been trying to fucking kill you? *He's* the reason I was fucking shot? Why Seb was shot? Fuck. FUCK," he barks, lifting his hands to his hair, pulling on the short lengths until I swear he's about to rip the strands clean from his head.

315

We all sit there for a few tense minutes, just watching as he paces back and forth, trying to come to terms with what Theo's just told him.

"Toby," I say softly, scooting to the end of the chair, ready to go to him if he needs it. "There's more."

He pauses and looks up, his eyes colliding with mine.

My breath catches at the pain in his depths.

"None of this is your fault, Toby," I tell him, hating that I can see the guilt that's etched into every inch of his face.

"Of course it fucking is," he barks, swiping his arms across the counter and sending plates and food flying. "I should have fucking killed him when I first discovered the kind of man he was. I should have stopped him. I should have stopped him hurting my—our—mum. I shouldn't have given him the chance to get anywhere fucking near you."

The pain in his voice fucking wrecks me, and I rip my other hand out of Seb's tight grip and walk toward my brother.

"None of this is on you, Toby," I say before colliding with his body and wrapping my arms around him, giving him little choice but to return my embrace.

He sucks in a shuddering breath as he tightens his arms around me.

"I'm so sorry," he breathes in my ear.

"Not your fault, Toby. No one blames any of this on you. All you've done is what you thought was best for Mom."

His breath catches as he realizes that I've just called her that for the first time.

"I've just wanted to do right by her. She deserves so much more than him."

"Too fucking true. We're gonna do it. Okay? Together."

"Fuck, I don't deserve to have a sister as fucking cool as you." I can't help but smile at his words as he wraps his hand around the back of my head and drops his lips to my forehead as if he's literally soaking up my strength.

"Nah, you just needed a Bonnie to your Clyde."

"We're not fucking dying, Princess. And I'm pretty sure you and Seb already claimed those titles."

"Meh, we make our own rules here." I take his hand in mine and lead him back to the table. "You need to listen to the rest."

"Fuck me." He scrubs his hand over his face.

"Sorry, bro," Theo says with a wince. All of them watch us closely as we rejoin them.

"Go on then, hit me with it," Toby demands once we're seated again.

"You're not Jonas's only son."

A bitter laugh falls from Toby's lips as he presses his fingertips into his temples.

"Of course I'm not," he mutters, his voice empty, like he's got nothing left to give. "Let me guess. He's a Reaper."

"Bingo," Seb says.

"Jesus." Toby sucks in a couple of deep breaths before he sits forward and looks Theo dead in the eyes.

"So what's the plan? How and when are we killing these motherfuckers?"

And just like that, Toby sheds his soft skin and pulls his mask down.

"Waiting for word from the boss on when to strike. We'll take Joker out—"

"Wait," Alex says, lifting a hand to pause Theo. "Joker?"

"Yep."

"He was at Helen's funeral," Nico adds.

"Right under our fucking noses," Theo hisses.

"He even spoke to me," I confess, making Seb jolt in surprise.

"He fucking what?"

"When I was coming out of the bathroom with Calli and Emmie. We walked into him and he spoke to me. Normal as fuck. Didn't really think anything of it. Can't even remember what he said."

"Cheeky fuck."

"I saw him the night of the fight, too."

"Is there any times you haven't fucking seen him, Hellion?" Seb snaps, clearly pissed that I didn't confess to all of this.

"It didn't seem important. He was just a no one. If I suspected anything then—"

"We know, Stella," Theo assures me, cutting Seb off before he can argue. "What happened before doesn't matter. The only thing we need to focus on is what happens next. This ends. Right fucking now."

My dad joined us a few minutes later, telling Theo and Nico that Damien wanted them, and after checking that both Toby and I were okay, he disappeared behind them, leaving the rest of us to sit and wait it out. And tidy up, because Toby had made one hell of a fucking mess.

I swear to God that it's one of the longest days of my freaking life.

We had a good clue as to what they were all discussing, but fuck, it took forever. As far as I could see, all we needed to agree on was that we were going to find the two fucks and put a bullet between each of their brows.

I guess it wasn't actually that simple.

Calli came back at some point, looked between us all and correctly read our grim expressions.

When Selene suggested they take the kids back to her house to get them away from all the men who were coming in and out, she reluctantly agreed and took them out for a playdate with her mom. She wasn't happy about leaving, but she's more than aware of how this all works. And the second I can talk, I'll tell her everything, because her days of being kept in the dark are over.

The door opens when the sun is just about to sink behind the trees at the end of the yard and someone I've been expecting to see all day joins us.

"You got yourself in a right mess here, hey Doukas?"

"Fuck off, Daemon," Alex barks, his top lip curling in disgust as he runs his eyes over his suited brother.

"Nice. I've been out all fucking day getting intel for you fuckers and that's how you thank me."

"Whatever," Alex mutters, pushing from the couch and storming across the room.

"What's his problem?" Daemon asks, looking genuinely confused.

"It's been a long day," I tell him. "Coffee?"

"Sounds good," he says, dropping into the seat his brother just vacated.

"Don't tell me. You take it black?"

"How'd you guess, Princess?"

"I dunno," I joke. "Something about your aura."

Right as Daemon takes the first sip of his still boiling coffee, the door swings open and Damien and Evan stand side by side. Charon slips into the room behind them and comes to stop beside his grandson, placing a supportive hand on his shoulder.

I smile at the two of them, glad that Toby has someone he can actually trust and look up to in all of this.

"The Reapers have a party happening at their compound tonight. Everyone is there. *Joker* is there," Damien says more specifically.

"Jonas?" Theo asks.

"I've got him out on a job. His whereabouts aren't in question."

Theo nods while Toby swallows somewhat nervously. I have no doubt he's got what it takes to finally get this done, but I can only imagine how he feels right now.

"Theo, Seb... Stella," he says, holding my eyes. Pride swells within me, because I can't imagine he instructs women to get involved in this kind of shit often, and I'm so fucking relieved that he isn't going to attempt to keep me here safely with his wife and kids.

That's not the kind of person I am.

"You three and Daemon go to the Reapers. Toby, Nico, Alex—you're with us."

A rumble of agreement goes around the room before Damien walks toward us and lowers his ass to the coffee table.

"I shouldn't need to tell any of you this but... keep the death count to a minimum. The Reapers have toed the line for years. I'd prefer not to completely fuck that up in one night.

"Ram knows that something is coming, but he doesn't know what, so you're going to be taking the entire club by surprise. Or at least that's the hope.

"Take that motherfucker out however you see fit, but do not leave until you're confident he's taken his last breath and every other fucker knows not to touch my family."

Damien meets all our eyes until we each agree.

"You've got it, Boss," Theo states. "We've got this. Right, Princess?"

"Joker's played his final card. Time to wipe the fucking floor with him," I agree.

"Ten PM. And not a second sooner. I'm trusting that you can handle this."

Then as fast as he appeared, he's gone, leaving the weight of the job at hand pressing down on all of us.

"I'm hungry," Alex says from the corner of the room where he retreated to earlier. "Shall we order pizza?"

"Is he for real?" I ask Seb, who just shrugs as if this shit is fucking normal.

CHAPTER TWENTY-NINE

Sebastian

"Stop looking at me like that," Stella hisses from beside me in the back of Daemon's car.

"What?" I ask innocently, but I'm unable to keep my eyes locked on hers, instead favouring dropping them down her body.

She looks sensational in her black pencil skirt, lace, almost-see-through corset and her black jacket. Add the gun holster and the knife I know she's got strapped to her thigh and I'm fucking harder than I can ever remember being.

My girl looks like the bad-arse that she is, all wrapped up in a sexy fucking package.

"Don't even think about fucking in the back of my car," Daemon barks.

"About the only place they haven't christened yet," Theo mutters.

"Ignore him, he's just jealous."

"Of getting laid every twenty minutes? I have no idea why," Daemon deadpans.

"Shut up and just fucking drive," I bark, although with those two in the front I have no chance of anyone taking orders from me.

"Seriously," Stella hisses.

"I can't help it," I say, holding her eyes this time. Her makeup is dark, her lips blood red. The same colour I intend on painting the town with tonight. Okay, maybe not the town, but the Reapers' floorboards at least. "The bloodlust burning in your eyes, and that outfit... fuck, baby. I'm so fucking gone."

"You need to get your fucking head in the game, Papatonis, or you'll be left behind with only your hand for company while your girl takes this cunt out," Theo barks.

"He's got a point."

I scoff, pulling at the fabric of my trousers in the hope of giving my cock some space.

"Why did Calli even think that was a good idea?" I mutter, eyeing her outfit again.

"Because she knows me well. I think I fit in perfectly."

"That's half the problem," Daemon adds, still eavesdropping on our conversation.

"Did you see Dad's face when she appeared? I thought that vein in his forehead was finally going to blow," Theo asks, sounding a little more relaxed all of a sudden. "Bet he never thought he'd see the day he'd send a female soldier out on a job."

"I'm just glad he didn't try keeping me away," Stella adds.

"Dad's old fashioned, not stupid, Princess."

"Good to know," she laughs.

Silence falls over the car as we take the final turn toward the Reapers' compound.

Another black car appears at the other end of the road that I recognise as one of ours. Boss didn't say that we'd have backup, but I'm hardly surprised. The Reapers have enough man and firepower to overpower the four of us. I'm just hoping Ram, their prez, knows what's good for him and holds fire. We don't need this turning into war just because one of his members decided to break the fucking rules and go up against us, Jonas's son or not. Cunt deserves to die for the shit he's pulled.

The Reapers, the Italians and us are meant to have a fucking agreement to save the kind of bloodshed that occurred in the past, as we've all fought for power and territory. But it seems to only be us right now who are following the rules all gangs agreed to.

Daemon pulls up on the side of the road outside the compound gates as the other car does the same.

The gates open for us, proving that Boss was right—Ram is expecting us in some way.

"This seems entirely too easy," Stella mutters from beside me, running her eyes around the mass of bikes and trucks littered around.

Daemon brings the car to a stop, and without saying a word, he and Theo climb out.

"Ready?" I ask Stella.

She doesn't need to answer. I can see it shining in her eyes.

"So ready." Her smile is pure violence, and it makes me hard as steel.

"Fuck, I love you, Hellion."

"Come on, let's go send this motherfucker to hell."

She climbs out, smooths down her tight skirt and slams the door behind her.

By the time I've rearranged my dick and joined them, she's standing with Theo and Daemon, all three of them with fierce determination written all over their faces.

Theo nods at me, spins on his heels, and marches toward the main entrance, pulling his gun from his waistband.

There are suspiciously few people out here, but the second we walk inside and come to a stop inside their clubhouse, we discover where everyone is.

Silence ripples for a beat before every member of their club pulls their guns on us.

I sense people step up behind us, but a quick glance tells me that it's just Carl and Cass, our backup.

"Theo Cirillo, what a pleasant surprise," Ram, Emmie's grandfather, states. His lack of actual surprise shows on his face.

"We're not here for trouble, Ram," Theo states, his voice hard, inviting no argument. "We're just here to right a few wrongs."

Ram's eyes narrow on Theo. A scuffle in the corner of the room catches my eye, making my finger twitch on the trigger of my gun, but I don't see anything of concern when I scan the area.

The sound of heels clicking on the old wood floor drags my eyes back, and I watch as Stella stalks deeper into the room, her attention locked on a single person sitting at the bar.

Shifting my gaze to him, I instantly recognise him, although he looks a hell of a lot better now the injuries he picked up on fight night are almost healed.

She steps right up to him, not an ounce of fear in the way she holds herself. The same can't be said for Joker, who swallows nervously and shifts on his seat. "Been expecting us?" she asks, her tone mocking.

"Joker?" Ram barks, his brows pulled tight in confusion.

"It's n-nothing, Prez. Just a misunderstanding."

"Perhaps you might want to start explaining then," Cruz pipes up, appearing from one of the back rooms.

"I-I... umm..."

"He's been trying to kill me," Stella says, not a single crack in her voice. "Isn't that right, Joker?" she sneers.

Ram just throws his head back and laughs, as if it's the funniest thing he's ever heard.

"Joker might not be the sharpest, but he's not that fucking stupid."

The dumb cunt glances at his prez and swallows once more, beads of sweat appearing on his brow before looking back at Stella.

"Aw fuck," Ram groans, running his hand down his face and rubbing his beard. "You went after a Cirillo princess, you dumb fuck?"

"Ask him why," I bark.

"Should we take this out the back, Prez?" Cruz asks, aware of the entire fucking club watching us.

"No," Theo states. "I think this is a lesson that all your members need to learn."

"Cirillo, they don't—"

"Don't they? Clearly, the rules haven't been laid down strong enough, *Prez*. Your leadership isn't solid enough, because this sick fuck has been running all over town following the orders of another and breaking all your rules."

"Who?" he barks in a deadly voice that would make most others cower.

Joker holds his eyes, silently begging his prez to get him out of this.

Joker is fucking delusional. No wonder it was so easy to corrupt him.

"His father," Stella seethes. The click of the safety cuts through the silence of the room as everyone waits to hear who that might be.

An amused chuckle falls from her lips as she lifts her gun, training it right between his brows.

"But don't worry, Joker. You're both going to hell together. He isn't going to be here to help you this time."

"I-I never wanted to hurt you," Joker pleads like a fucking pussy.

"Well that's a real shame, because you did. And

more than that, you hurt people I care about, and that is something I can't let go of."

To my surprise, Stella takes a step back from him and both Ram and Cruz breathe a huge sigh of relief.

"You get one chance," Stella tells him.

"Stella, what the hell are you—"

"One chance to show your entire club what you're made of," Stella continues, ignoring Theo's question.

"Are you going to be a man like you're trying to prove to your father, or are you just a weak, pathetic—"

He scrambles from the stool he was on, effectively answering Stella's unasked question.

He makes it all of five steps before the loud crack of her gun rings through the vast room, followed by the recognisable sound of a body hitting the floor with a dull thud.

"Fucking hell," Ram mutters as blood begins to pool on his floor.

Taking off toward her victim, Stella comes to a stop above him and stares down as he fights to drag in the breaths he needs.

"You lost, Joker. Nice try though. It was fun while it lasted."

She lifts her gun again, and this time instead of hitting him in the chest, her bullet lands right between his brows.

Holy fuck, my girl is epic.

Lowering her weapon, she looks around the room at the shocked faces of the club members and their ol' ladies who just watched the show.

"Anyone else want to have a go?" she asks, raising

her arms from her sides, offering herself up as an easy target.

Panic floods me that there could be more than one stupid motherfucker in here, and I take a step forward, only to be stopped when Theo's arm shoots out and hits my stomach.

"She's got this," he whispers.

"Good." She turns to look Ram right in the eyes. He's a scary motherfucker, and Joker aside, he runs this club like a well-oiled machine. His reputation is everything, and Stella just put a massive fucking dent in it.

Closing the distance between them, Stella makes a show of holstering her gun once more. I, however, keep mine at my side, ready to go. I don't trust anyone in this building right now.

"Keep your boys in check, *Prez*. And maybe your girls too, for that matter." Ram frowns for a beat, but then his lips part as he realises who Stella is talking about. "And don't forget who really runs this side of the city. Everyone else is... expendable."

Spinning on her heels, she turns back to the three of us. Her face is blank, but I see her excitement, her sense of accomplishment, her hunger, in her eyes.

I'm sure the only thing on mine right now is shock, and if I were able to look away from her, I might even see a crack on both Theo and Daemon's usually impenetrable masks.

She sidesteps us as Ram speaks once more.

"Wait, who was his father?"

"No one you need to be worrying about," Stella

answers, continuing toward the door. "You guys coming or what?" she snaps when she gets there.

She yanks it open and disappears outside with her head held high and a confident sway to her hips.

It's such a fucking turn on.

With one more look between Ram and Cruz, I spin around and follow her. Daemon and Theo follow a few seconds later.

The moment I catch up with her, I grab her around the throat and pin her back against Daemon's car.

"That," I growl, "was fucking insane."

Her pulse thunders against my fingers as she holds my eyes.

We hadn't agreed how we were going to play that. Well, not entirely. But *that,* my girl handing the Reapers their arses on a platter quite so spectacularly, wasn't what we'd talked about.

"Nice work, Princess. I'm impressed," Daemon says, stopping beside us.

My eyes widen. No one ever impresses that cunt.

"But if you get any kind of bodily fluids in my car, it'll be your last fucking kill," he warns us.

He pulls the driver's door open and is about to drop inside when Theo speaks.

"You guys go without me. I've got something to finish up here."

We all turn to him.

"You need backup?"

"Nah. I think Stella made our point pretty well. I'll only be a few minutes."

Daemon nods, clearly happy that he's not about to walk back into a trap after that.

"Come on then. I've got something I want to show you, anyway," I tell Stella, opening the door and gently pressing my hand to her lower back.

"Princess sits in the front," Daemon barks.

"What?"

"She's in the front, or I'll leave you both here too."

"Fine," I concede, not wanting to be left.

Walking her around the car, I pull that door open for her instead.

"I can do this myself, you know. I thought I just proved that I can handle myself."

"Oh baby, you more than did. I'm so fucking horny right now."

Grabbing her hand, I press it against my painful dick. I can't fight the growl when she squeezes.

Her tongue sneaks out and wets her lips, my eyes following the trail.

One side of her mouth curls up in a smile as her eyes drop to mine.

"For fuck's sake, come on. I've got shit to be doing," Daemon barks from inside the car.

"You'd better hope that whatever you've got to show me is good." Stella shoots me a seductive wink before dropping into the car.

CHAPTER THIRTY

Stella

The second my ass hits the chair, a violent shudder rips through me. Curling my fingers, I tuck my fists into my body in an attempt to hide my reaction to what I just did.

I blow out a long, slow breath and fight to calm my racing heart.

"Shock is pretty normal," Daemon tells me before Seb has a chance to join us. "Just ride it out, you'll be okay."

I turn to look at him, surprised by his understanding. I know he's not a complete cold-hearted monster, but I still wasn't expecting *that* from him.

"I'm good," I lie quietly.

I didn't walk in there with the intention of just

stepping up and blowing Joker's brains out. I thought Theo, or Seb even, would lose their shit and just take over. I wasn't expecting them to allow me to take charge and deliver the revenge that fuck needed for everything he's put us all through. I just hope that Toby is getting the vengeance he needs with his cunt of a father on the other side of town.

"You need to get laid, you know that, bro?" Seb hisses as he joins us.

Daemon rolls his eyes and presses his foot to the gas, quickly getting us away from the Reapers' compound.

"Still the same place?" he asks Seb cryptically.

"Yep," Seb confirms but doesn't elaborate.

I glance back at him over my shoulder, happy to focus on whatever he's hiding instead of the reality of what we're leaving behind, but the smug fuck just smiles innocently at me.

"What's Theo doing?" I ask, needing to keep talking. I have no idea what's going to happen when I allow myself to actually process the fact that I killed someone tonight, and I'd rather not find out while sitting in Daemon's car.

"No fucking clue. Boss probably set him up to debrief with Ram or something."

"Won't he retaliate? We—I—just shot one of his members."

"One of his members who broke one of Ram's rules," Seb points out.

"He'll just be pissed he didn't get to pull the trigger

himself. Ram doesn't take well to disobedience. And," Daemon continues, "as you probably just saw, the whole club knows who's really in charge. Ram will need to grovel if he doesn't want any more repercussions from this."

"Can't imagine Joker stood a lot of chance against Jonas," I mutter.

"No. But he also didn't need to go against his prez."

"Does he have any other kids we should know about?"

Daemon chuckles. "We're looking into it."

"I hope that they make it hurt, whatever they've got planned for him," Seb says, sitting forward and wrapping his hand around my waist.

"I can almost guarantee it."

"You're heading to where they're taking him next, huh?" I ask Daemon.

"I wouldn't miss out on that kind of fun."

"Don't you want to be a part of that?" I ask Seb, genuinely curious.

"I've got something much better in mind."

Only a few minutes later, Daemon pulls his car to a stop on the side of the road.

I look out, seeing nothing that grabs my attention. It's just a street with stores and apartment buildings deep within the Cirillo territory.

"What's this?" I ask as Seb pushes the door open behind me and climbs out.

"Have a fun night." Daemon winks at me as the door beside me opens and Seb reaches in.

"You too. Make him scream." Daemon chuckles at my words before I'm hauled from the seat.

Seb takes my hand and drags me onto the sidewalk before pressing me up against the wall of the building.

"Can't fucking wait any longer," he groans, once again wrapping his fingers around my throat, tilting my chin up a little so he can crash his lips down on mine.

I barely get a chance to register his move before his tongue is pushing past my lips and his hand is snaking up my thigh, wrapping my leg around his waist and allowing him to grind himself against me.

"You're fucking incredible," he groans as he kisses down my throat.

"S-Seb, we're... *fuck*," I hiss when his length grazes my clit just so that it makes me lose my train of thought.

Thankfully, or maybe not, some douchebag across the street wolf whistles. I can only assume it's for our benefit, but it's enough to remind me that we're currently out in public.

"Seb, we need to stop," I say, finally finding my brain. My hands stop on his chest to push him back.

"Why? I have no problem showing the world who you belong to, Hellion. You know that every guy who'd see us would be crazy jealous of me."

My pussy clenches at the thought of him taking me somewhere so public.

He fucking knows it too, because his smile turns wicked.

"You'd fucking let me, wouldn't you, Hellion?" he

growls, sliding his hand down my leg until his fingertips brush the soaked lace of my panties.

His fingers tighten around my throat, enough that stars begin to flicker in my vision.

"You're a dirty fucking whore, Hellion," he says, holding my eyes as he rubs my clit. "And you're my whole fucking world."

I don't realize we've moved until warmth hits me, and when I pull back from Seb's lips and open my eyes, I find that we're inside and standing in front of an elevator.

"W-where are we?" I ask, my voice rough with desire.

"Your surprise, Hellion."

The doors part, and after Seb taps something against the control panel, we start rising through the building.

"Have I told you yet how fucking incredible you look tonight?" he growls, taking a step toward me as his eyes eat me up.

I move back, teasing him, but my back soon hits the wall, stopping my retreat.

"Once or twice," I quip.

"Not enough, then."

He drags his bottom lip between his teeth, his eyes raking over every inch of me and setting my skin on fire.

He isn't even touching me and I'm standing here with weak knees, damn near panting for him.

"You're so fucking beautiful, Hellion. And not just on the outside."

He closes the space between us, his hand wrapping around the side of my neck.

"You saved me, baby. You know that?"

I shake my head. "You didn't need me, Seb."

"Not true. I'd have gone under by now."

He leans in, brushing his lips against mine, but before he can deepen it, the elevator dings, announcing our arrival.

Taking my hand, Seb pulls me from the elevator and drags me out into an empty hallway. The scent of fresh paint hits my nose as my feet sink into the plush carpet. There are four black doors set in the fresh cream wall, from what I can see.

"Where are we?" I ask, and we pass one door and head toward another a little farther down.

"Press your hand to that pad," he says, pointing to a familiar square black box on the wall.

Some of the houses Dad and I have lived in have had this fancy tech shit, so it isn't new to me.

"Seb," I warn, my heart fluttering while my head gets carried away with what could be behind this door.

"If you want to finish what we started then—"

I press my hand to the pad, effectively shutting him up.

There's a click, and when I push the handle down, the door opens for me.

There's a soft glow from side lamps as I step inside.

The apartment is fully furnished. The walls are a soft cream, the furniture is all wood. The whole place is so warm and homely, the complete opposite of all the places I've lived with Dad. There's a huge cream sectional with an array of cushions and floor-to-ceiling windows behind which showcase the twinkling lights of the city in the distance.

"Wow, this place is gorgeous," I say, walking farther inside and finding a huge, fully kitted-out kitchen complete with an island and giant breakfast bar.

It's incredible, and the exact kind of thing I'd choose for myself.

"Y-yeah?" Seb asks from somewhere behind me.

The slight hesitation in his voice makes me turn around and look at him.

He's got his arm up, his fingers twisted in his hair, and there's a slight frown marring his brow. Yet still, he looks insanely hot in his suit. Butterflies continue to flutter from what we started earlier.

"Thought we should give Theo some peace for the night, huh?" I ask, assuming he's rented or borrowed it. I lock down any other options, because I refuse to get carried away with myself.

His hand drops to the back of his neck.

"Yeah, the night... forever." His eyes hold mine as he takes a step forward.

Something explodes in my belly... the excitement that I was trying to keep a lid on at thinking this could be something beyond serious.

"Seb, what have you done?"

His hand slips around the back of my neck, dragging me forward until our heads touch.

"Welcome home, baby," he whispers.

My heart pounds so hard in my chest I can feel it in

the tips of my fingers as his eyes hold mine, waiting for my reaction.

"Seb," I breathe.

"It wasn't meant to be ready for a few weeks. It's *not* entirely ready. But Damien pulled some strings last night and there have been people here all day and night trying to get it sorted. Maybe... don't touch the paint," he chuckles.

"This is crazy," I tell him, my head starting to spin.

"Suits us, huh?"

"I... I don't know what—"

"It's a Cirillo building. These apartments have had our names on them for ages. Daemon actually already lives down the hall. The rest of us just didn't feel the same need to rush. Well, until—"

"That asshole blew up our home."

"Yeah," he agrees. "Theo and Nico have the penthouses above us. Alex, Toby and Daemon are on this floor too. Or they will be when their flats are done."

"This is ours. Just... ours?" I ask, just to confirm.

"Yep."

"Does my dad know?"

A smile pulls at Seb's lips, excitement and anticipation twinkling in his eyes.

"Who do you think helped me furnish it?"

"It... it's perfect."

"No. That's you, baby. You're perfect. Watching you tonight. Hellion... do you realize just how fierce you were?"

I shrug like it was nothing, when in reality, images of me shooting that fuck in the head are right on the edge of my conscience, desperately trying to be at the forefront. Something I suspect Seb knows.

"Just protecting my family. I'm fed up with watching my back. Of worrying about you, about them." My eyes shoot up to the ceiling to indicate the guys. "It shouldn't be like this."

"We're dangerous people, Hellion. There's always an element of looking over our shoulders, but it shouldn't be this bad."

His hands slip down my body until he finds the clasp of my shoulder holster, and in seconds he has it and my gun on the counter beside us. "You earned this tonight, huh?" he says, eyeing my Cirillo family Glock.

A smile twitches at my lips. I probably shouldn't be proud of that fact, but fuck it, I am.

"Time to celebrate?" I ask, noticing the bottle of champagne sitting in an ice bucket on the counter with two flutes beside it.

"That was the idea." He reaches for the bottle and pops the top, immediately lifting it to his mouth for a sip.

He swallows, licking his tongue across his lip, collecting up the drops. My mouth waters for a taste as I watch him do it again, the muscles in his neck rippling and his Adam's apple bobbing.

"Seb," I groan.

His hooded eyes find mine and he tips the bottle in my direction, asking if it's what I want.

Reaching out, I wrap my fingers around his, bringing it closer to my lips.

"Desperate, baby?" His voice is so low, so rough that

it sends a shiver of desire racing down my spine that ends at my clit.

"You have no idea."

Humoring me, he moves the bottle to my lips, tipping it enough that a small trickle fills my mouth, the bubbles exploding on my tongue.

I swallow, expecting him to stop, but he doesn't, and the champagne runs from my mouth and down my chin, the ice-cold liquid hitting my chest.

"Sebastian," I moan when he dips his head and licks up my flushed skin.

"You taste like sin and death, Hellion."

"Exactly as you like it."

Abandoning the bottle on the side, he pushes my jacket from my shoulders, allowing it to fall on the counter.

Dragging my feet up the back of his legs, I pin his waist against me, moaning when his hard length presses against my core.

"Whore," he mutters against my chest, his hand gliding up my bare leg until he finds my thigh strap, or more specifically, my knife.

He pulls it free and presses the cool flat of the blade against my cheek.

My chest heaves as we stare at each other, my nipples like bullets behind the cups of my corset.

"You wanna play, Hellion?" Seb drawls, dragging the knife over my jaw and down my neck.

"You know I do," I whisper, trying to slow the movements of my chest when the point of the blade lowers.

He doesn't cut me—I trust him implicitly not to hurt me—but I feel the slight scratch.

I know just how sharp that thing is, how quickly it could slice me up and leave me bleeding out on this countertop.

"I really love this," he breathes, running the top of the blade along the edge of the corset. "Sadly, not enough." He tucks the tip under the fabric covering my breast and tugs.

The lace tears with ease, exposing my heavy breasts.

"Oh God," I moan, resting back on my palms and arching my body, offering myself up to him.

Moving the knife away, he dips his head, sucking my hard nipple into his mouth and biting down until I cry out.

"Yes. Seb, yes."

With his mouth still on me, he cuts the rest of my corset away until it falls to the counter as ruined scraps.

Dragging his lips to the other side, he gives that one the same treatment until I'm writhing on the counter, digging my heels into his ass as I fight for the friction I need to get myself off.

"Seb, please. I need—"

"Trust me, Hellion. I'm going to give you exactly what you need."

Kissing down my belly, his fingers find the little zipper at the base of my spine and he drags it down painfully slowly.

The second it's open, I lift my ass from the counter,

allowing him to drag it down my legs. He discards it at my knees, letting me kick it off.

"So fucking perfect."

He kisses a line along the scar on my belly before licking all the way back up it.

"Fierce." Kiss. "So fucking strong." Kiss. "My world." Kiss. "My weakness." Kiss.

My panties suddenly fall from my body, courtesy of my knife, once more leaving me writhing naked on the counter.

"Died and gone to fucking heaven," Seb mutters, rubbing his thumb across his bottom lip as he studies me.

His fingertip trails around the strap on my thigh, making me shudder. I widen my thighs in the hope it'll entice him higher.

"Whore," he says with an amused chuckle.

"I'll be whatever you want me to be—"

"If it gets you what you want?" he finished for me.

"Problem?" I gasp as he releases the strap, dropping it so it joins my skirt.

"Not at all."

He shrugs out of his jacket, throwing it on the counter before undoing his tie and shedding his shirt, leaving him standing in just his black dress pants that hang low on his hips, showing the band of his boxer briefs and his deep V lines.

"Seb," I breathe, my eyes locked on his body, my fingers wrapping around the edge of the counter to stop me from taking things into my own hands.

"Tell me what you want, baby," he growls, taking a step closer.

My cunt aches at his words, and my eyes drop to the tent in his pants.

I want that, fuck. But I also...

"Mouth," I pant, spreading my legs wider.

His brow quirks as he stands before me, not freaking moving.

"Seb," I groan as if I'm in actual pain, "I want your mouth on my cuuu— YES!" I scream as he drops to his knees, drags my ass off the edge and eats me as if he'll die without it.

My fingers twist in his hair as his tongue assaults my clit, making my entire body tremble with my need for release.

He pushes two thick fingers inside me and curls them just so. Only seconds later I'm detonating around him, my body convulsing on the hard counter as I ride out each powerful wave of pleasure.

When he pulls back, his face is glistening with my release and he's got a smug-as-shit grin on his face.

My lips part to bark out a cutting remark about it, but I swallow the words when he rips the fly of his pants open and frees his aching cock.

The tip glistens with precum and my pussy clenches, more than ready to feel him moving inside me.

"Please," I whimper so quietly even I don't hear it over the pounding of my heart and the blood rushing past my ears.

But the second his eyes lock with mine, I know he did.

He brushes the tip of his cock through my wetness, coating himself in my juices before his hand wraps tightly around my hip, dragging me farther off the counter before he pushes his cock inside me.

"Please, I need—"

He responds by thrusting up inside me harshly, filling me to the hilt in one move and making my breath catch in my throat.

His fingertips dig into my ass as he fucks me like a fucking demon. The bite of pain from his grip only adds to the pleasure that builds within me faster than I thought possible.

"You're as fucked up as the rest of us, aren't you, Hellion?"

"Seb," I groan, my head falling back as his lips find my neck.

"Blood and violence get you as horny as the rest of us."

"Harder."

"Fuck, baby."

He pulls out of me and I shout my displeasure at losing him, but I quickly figure out his plan before my bare breasts connect with the marble counter I was lying on. He tells me to hang on and drags my ass back until I'm exactly where he wants me.

With my heels still on, I'm the perfect height for him, and not a breath after I feel him shift closer is he fully seated inside me once more—only with this position, it feels so much deeper.

My head spins as he fucks me so hard, hits me so deep, I have no idea where the pleasure ends and the pain begins.

It's fucking everything.

My chest slides against the counter, my skin slick with sweat as he fucks me until I'm a boneless, panting mess.

"Again," he demands after another mind-blowing release.

His hand slips around my belly, relying on my legs taking a little of my weight. Risky.

"Oh God," I gasp when his fingers brush against my clit. I'm so fucking sensitive I can hardly stand it.

But then he rolls his hips, grazing my G-spot again, and it lights something up inside me.

Arching my back, I allow him to take me even deeper as he strums my clit like he's got a fucking instruction manual to it.

"Come for me, Hellion. Let me hear you screaming my name," he demands, his thrusts getting rougher as he nears the end.

My voice is already hoarse from doing just that.

The second he pinches my clit, it sends me tumbling headfirst into another release and I cry out as he groans and stills behind me, his orgasm hitting.

"Stella, fuck. FUCK," he booms, his cock jerking violently inside me.

"Oh my God," I breathe, collapsing on the counter with his weight against my back.

His chest heaves, his breaths racing across my neck and making me shiver.

"You're a fucking goddess, baby."

"Not so bad yourself."

He chuckles lightly before lifting from my body and scooping me up in his strong arms as if I weigh nothing.

"Hey," I breathe, a lazy, sated smile on my lips.

"Hey," he replies, his eyes sparkling with mischief still, telling me that our night is far from over.

Bring it on, baby.

CHAPTER THIRTY-ONE

Sebastian

My phone ringing somewhere in the flat drags my attention from my girl sleeping in my arms.

I took her again against the wall in our huge walk-in shower, and then again, only slower, after I lowered her to our bed.

I didn't want to fuck her in there the first time. I wanted to take my time, savour her, show her just how fucking incredible she was.

And after I made her come another handful of times, she curled up on my chest, her hair still wet from our shower, and passed the fuck out.

I got it. I was fucking exhausted too after the past twenty-four hours. But I was still buzzing. The memories of our place going up, the fresh images of

Stella delivering our message fucking perfectly to the Reapers, concern over what Theo went back for, and how Toby and the others got on stop me from relaxing at all, even after all those releases.

Slipping out from beneath her, I silently pad across the room in search of the noise.

I find my phone still in my trousers pocket on the kitchen floor.

Pulling it out, I stare at the island with a smile on my lips.

Fuck, she looked insane laid out on there, waiting for me.

My cock swells just from the memory, although that high soon dies a little when I see Theo's name lighting up my screen.

"Hey, bro. How'd it go?" I ask the second the call connects.

"Yeah, it's good. Dad's got Jonas. Stubborn fuck isn't talking, so he's giving him a little time to think about his actions." I can't help but smile at the amusement in Theo's tone.

"How's Tobes?" I ask, knowing that it's going to be one of the first things Stella is going to want to know when she wakes up.

"He's good. Little fucker is drowning in bloodlust right now."

"Good. Tell him to make it fucking hurt."

"Don't worry. He's well on board with the plan. How's Stella?"

"She's good, man. I've been... taking her mind off it all."

He scoffs, and I can imagine him shaking his head.

"Of course you have. I wouldn't expect anything else from you two. Keep an eye on her though, bro. Remember your first kill?" he asks. The image of the first life I took slams into me and a shudder runs down my spine. I was so young. Too fucking young. It wasn't just the lying cunt at the other end of my gun who died that day; so did the shreds of my innocence I was still holding onto. I never really got a chance to be a kid, but that moment, that was the final straw. The day I became a man. I just needed my body to catch up with my mind.

"Yeah, like it was yesterday. I've got this. She's gonna be good."

"I know. She's a fucking goddess."

I scoff.

"I'm going nowhere near her, man. Don't start on that bullshit. Unless of course... you're not man enough."

"You fucking well know I am. So are you—" I'm about to ask if he's gonna go and find a willing girl to celebrate with tonight when a blood-curdling scream fills the flat. "Fuck. I gotta go."

"Go be with her," I hear Theo say before I cut the call and run through our new home.

I don't slow as I get to the bedroom door and fly into the room, but the sight before me stops me in my tracks.

Stella is sitting in the middle of the bed, her arms wrapped around her legs, her entire body trembling as silent tears stream down her cheeks.

"Stella, baby," I whisper, not wanting to startle her if she hasn't heard me.

Crawling onto the bed with her, I wrap her in my arms in the hope it'll break through whatever has her so terrified.

She turns into my body and tucks her face into my chest, her tears dripping down and landing on my stomach.

"Hey, baby. It's okay."

I rub my hand soothingly up and down her back as I whisper how much I love her and how fucking insane she is.

She never says a word as she cuddles into me, but her body doesn't stop trembling. Her skin is flushed with sweat but goose bumps cover her.

"Baby, what's—"

I don't get to ask what's going on. Probably a good thing—it's a fucking dumb-arse question anyway—because she pushes me away and races toward the bathroom.

When I rush in behind her, I find her on her knees, vomiting in the toilet.

Gathering up her still damp hair, I rub her back until she's done.

Sitting on her heels, she pushes a few loose strands of hair from her face, keeping her eyes locked on her knees.

"I-I'm sorry. I'm okay," she says weakly, her hands still trembling in her lap.

Moving quickly, I start the bathtub, running and pour in some bubbles from the fancy bottle on the side.

Leaving it to fill, I drop to my knees before my girl and take her face in my hands.

"Never apologise for needing me, baby."

A sob rips up her throat.

"I-I thought I was okay," she confesses quietly.

"You are. The adrenaline has just run out and you're in shock," I say confidently, more than recognising the signs. Hell, I've lived them more than once over the years. I've witnessed it in others too. "But it's going to be okay. I've got you, okay? And I'm not letting go. Ever."

Finally, her tear-filled eyes lift to mine.

"I killed him," she whispers so quietly that I'd probably have missed it if I didn't see her lips move.

"Yeah, baby. You did." I want to tell her that it was fucking beautiful too, but I don't think she'd appreciate that right now. "Because he hurt you. He hurt me," I say, pointing to the scar on my shoulder. "Because he hurt Toby."

Her eyes harden with anger as I point each of those out, and I know that she's beginning to claw out of the worst of her darkness.

"We're all safe now, because of you."

Unlinking her own fingers, she reaches out and takes mine.

Brushing my thumbs over her knuckles, I wait for her to form her words.

"W-what will happen now?" Another violent shiver rips through her despite the fact that we're sitting on a heated floor.

"Hold that thought."

Climbing to my feet, I pull her up with me. "Come on, let's warm you up."

With my hands on her hips, I walk her over to the now almost full bathtub and help her get in.

The second she lowers down in the water, I step in behind her, wrap my legs around her and pull her back against my chest, encasing her in my arms.

She wiggles to get comfortable and I sigh in contentment. I know she's struggling right now, and I fucking hate that, but man, I needed this.

"So?" she asks, reminding me that she wanted some answers.

"Nothing will happen now, baby. Joker betrayed Ram with what he did, and in turn, that means Ram and the entire club betrayed their agreement with Damien. That isn't something Ram will take lightly."

"So... the Italians, the Reapers and us... we all have an agreement to stay out of each other's way?"

"Yeah, in layman's terms. But ultimately, we're in charge. We control the shipments that get into this part of the city which means we control the money. The Reapers or the Italians fail to get their shipments and they'll go under. We have the power to cut them off. We pull the strings, so—"

"They break the rules and they're fucked."

"Pretty much. And by putting those hits on you, on us, whether he was working for Jonas or not, Joker shattered those fucking rules. If you didn't put that bullet in his head, then Ram would have done it himself when he found out what his prospect was up to."

"Okay," she whispers, nodding.

"The second he decided to try to impress Jonas, he signed his own death certificate, baby."

"And Jonas knew that?"

"Of course he did."

"I hope Toby is having fun with him."

I can't help the chuckle that rumbles in my chest. "Oh, he is."

She twists to look up at me, sloshing water all over the side of the tub in the process.

"You've spoken to him?" she asks, her eyes hopeful.

"I've spoken to Theo. That's where I was when you..." I trail off, not wanting to remind her of whatever happened there. "He's with the others where they're holding Jonas."

"O-okay. Good. Theo's okay too?" she asks, concern pulling her brows tight.

"Yeah. The Reapers wouldn't have touched him, baby. Everyone who should be okay *is* okay. You can relax."

She nods and sinks back against me.

"This is nice," she whispers after a few silent minutes.

"Yeah. I had big plans for this bathtub when I chose it," I confess.

Her thigh brushes against my semi. "You're insatiable."

"You're naked."

She shakes her head and rests it back against my chest.

"Thank you," she whispers.

"You have nothing to thank me for, Hellion."

She nods against me before pressing a kiss to my scar.

"I love you," she whispers, her exhaustion and emotion making her voice crack.

"I love you too, Stella. More than you could ever know."

I press a kiss onto the top of her head and sink us both lower into the water.

Thankfully, both of us actually get some sleep, and when I wake up to the sound of a buzzer I don't recognise, Stella is still out cold.

Releasing her, I tuck the sheets around her to keep her warm, drag a pair of joggers from the drawer and pull them up my legs to see who's come to visit.

It's hardly a surprise to find an anxious little brunette bouncing on the balls of her feet with four annoyed-looking guys behind her when I bring the screen to life.

Unlocking the door, I pull it wide and press my finger to my lips, instructing them to be quiet before letting them all in.

"Is she okay?" Calli whispers the second she's over the threshold.

"Yeah, she's good."

Memories from her freak-out the night before flicker in my mind, but I know deep down that she's going to be okay. It might take a few weeks, or months even, but my girl's strong and she'll deal with the events of the last night in her own time and come out even fiercer than before.

"We brought coffee and breakfast," Theo says, holding up the tray of coffees in his hand and nodding to the bag Alex is carrying.

"Good. You know you'd have been kicked straight back out if you'd turned up empty-handed," I lie, plucking out a coffee from the tray.

"Bellend," Theo mutters.

"This place is nice, man," Toby says, looking around at the home I designed for my girl. "She likes it?"

"I mean, we didn't spend all that much time looking at the furniture, Tobes." He groans as if my words cause him physical pain. "But yeah, I think she approves. What about you? Have the best night of your life?"

He grimaces a little. "Yeah, it was... fun."

Theo sniggers. "Bro, you were a fucking demon, and you smiled the whole fucking time."

"Yeah, still not entirely sure it was as..." He narrows his eyes on me. "*Pleasurable* as Seb's night."

"Guys," I groan. "Don't tell me you didn't line up for pussy for our boy after all that torture?"

Nico scoffs. "Who the fuck do you think we are? Of course we fucking did. Not our fault he didn't go for it."

"She was a fucking ho," Toby argues.

"Didn't stop me," Nico barks.

"Yeah, man. We fucking know," Alex points out, making me wonder exactly what last night entailed.

"Ignore them," Theo says, mostly to Calli, who's watching everyone with wide eyes. Although I'm not sure why. She's learning fast what we've kept from her over the years.

"So now what?" I ask, propping my foot on the edge of the coffee table after grabbing a pastry from the bag Alex dropped on the centre.

"Back to normal life, hopefully," Theo says.

"Yeah, you say that, but your home just went up in a fireball."

He scowls at me.

"My place will be ready in a few days," he says, shooting a look at the ceiling where his penthouse awaits its master.

"You guys joining us too?" I ask Nico, Alex and Toby.

"Hell yes. Party central," Nico barks, while Alex shakes his head.

"Does that mean I get your basement?" Calli pipes up.

"Uh..."

"You've said it now. It's time for the queen to take over your palace, Cirillo."

All of us but Nico bark out laughs at the serious expression on Calli's face. Girl's not messing about.

And something tells me she's about to cause her big brother—us—some fucking trouble in the near future.

"The princess has spoken," Alex says with a wink in Calli's direction.

She rolls her eyes at him and changes the subject.

"Anyone spoken to Emmie? She's not answering her phone."

All eyes turn on Theo, making him rear back.

"What? Why would I have spoken to her?" he asks, completely affronted. But the second his eyes lock on mine, I read the truth. Cheeky fuck is lying through his teeth.

"She's fine," I answer for him.

"Yeah. So she managed to not get in the middle of your bullshit last night?"

I raise a brow at her.

"Our bullshit?" Theo asks. "Did you, or did you not, ask to become a part of this?" Her lips part to answer, but he beats her to it. "Our *bullshit* is now your bullshit. You might not have had your finger on the trigger, baby C, but you're a part of this now, so suck it up."

She swallows somewhat nervously at the serious tone of Theo's voice.

"O-okay. Jeez. I just wanna know if my friend is okay."

"She's fine," he says coldly, making me wonder if she actually is.

My eyes narrow at him, trying to read between the lines.

He went back in there last night because of her, I'd put fucking money on it.

Subtly, he shakes his head at me.

"I'm going to the toilet," Calli huffs, taking off down the hall. She doesn't need to ask where to go seeing as it was she and Selene who filled this flat yesterday with everything we'd need. It wasn't only Stella's outfit they went shopping for.

"Who's got her knickers in a twist?" Alex asks.

"*Don't* talk about my sister's knickers," Nico barks.

"Jesus," Theo mutters, throwing a croissant at him. "Stuff that in your face and stop fucking talking."

The buzzer rings out again and I push from the couch. There are only a handful of people who know about this place, so it's not hard to guess who might have come to join us.

Checking the screen, I find exactly what I was expecting.

The devil of death himself.

"Morning, sunshine," I sing.

Daemon stares back at me with his cold, empty eyes and doesn't even crack a smile.

Weird fuck.

"How is she?" he asks, inviting himself in.

"Still sleeping, but she's going to be okay."

"Yo bro," Alex says when I appear ahead of him. "Satan let you out to play today, huh?"

Daemon flips him off before stealing his coffee and perching himself on the arm of an empty chair as Calli reappears down the hallway.

Her footsteps falter a little before she nods at something, or more so someone behind me.

Twisting around, I find my girl standing in the doorway, wearing just my shirt from last night and a lazy, sleepy smile on her face.

"Stel," I breathe, my heart tumbling in my chest as I take in her beauty, her strength, her fucking resilience.

Pushing from the sofa, I make my way over to her, taking her face in my hands and staring right into her eyes, searching for any signs that the effects of her panic attack last night might still be lingering.

"I'm okay," she whispers so that only I can hear her. "I promise."

"Sorry I left you. These arseholes turned up."

She smiles at me before looking over my shoulder at our visitors.

"Wouldn't have it any other way."

"Come and get your coffee before it gets cold, Princess," Theo says, pride evident in his tone.

Taking her hand in mine, I turn away, ready to lead her toward the guys, but she tugs on my hand, pulling me back.

I crowd her against the wall, pressing the length of my body against hers, resting my forearm beside her head.

"I think you forgot something," she purrs.

"Fucking hell, not again," someone complains, but I'm too lost in my girl's eyes to acknowledge who it is.

"Yeah, I think I did," I murmur, dropping down and brushing my lips against hers. "Morning, baby."

She arches into me the second I claim her lips, grip her hip in my hand and hold her tighter against me.

Someone wolf whistles as my tongue plunges into her mouth, and I flip whoever it might have been off as I drown in her.

The temptation to drag her back down to the bedroom is strong, but she makes the decision for me when our kiss ends.

"Come on, I need that coffee."

With my arms around her waist, I hide my raging

hard-on behind her body as we make our way back to the sofa, a move that none of the guys miss. Calli just looks at us through soppy, teenage girl eyes. Something tells me that sometime soon, she's going to really experience what being a part of this life entails, and that innocence that lingers in her eyes, the one Nico has tried to protect for so long, is going to shrivel up and die. I hope for her sake it doesn't, but I know that realistically, it's inevitable.

Stella settles herself on my lap and accepts her coffee from Theo and a pain au chocolat from Alex, and we all settle into our new normal in our new home, while they all look at her with pride and awe in their eyes—but no one more than me, because none of them can truly appreciate just how fucking incredible the woman in my arms is, how she brings me to my knees every single second of every fucking day.

Leaning forward, I press a kiss to the soft skin behind her ear and breathe in her addictive scent.

Turning away from Calli, who she's having a conversation with, her eyes lock on mine.

"You okay?" she asks.

"Yeah. Just needed to..." Her brows pinch as she waits for me to finish. "I love you, Hellion." Her face softens, a content smile pulling at her lips. "I can't wait to burn the rest of hell down together."

EPILOGUE

Stella

"**M**an, I really needed that," I say as Calli and I step out of her mom's spa, the low winter sun making us squint.

Tugging the zipper of my coat up, I snuggle into its warmth as the freezing temperature threatens to ruin my mood.

"What next?" I ask, remembering her telling me when she came to pick me up this morning that she had plans for our whole day.

She pulls her cell out and taps on the screen, shooting off a message to someone as we make our way down to her car.

She doesn't respond for a few seconds, as if she's waiting for confirmation about something. Then, after her cell has pinged and she's got her answer, she drops it into her purse and looks over at me.

"I think we should probably just head back. I'm wiped."

"Oh... uh... okay. We can just hang, order takeout?" I ask, knowing deep down that she's right. I fell asleep during my massage up there. I'm more than exhausted.

Things since the night I killed Joker, or Joseph as I've since learned, have been weird.

Most nights I wake up in a cold sweat, having just relived the moment I shot him in cold blood.

But every time, Seb is right there, dragging me from the moment and reminding me that everything is okay.

I hate it. I hate questioning what I did, especially when I know I did the right thing. But taking someone's life, no matter how much they might have deserved it for hurting those I love, has still fucked with my head.

It'll get better, I know it will. I also know that while Joker might have been my first, he won't be my last, because if anyone, and I literally mean anyone, threatens or hurts any of my family again, I'll be the first there with my fucking gun to prove a point.

Damien might be a little unsure about his leap into the twenty-first century by allowing me to stand beside the boys as one of his soldiers, but fuck it. My dad trained me my entire life for this, and I'm damn well taking my place.

I won't be a woman who stays behind while the men go and fight our battles. I want to be a part of it. I want to play my part. I want to stand beside my man, my dad, my brother, my family with my head held high and my pink blade poised and ready to protect those I love.

I glance over at Calli as she pulls away from the curb, and the sight of the frown pulling at her brow makes me pause.

Something's up with her. It has been for a while.

At first, I thought that the events of Halloween were just a little too much for her to handle and she backed away.

I got it. Hell, I more than got it. Knowing that some crazed lunatic was chasing me through the backyard of that place with a gun would be enough to put anyone off this life, but I'm starting to think it's more than that.

"You wanna talk about it?" I ask, hoping that she might finally open up now she's all relaxed from the spa. Hell knows that getting her drunk last weekend didn't work.

"What? I'm fine. Nothing to talk about," she argues.

"Right," I mutter, totally unconvinced. "Whatever it is, you know I'd never judge you for it, right?"

"Of course I know that." She glances over at me. "I'm really okay."

"Okay," I concede, knowing that I'm not going to get anywhere by continuing to poke her.

She'll talk when she's ready and not a second sooner.

The journey back to our apartment building takes forever with the busy afternoon traffic, and I almost fall asleep again as we stop and start, but eventually, Calli pulls her car into the almost empty parking lot in front of our building.

Daemon had already moved in before us, and now Theo is upstairs, but as of yet, the others' apartments aren't ready. The rest of the building is currently empty and mostly a building site, so we have our choice of parking spaces right now.

"Are the guys here?" I ask, glancing at the other cars.

"No idea."

It's hard to know where any of them are just by their cars because they're always driving each other's—Theo's Ferrari the exception, of course. As it stands, only Seb and I have had the pleasure of racing that through the city.

We're currently borrowing cars from Damien, seeing as both my Porsche, my poor baby, and Seb's Aston were completely destroyed in the explosion.

We've both got new ones on order though, and I can't wait to get back behind my own wheel.

"Come on, I'm starving."

We make our way through the entrance and step into the elevator that's waiting for us.

I study Calli with suspicion when she starts chewing on one freshly-manicured nail as we climb through the building.

"You're hiding something."

"What? No, I'm not," she argues unconvincingly.

I narrow my eyes at her but let it go.

The second we step out of the elevator, I breathe a sigh of relief as my feet sink into the carpet. I love it here. I love having a home with my man.

Who would have thought that I'd be living with that boy from the graveyard that night only a few months into my life here? And not only that, but that I'd be totally head over heels in love with him.

Pressing my palm to the biometric pad, the locks disengage and allow me to push inside.

At first, as I kick my shoes off and hang my coat up on the row of hooks, I don't realize that anything is amiss. But the second I step into our living area, I soon discover that Calli was very much hiding something.

"Happy Thanksgiving," everyone shouts, making me pause as a giant lump crawls up my throat.

Seb steps forward, taking both of my trembling hands in his.

"Surprise, Hellion."

I blink at him a couple of times as I fight with the tears that are blurring my vision.

"You did all this?" I ask, looking around at the decorations and the perfectly laid table.

"Well," he says a little nervously, shooting a look over his shoulder, "I had a little help from the experts."

I follow his gaze, scanning the mass of people standing behind him, and find my dad, Calvin and Angie smiling at me.

That lump in my throat only grows bigger at the sight of them.

"Thank you," I croak out. "Thank you so much."

"Anything for you, baby. You know that. Did you really think we'd let it pass you by?"

I nod as my first tear drops, because yeah, I didn't think he'd even realized what day it was.

Swiping the tear away with the back of my hand, I curse myself for being so emotional. Before falling for Seb, I can't even remember the last time I cried. He's softened a part of my black heart, and secretly, I love it.

"Hey, sweetheart," Dad says as I step up to him and wrap my arms around his waist. "Surprised?" he asks with a laugh.

"Just a little."

Maria—Mom—is standing right at his side with a wide smile on her face as she watches me.

"Hi, sweetie," she breathes as I lean in for a hug. It's still early days for us, but we're starting to get to know each other, and hopefully we'll fully embrace our mother/daughter status soon. She's moved in with Dad now that Jonas's reign of terror over her has come to an end, and I've never seen my dad happier. There's a constant smile on his face and a twinkle in his eye that I didn't even realize existed until the first time we visited them.

I say quick hellos to Calvin and Angie before turning to another person who I know will have had a big hand in organizing this surprise.

"Hey, Bro," I say, turning to Toby.

"Hey, Sis."

He pulls me in for a hug, and I hold him just that little bit longer than I probably should, just soaking up his strength.

It turned out that discovering that Jonas had another son wasn't the only secret that cunt was keeping, because after doing a little more research and then some DNA testing, it turned out that everything Toby and Maria suffered over the years was for nothing. Toby isn't Jonas's son.

He's my dad's first born. My real brother.

Something that we're all convinced Jonas was well aware of. He was so fast to DNA test me as a baby that there's no way he wouldn't have done Toby, but he was so damn desperate for control, for an heir, that he claimed him as his own and spent the next nineteen years torturing him for something he had no control over.

Safe to say that revelation fucked with Toby's head more than he was expecting. I hate seeing him suffering. I wish there was more I could do for him other than offering a shoulder to cry on and a sympathetic ear when he wants to talk.

But I have every confidence that he'll be okay, just like I will. Jonas, despite his best efforts, will not break us.

I have no idea what's happened to him since they captured him, and quite frankly, I don't need to know.

He's out of our lives now, and we're all able to put him behind us. That's all that matters.

"You ready for your first Thanksgiving?" I ask him, butterflies fluttering in my belly, knowing that I'm about to have my first holiday with my family. My real family.

"Have you seen the amount of food Angie and Mum have been preparing? Hell yeah, I'm ready."

I laugh at him before two people approach me from behind.

Turning around, I find a sheepish-looking Calli.

"I'm sorry. I almost told you so many times. I'm not good with secrets."

"No shit," I laugh, pulling her in for a hug.

"Come on, dinner's ready," someone shouts, and everyone moves toward the extended dining table.

I search the room, looking for the person who's obviously absent from this little gathering. and my heart aches for her.

Emmie has kept herself away from us after what went down at her grandfather's clubhouse. I understand why. She feels guilty for not knowing what was going on under her nose. But I get it, and I don't blame her at all.

I just wish she could stop blaming herself so she didn't feel she had to miss out.

Seb takes his place at the head of the table, with Theo at the other end. I can't help but laugh at the pair of them.

The food is incredible, the company is amazing, and we all have the best afternoon. At some point, Seb brought his tablet to the table and we were able to video chat with everyone in America and properly introduced them to the rest of our family. As expected, the guys spent most of the call arguing about the correct shape of a football. Seb had backup this time, so it went on way longer than necessary.

"Hey, baby. Can I steal you for a minute?" Seb asks

after finding me on the couch talking to Dad, Maria and Toby.

"Yeah, of course. Excuse me," I say to them, taking Seb's hand and allowing him to drag me through to our bedroom.

"Seb," I warn. I might be open to screwing his brains out when our friends are close by, but I draw the line at my entire family. It's already bad enough that Toby has heard—and seen, for that matter—way too much. I don't need to extend that to Dad and Maria. "We can't."

"You've got a one-track mind, Hellion. I haven't brought you in here to fuck your brains out. Although," he says, taking a step toward me, "now you've mentioned it..."

"Behave, Sebastian."

"Me? Never."

"Nightmare." I roll my eyes dramatically at him.

He tugs my hand so I have no choice but to fall down on the edge of the bed beside him.

"I've got something for you," he confesses.

"Oh?"

Reaching into his pants pocket, he pulls out a box.

"Uh... you do know it's not Christmas, right?"

He laughs at me. "Yeah, Princess. I'm aware. Just wanted to show you how thankful I am for you."

I swoon so fucking hard it almost hurts.

"Open it."

A wide smile spreads across my face as I rip the silver paper from the small gift and find a black jewelry box inside.

My heart damn near stops in my chest, and my wide eyes meet his.

"Uh... n-no, it's not what you're thinking. But I'm glad I know where you stand on that," he jokes.

We haven't talked about the future. We spent so long fighting to ensure we even have one that we've just been living in the moment.

"I do... I mean, I want that... o-one day... I—"

"Stella, it's okay. I was joking. We're too young for all that shit." I breathe a sigh of relief. It's not that I don't want to marry him. I just... I want a chance to settle into life with him. I want to just be us without constantly looking over our shoulders. "I will ask one day, though. Because this," he says, wrapping his hand around the back of my neck. "It's a done deal."

"Oh yeah?" I ask with a smirk.

"Yep. I wrote my name on you, so you're mine now."

"Oh my God," I laugh.

"What? It's true."

Shaking my head, I focus back on my gift and flip the lid.

Sucking in a breath, I stare down at the necklace before me.

"Seb," I breathe. "It's..." I can't help but laugh. "Perfect."

"I thought so," he states proudly.

Lifting one hand, I run my fingertip over one of the delicate chains and down to the first charm. A platinum heart with a black diamond in the center.

"Only you would get me a black heart," I joke.

"Because I know you better than anyone else."

I nod, silently agreeing with him as I move down the longer chain to the second charm.

It's a dagger. Well, no, not just a dagger—a pink diamond-encrusted dagger mimicking my own."

"I love it."

"Can I?" he asks, taking the box from me and pulling the necklace out.

Lifting my hair from my shoulders, I allow him to place it around my neck.

The heart falls right on my breastbone while the dagger hangs teasingly in my cleavage.

Twisting back around to him, I show him how it looks.

"Even better than I could have imagined," he mutters, his own fingers trailing down the chain, causing goose bumps to erupt across my body.

"Yeah, I was thinking the same about you."

"Nah, baby. I'm worse. So, so much worse."

His hand finds its home around my throat, and he kisses me entirely too thoroughly and dirtily, considering our family is right outside the door.

"I love you, Hellion. Never change."

"Never. I love you too."

Extended Epilogue

Theo

Her shriek of fright as I slam the door behind me makes a smirk curl at my lips.

Shaking my head, I step farther into the dark room.

Her wide, terrified eyes track my every step as I get closer to her.

"What do you—"

I don't give her a chance to finish her dumb fucking question. Instead, my fingers wrap around her throat and I slam her back against the wall behind her.

"You think you're so fucking clever, don't you, Ramsey?"

My eyes narrow as I stare down into her dark ones, and my jaw tics in frustration.

The others seemed to miss the flash of dark hair that bolted from the corner of the room the second we stormed the Royal Reapers clubhouse. But I didn't. I saw every second of Cruz dragging her away and hiding her in here to keep her safe.

A sneer pulls at my lips.

Fucking idiot.

If he wanted her safe, he shouldn't have let her inside this compound in the first place.

"I-I don't—"

"Don't fucking lie to me." My fingers tighten around her throat as her pulse thunders beneath them.

She likes to pretend that she's not scared of me, that she's immune to what everyone sees when they look at me. But I can see past that mask she puts on. I feel the tremble of her body when I touch her.

She's not stupid, despite how she tries to act.

She knows she's in the wrong here, and she's fucking petrified.

"I'm not," she snaps, trying to cling to her brave façade. "I had no fucking clue that you'd all be here tonight. That you'd..." She waves toward the wall that leads to the main clubhouse where Stella just put an end to one of the Reapers' lives. The wall has a window in the middle of it, and despite the fact that we couldn't see her hiding inside here, I just fucking knew that she could see everything.

And I was proved right the second I stepped in here and had a clear view of the chaos we left behind as Ram and the rest of his men scrambled around to remove the dead body from their floor.

Fucking idiots didn't even see me slip back inside here, let alone hunt down their little princess.

A laugh rips from my throat.

Princess.

Un-fucking-likely.

"S-Stella killed him," she states coldly as she recalls what she saw.

My fingers tighten once more, forcing her eyes back to me.

"What did you have to do with this, Emmie?"

Her eyes widen in shock. "W-what?"

"Emmie," I growl.

"I didn't... I had no clue that—"

"So you knew nothing about fight night? You had

no clue that that sick fuck was going to try to blow my girl up the second you left the coach house last night?"

Her entire body tenses at my accusations, her eyes narrow to slits as she glares at me.

"You really don't think much of me, do you, *Boss?*" she hisses, a condescending smirk on her lips.

"The only thing I think right now, *Princess,* is that you're an untrustworthy cunt."

"Ouch, careful. You might hurt my feelings."

I bark out a laugh at her words, although my face shows zero happiness as I do so.

"Your feelings? What about Stella's? She thinks you're her friend, yet the person who's been trying to kill her has turned out to be connected to you. Coincidence?"

"Yes," she spits. "It's a fucking coincidence. I had no idea last night was going to happen. And you really think I'd have gone to that fucking fight if I knew the place was going to go up?"

I shrug. "You haven't shown yourself to be the most intelligent, so I wouldn't put it past you."

"Fuck you, Theodore." Her use of my full name makes my teeth grind so hard I'm sure I'm about to fucking crack one. "Stella *is* my friend. I'd never do anything to hurt her."

I glare at her, not believing her words for a second.

Shifting my grip on her neck slightly as I take a step closer, I tilt her face up so she has no choice but to hold my eyes.

"Decide where your loyalties lie, Ramsey. And if it's not with us, then walk away. We both already know that I don't want you in my fucking life, so maybe do Stella a solid and let her get on with hers without a traitorous bitch like you in it."

She gasps at my harsh words, but she doesn't even try to argue. Instead, her chest just heaves as she fights to breathe with me constricting her windpipe. Her shallow breaths rush past her slightly parted lips as she stares at me in disbelief.

"What?" I ask innocently. "Did you think I was going to what... barge in here, kiss you, and take you back to my bed? Newsflash, Ramsey. My bed is in ashes, and I want to know for fucking sure that you had nothing to do with it."

Her jaw flexes like she's about to come back at me with some cutting remark, but I don't give her a chance.

Releasing her, I take a huge step back, finally breathing in some air that isn't filled with her scent while she sags back against the wall, her hand brushing over her tender throat.

The sight of the red marks my firm hold left behind does things to me that I refuse to register or acknowledge.

"Is that all you wanted, Cirillo?" she finally heaves out once my fingers are around the door handle, more than ready to make my escape.

"This," I say, pointing between the two of us. "That," I spit, gesturing to what she saw beyond the one-way glass tonight. "Never fucking happened."

"Or what?"

I suck in a calming breath at her question,

reminding myself of the Boss's words from earlier. *"Keep the death count to a minimum."*

My lips curl at one side as I continue to hold her eyes.

"Try me, Princess. I fucking dare you."

Emmie and Theo's story continues in DEVIANT KNIGHT.

Coming 13th January 2022!

THORN

CHAPTER ONE
Amalie

"I think you'll really enjoy your time here," Principal Hartmann says. He tries to sound cheerful about it, but he's got sympathy oozing from his wrinkled, tired eyes.

This shouldn't have been part of my life. I should be in London starting university, yet here I am at the beginning of what is apparently my junior year at an American high school I have no idea about aside from its name and the fact my mum attended many years ago. A lump climbs up my throat as thoughts of my parents hit me without warning.

"I know things are going to be different and you might feel that you're going backward, but I can assure you it's the right thing to do. It will give you the time you need to... adjust and to put some serious thought into what you want to do once you graduate."

Time to adjust. I'm not sure any amount of time will be enough to learn to live without my parents and being shipped across the Pacific to start a new life in America.

"I'm sure it'll be great." Plastering a fake smile on my face, I take the timetable from the principal's hand and stare down at it. The butterflies that were already fluttering around in my stomach erupt to the point I might just throw up over his chipped Formica desk.

Math, English lit, biology, gym, my hands tremble until I see something that instantly relaxes me, *art and film studies.* At least I got my own way with something.

"I've arranged for someone to show you around. Chelsea is the captain of the cheer squad, what she doesn't know about the school isn't worth knowing. If you need anything, Amalie, my door is always open."

Nodding at him, I rise from my chair just as a soft knock sounds out and a cheery brunette bounces into the room. My knowledge of American high schools comes courtesy of the hours of films I used to spend my evenings watching, and she fits the stereotype of captain to a tee.

"You wanted something, Mr. Hartmann?" she sings so sweetly it makes even my teeth shiver.

"Chelsea, this is Amalie. It's her first day starting junior year. I trust you'll be able to show her around. Here's a copy of her schedule."

"Consider it done, sir."

"I assured Amalie that she's in safe hands."

I want to say it's my imagination but when she turns her big chocolate eyes on me, the light in them diminishes a little.

"Lead the way." My voice is lacking any kind of enthusiasm and from the narrowing of her eyes, I don't think she misses it.

I follow her out of the room with a little less bounce in my step. Once we're in the hallway, she turns her eyes on me. She's really quite pretty with thick brown hair, large eyes, and full lips. She's shorter than me, but then at five foot eight, you'll be hard pushed to find many other teenage girls who can look me in the eye.

Tilting her head so she can look at me, I fight my smile. "Let's make this quick. It's my first day of senior year and I've got shit to be doing."

Spinning on her heels, she takes off and I rush to catch up with her. "Cafeteria, library." She points then looks down at her copy of my timetable. "Looks like your locker is down there." She waves her hand down a hallway full of students who are all staring our way, before gesturing in the general direction of my different subjects.

"Okay, that should do it. Have a great day." Her smile is faker than mine's been all morning, which really is saying something. She goes to walk away, but at the last minute turns back to me. "Oh, I forgot. That over there." I follow her finger as she points to a large group of people outside the open double doors sitting around a bunch of tables. "That's *my* group. I should probably warn you now that you won't fit in there."

I hear her warning loud and clear, but it didn't really need saying. I've no intention of befriending the cheerleaders, that kind of thing's not really my scene. I'm much happier hiding behind my camera and slinking into the background.

Chelsea flounces off and I can't help my eyes from following her out toward *her* group. I can see from here that it consists of her squad and the football team. I can also see the longing in other student's eyes as they walk past them. They either want to be them or want to be part of their stupid little gang.

Jesus, this place is even more stereotypical than I was expecting.

Unfortunately, my first class of the day is in the direction Chelsea just went. I pull my bag up higher on my shoulder and hold the couple of books I have tighter to my chest as I walk out of the doors.

I've not taken two steps out of the building when my skin tingles with awareness. I tell myself to keep my head down. I've no interest in being their entertainment but my eyes defy me, and I find myself looking up as Chelsea points at me and laughs. I knew my sudden arrival in the town wasn't a secret. My mum's legacy is still strong, so when they heard the news, I'm sure it was hot gossip.

Heat spreads from my cheeks and down my neck. I go to look away when a pair of blue eyes catch my attention. While everyone else's look intrigued, like they've got a new pet to play with, his are haunted and angry. Our stare holds, his eyes narrow as if he's trying to warn me of something before he menacingly shakes his head.

Confused by his actions, I manage to rip my eyes from his and turn toward where I think I should be going.

I only manage three steps at the most before I crash into something—or somebody.

"Shit, I'm sorry. Are you okay?" a deep voice asks. When I look into the kind green eyes of the guy in front of me, I almost sigh with relief. I was starting to wonder if I'd find anyone who wasn't just going to glare at me. I know I'm the new girl but shit. They must experience new kids on a weekly basis, I can't be that unusual.

"I'm fine, thank you."

"You're the new British girl. Emily, right?"

"It's Amalie, and yeah... that's me."

"I'm so sorry about your parents. Mom said she was friends with yours." Tears burn my eyes. Today is hard enough without the constant reminder of everything I've lost. "Shit, I'm sorry. I shouldn't have—"

"It's fine," I lie.

"What's your first class?"

Handing over my timetable, he quickly runs his eyes over it. "English lit, I'm heading that way. Can I walk you?"

"Yes." His smile grows at my eagerness and for the first time today my returning one is almost sincere.

"I'm Shane, by the way." I look over and smile at

him, thankfully the hallway is too noisy for us to continue any kind of conversation.

He seems like a sweet guy but my head's spinning and just the thought of trying to hold a serious conversation right now is exhausting.

Student's stares follow my every move. My skin prickles as more and more notice me as I walk beside Shane. Some give me smiles but most just nod in my direction, pointing me out to their friends. Some are just downright rude and physically point at me like I'm some fucking zoo animal awoken from its slumber.

In reality, I'm just an eighteen-year-old girl who's starting somewhere new, and desperate to blend into the crowd. I know that with who I am—or more who my parents were—that it's not going to be all that easy, but I'd at least like a chance to try to be normal. Although I fear I might have lost that the day I lost my parents.

"This is you." Shane's voice breaks through my thoughts and when I drag my head up from avoiding everyone else around me, I see he's holding the door open.

Thankfully the classroom's only half full, but still, every single set of eyes turn to me.

Ignoring their attention, I keep my head down and find an empty desk toward the back of the room.

Once I'm settled, I risk looking up. My breath catches when I find Shane still standing in the doorway, forcing the students entering to squeeze past him. He nods his head. I know it's his way of asking if I'm okay. Forcing a smile onto my lips, I nod in return and after a few seconds, he turns to leave.

THORN and the rest of the ROSEWOOD series are now LIVE.

DOWNLOAD TO CONTINUE READING

ABOUT THE AUTHOR

Tracy Lorraine is a *USA Today* and *Wall Street Journal* bestselling new adult and contemporary romance author. Tracy has recently turned thirty and lives in a cute Cotswold village in England with her husband, baby girl and lovable but slightly crazy dog. Having always been a bookaholic with her head stuck in her Kindle, Tracy decided to try her hand at a story idea she dreamt up and hasn't looked back since.

Be the first to find out about new releases and offers. Sign up to my newsletter here.

If you want to know what I'm up to and see teasers and snippets of what I'm working on, then you need to be in my Facebook group. Join Tracy's Angels here.

Keep up to date with Tracy's books at
www.tracylorraine.com

ALSO BY TRACY LORRAINE

Hate You #1

Trick You #2

Defy You #3

Play You #4

Inked (A Rebel Ink/Driven Crossover)

Rosewood High Series

Thorn #1

Paine #2

Savage #3

Fierce #4

Hunter #5

Faze (#6 Prequel)

Fury #6

Legend #7

Maddison Kings University Series

TMYM: Prequel

TRYS #1

TDYW #2

TBYS #3

TVYC #4

TDYD #5

TDYR #6

TRYD #7

Knight's Ridge Empire Series

Wicked Summer Knight: Prequel (Stella & Seb)

Wicked Knight #1 (Stella & Seb)

Wicked Princess #2 (Stella & Seb)

Wicked Empire #3 (Stella & Seb)

Deviant Knight #4 (Emmie & Theo)

Ruined Series

Ruined Plans #1

Ruined by Lies #2

Ruined Promises #3

Never Forget Series

Never Forget Him #1

Never Forget Us #2

Everywhere & Nowhere #3

Chasing Series

Chasing Logan

The Cocktail Girls

His Manhattan

Her Kensington

Printed in Great Britain
by Amazon